Downsized or Dead

by

S.E. Greco

Downsized or Dead

Cover Art by *The Wild Rose Press, Inc.*

The Wild Rose Press, Inc.
PO Box 708
Adams Basin, NY 14410-0708
Visit us at www.thewildrosepress.com

Publishing History
First Edition, 2023
Trade Paperback ISBN 978-1-5092-4760-8
Digital ISBN 978-1-5092-4761-5

Published in the United States of America

I know that the person with the gun is both determined and very pissed off, and I can see an index finger taut against the trigger. I'm worried about the gun going off accidentally, but maybe it's not accidents I need to fret about because it's one of those old-fashioned revolver pistols with the wheely thing that holds the bullets, and now I can see the hammer part being pulled back. I know squat about guns, but I've watched some Clint Eastwood westerns, and I recall that when the hammer goes back, that's bad news because pretty soon a bullet comes out the front.

But there's actually no need to shoot me. I'll probably croak right here, no assistance required because my ticker is racing from fright like I'm a hummingbird on speed, so I'm sure I'll blow out an artery any second...then this wacko can just sneak my carcass into my shitty little chicken-coop sized cubicle at Fleener Plastics after hours and plop me in my chair, slump me down so that my head is on the desk, put a pen in one hand and a coffee cup in the other and that's it, job done. Because who the hell is going to question one more employee being worked to death by that crappy company?

Hot flashes are coming in waves now.

I feel dizzy, faint, peripheral sight shutting down, and... and now, I'm looking out the window and...

I see a vision.

A vision of...

Death.

Dedication

To my wife, Shelley.
For the endless supply of love, support, encouragement,
and applause.

Prologue

My eyes are locked on the gun that's pointed at me, at a spot right in the middle of my forehead, I think. Not good, because it's held by a sicko who I know for sure wants me dead.

And I'm just an accountant.

That's right, an accountant at a decaying old company that makes shitty plastic products. Not a cop, a CIA operative, a Navy SEAL, not even a ninja. I don't have any superpowers or a secret identity. And my name isn't agent triple X or anything like that.

It's June. My name, I mean. Don't get confused because my parents named me after a month. I'm just a mom, a wife, and a goddamn accountant, but I think I need to add imbecile to that list for getting myself into this royal mess. On Saturday I was counting out carrot sticks and clementine sections to put into little baggies because I was the snack mom for my son's soccer game.

And now I'm counting the minutes left in my life.

On one hand.

Because I know that the person with the gun is both determined and very pissed off, and I can see an index finger taut against the trigger. I'm worried about the gun going off accidentally, but maybe it's not accidents I need to fret about because it's one of those old-fashioned revolver pistols with the wheely thing that holds the bullets, and now I can see the hammer part being pulled

S.E. Greco

back. I know squat about guns, but I've watched some Clint Eastwood westerns, and I recall that when the hammer goes back, that's bad news because pretty soon a bullet comes out the front.

But there's actually no need to shoot me. I'll probably croak right here, no assistance required because my ticker is racing from fright like I'm a hummingbird on speed. So I'm sure I'll blow out an artery any second...then this wacko can just sneak my carcass into my shitty little chicken-coop sized cubicle at Fleener Plastics after hours and plop me in my chair, slump me down so that my head is on the desk, put a pen in one hand and a coffee cup in the other and that's it, job done. Because who the hell is going to question one more employee being worked to death by that crappy company?

Hot flashes are coming in waves now.

I feel dizzy, faint, peripheral sight shutting down, and...and now, I'm looking out the window and...

I see a vision.

A vision of...

Death.

Chapter 1

Eight Days Earlier

My name's June Bloom.
It's Monday morning.
The start of another lousy week toiling away at my crummy job at the Fleener Plastics Company in Bridgeport, Connecticut, where I'm the bottom level manager of a business accounting group, working for a moron of a boss who claims to be an accounting genius but doesn't know enough math to count his own nuts.

And I hit forty a few months ago. And I don't really care for my first name because it sounds so matronly. And my whole name, first and last together, makes me sound like some kind of spring flower.

Other than all that, everything's just swell.

Today I start my day in the usual way. I get my two little boys on the school bus, kiss my husband Darryl goodbye, and back my sixteen-year-old junker of a station wagon out of the driveway of my modest raised-ranch home in suburban Norwalk to leave for work.

And even though it's a beautifully sunny spring day, the air cool and crisp, I begin to feel that dull ache in my temples that I always get when I head to work on Monday morning, the one that morphs into a migraine a few hours later. But otherwise, I feel okay, and this morning I'm wearing my slick navy-blue pantsuit with a white blouse and a paisley bow. It's the outfit I often wear on Mondays to raise my mood, and it's working today, at least until I reach the end of our tree-lined street and see Abbey on her morning jog, which takes all the hot gas right out of my balloon.

Abbey Tate is the *better than you* woman on our block. Every neighborhood has one. You know, she's single, blond, statuesque, good looking. Okay, let's say gorgeous, perhaps even ravishing. She has no children, and she's younger than all of the moms around here like me. Abbey has an incredible figure with super-toned abs, thighs, and calves. An ass so firm and tight she could open champagne bottles with it. She has her own business, some type of bullshit holistic mind and body wellness thing, I think. And I'm sure she sets her own hours and does all her work from home because she has plenty of time to jog around the neighborhood in her little white shorts and semi-transparent sports bra, her ponytail swaying back and forth beneath her hundred-and fifty-dollar designer headband and her eye makeup in perfect condition, and who the hell does their makeup before jogging anyway?

As I putter by her, with my own marshmallow ass gradually compressing and sinking me ever further down into the car seat, she waves to me. It's just a little waggle of her hand, Queen Elizabeth style, and she also gives me her insincere little smile, which conveys a chummy greeting on the surface, but I know that the real message behind that smile, to all the women on the block, is this: *I could take your husband away from you any time I want.*

And indeed, the behavior of our husbands, as influenced by Abbey, is as shallow and disgusting as you might expect. Many of the husbands on the block saunter down to the curb every morning at about the same time to put out the trash cans or put a letter in the mailbox or whatever, and they delay their return while they carefully evaluate the health of the lawn or check the driveway for cracks or examine the shrubs for any signs of leaf fungus, hoping and praying that Abbey will bounce on by. And if she happens to stop by the curb to do some stretches, the men tend to congregate around her and chat, and I think on one occasion my next-door neighbor Mona had to go out there and disperse the crowd with a cold-water garden hose.

Thirty-five minutes later, after battling the rush hour traffic on interstate ninety-five while inhaling my daily dose of eighteen-wheeler diesel fumes, I pull my car into the pot-holed parking lot at Fleener Plastics, where a bountiful crop of spring ragweed has already begun to sprout from the numerous cracks in the grimy asphalt. I walk toward the entrance of the building where I work, its crumbling, soot-covered façade framed by the two ancient smokestacks that are constantly belching God knows what horrible toxins into the air and eventually into my lungs. It's a good thing the company sends out those reports to us every month stating that the thirty-six known airborne carcinogens in my office space are happily all measuring at acceptable levels. And as for the yellowish water in the drinking fountains that the company swears is perfectly safe, I stopped ingesting it months ago, afraid I'd eventually grow a tail from it.

I make it to my cube and plop into my rickety but supposedly ergonomic chair. This is my little hovel, my personal Bob Cratchit workspace, my three by four-foot cell with drab gray walls that were engineered to let through every sound generated by every other person in the entire cube area—every spoken word, every squeak, sniffle, belch, and fart. It's where I'm supposed to be super productive even as I feel the blood clots growing in my legs because I don't have room to straighten them when I'm sitting at my second-grader-sized desk. There's not much space here to personalize, but I have a family picture on the desk. I also have a poster of some serene Caribbean beach mounted on the wall, but it's not like I can waste time gazing at it while I'm sitting because the cube is too small for me to get my eyes far enough away to focus on it.

I open my laptop, call up my e-mail, and I'm immediately assaulted by the urgent note at the top of my inbox, with the subject in red: *Human Resource Initiative.*

As I click on it, I gnash my teeth because I know what's coming. *Human Resource Initiative* has to be the company's newest euphemism for another layoff. Last time it was, I think, *Strategic Manpower Realignment*, and the time before that, *Personal Skills Redistribution.* There must be some asshole in HR whose sole job it is to sit around and dream up these cutesy phrases.

I skim through the usual two paragraphs of happy horse shit about how today's challenging business environment requires that we take drastic and sometimes unpleasant measures to remain competitive, and of course the only effective way to do that is to cut the headcount, a painful but necessary step which will adversely affect the lives of a limited number of employees, while ultimately ensuring the long term welfare of the company and therefore the livelihood of a much larger number of employees—*blah, blah, blah.*

Enough to make you puke, so it's a good thing I'd skipped breakfast.

The note contains nothing about the number of employees who would be getting the ax, or about the timing. It says that more information will be "forthcoming in a timely manner." I know that once they announce layoffs are coming, upper management will try to get all the dirty work over and done with as soon as possible to reduce the angst among the employee population. And this isn't for noble reasons. Worrying simply reduces productivity. The note emphasizes to us managers the importance of keeping this information secret for now. Yeah, right. This will spread like a fire in a match factory. Everyone in the plant will know by the end of the hour.

There is nothing mentioned in the note about managers losing their jobs, so I guess that my own job is safe, at least for now, but I'm not sure if I should be glad about that. Sometimes I think it would be best if they fire me before I have a stroke sitting at my desk, although it's true that if I die at work, my husband and kids will get a bigger life insurance payout. I've told Darryl that if I die at home, he should drive my corpse over to the Fleener Plastics plant at night and toss it in the bushes in front of the building.

My first command decision of the day is to get a significant amount of caffeine into my bloodstream before trying to deal with any of this crap.

I close my laptop, get up and walk to the employee snack area. I eye the coffee dispensers, looking for the flavor of the day when I see Faith walking towards me.

Faith works for me. She's a sweet and petite little single southern gal from Tennessee in her mid-twenties, with big puppy dog brown eyes and a cute little button of a nose. Her pretty face is framed by shoulder-length brown hair in a sixties wave. But upstairs she's six donuts short of a dozen.

There's always something going on with her. She's a self-proclaimed clairvoyant. Faith gets visions and I guess she sees dead people too, because I heard through the local gossip network that she saw Elvis last week when she was back home visiting her family, and this wasn't her first encounter with the King. I try not to talk about any of this with her because it always makes me a bit uncomfortable. I don't care for having to pretend that I believe her.

As she came up to me, I hoped that she wouldn't bring it up.

"June, did you hear?" she squeals in her precious Tennessee accent, waggling both her hands with excitement. "My word, ah saw Elvis again!"

"Oh, wow, is that right?" I give her a grin as sincere as I can make it.

"Yes, at a Piggly Wiggly store in Nashville! This is the second time, although ah don't like to make a big thing about it. This time ah saw the fortyish Elvis in his sequined white jumpsuit, whereas last time ah saw the younger Elvis in his Army uniform. A double sighting by one person is quite unusual you know, and seeing him at two different ages is even *more* unusual!"

"Oh yes, very unusual. Really something," I reply. I grin again and nod my head like an idiot, as I scramble for something relevant to ask. "Uhhhhh, well, when you see these…Elvises…or Elvi, I guess is the correct plural form…what are they shopping for?"

Faith's eyes are wide and bright as she answers with

complete sincerity in a sweet southern drawl. "Well now, you know those little round felt buttons that you stick on the bottom of table or chair legs, so they don't scratch the floor? This Elvis was gettin' a pack of those."

I give her a thoughtful nod and say, "Hmmm, of all the things you think you might need in the afterlife, who would have thought felt floor protectors would be at the top of the list? Go figure."

Faith smiles and nods in agreement. "Right! Oh, gotta go, June. There's Mary, I want to tell her about it. She's a *big* Elvis fan!"

"Okay, see ya."

I pay for my coffee and then head back to the cube area, taking a different route, one that will take me a few minutes longer. I always tell myself that I do this because I want a little extra exercise, but I know it's because I can delay starting my workday for another two minutes.

On the way, I pick up the sounds of my boss Larry and his entourage of brown-nosers, in one of the conference rooms off the hallway. Several times a week I see him practicing his stand-up comic routine, telling his crude jokes to his lackeys.

"Aaahh, my wife," says Larry. "She's a country girl, and I thought when I got engaged to her, that her father would give me a dowry, you know? But all she came with was a car loan, a student loan, and a couple of personal loans. I blame my friend Vinnie who fixed us up on a blind date. He *thought* I said that I wanted a farm girl with big debts! Yaghhh, Yagghh, Yaggghhhh!"

"You PIG!" I utter out loud, but not quite loud enough for Larry or the others to hear me. I despise Larry's laugh as much as his stupid sexist jokes. Up until a few years ago, I can honestly say that I never really hated anyone enough to wish them harm. Now it scares me that I have daydreams about smashing this guy's face in, even though I'd never actually try it.

It's amazing, he's a second-level manager, but he's not bright enough to even close the door to the conference room. I don't think he realizes that if someone hears that kind of talk at work and takes offense, he could get his ass shipped off to corporate diversity training class for two solid weeks, and he'd get a big black mark on his company personnel record. Believe me, I've thought about turning him in many times. The problem is, I know they wouldn't fire him, and being my boss, he has the power to make my work life absolutely miserable. I mean, more miserable than it currently is, assuming that's possible.

I walk past the conference room, anxious to get back to my cube where I'll take the first sips of my coffee. I hope that the extra dark roast I chose will cool my throbbing migraine a bit.

"June! June!" wails Larry at my back.

Crap. Larry caught me. Ignoring him is futile, I know he'd come running after me. He has a six-legged, four-winged bug up his ass almost every day. Usually, it has to do with some hare-brained business scheme that he has to bounce off me. I turn to face his pudgy frame. He barrels up to me like a rolling, sweaty shitstorm, half running like he always does because of the perceived urgency of whatever stupid idea he's about to bellow at me.

"Meat diapers, June, MEAT DIAPERS!" Larry barks, as if he were revealing to me the secret of eternal life. He sticks his finger in my face, about to make his important point. Larry is in his fifties, with a face as round as a cantaloupe and his skin has a cantaloupe texture too. The imbecile always wears white shirts that are two sizes too small, so that the buttons are holding on for dear life. He always sports a pair of greasy yellow stains under the armpits because he's continuously sweating buckets, even at nine in the morning. His cheesy striped polyester neckties are always pulled so tight that they appear to be choking off his air, the apparent reason for his bulging eyeballs.

"Meat diapers?" I ask with feigned interest. One of his bug eyes stares right at me, the other is off doing its own thing. I hold back a gag as I catch the putrid odor of his breakfast wafting from his mouth—unmistakably a garlic bagel with salmon cream cheese spread that was sitting unrefrigerated in the company snack bar for way too long.

"Yeah, that's right, meat diapers! You know, those pieces of plastic that they put under the meat in the supermarket, so it doesn't touch the Styrofoam tray? It looks kind of like a baby diaper. C'mon, you're a woman, you're supposed to know something about diapers, right? You got two kids, right? Sure, you do. You've got that kind of matronly look about you, you know, the child-bearing hips and all, and don't get me wrong, I mean that in a *good* way. You remind me of my mother, God bless her dead soul and her hairy upper lip. That woman was a saint. Changed a hell of a lot of diapers, you know?"

I nod my head, gritting my teeth, and give my boss a shit-eating grin while I size up the distance between us, wondering how many steps it would take for me to reach his fat head so that I could drive the heel of my palm into his face.

S.E. Greco

He continues with his usual egotistical bluster: "I've come up with something that's going to blow the lid off the meat diaper business, June. If we can tighten the size tolerance of the diaper, we can cut a full millimeter off the top and bottom edges and that will save a full fiftieth of a cent off the production cost of each and every meat diaper, and do you know what that will translate to in increased profits? This is big, June, *really big*!"

I take a step back from Larry, then I nod my head and give him a slight smile as if to acknowledge the depth of his genius. I wait for some asinine marching order. Maybe he'll send me into the manufacturing line to watch the meat diaper production process and collect all the pieces of waste plastic that are cut away and weigh them, or some such bullshit. But luckily his wandering eye spots another hapless victim, someone else to blather to about his genius idea. He grunts and runs off after them. I'm safe for the moment from having to do another one of his pointless, hamster wheel tasks.

When I get back to my cube, I open my laptop and check to see if there are any new e-mails, sent in the past ten minutes, about the workforce reduction.

Nothing.

Okay, so they're going to keep us in suspense for a while longer.

I try to put it out of my mind because I have work to do. Today I have to churn through the brain-frying experience of doing the quarterly consumables forecast. I guess that it will take maybe three hours of concentrated work. That means that with all the interruptions that come with sitting in a cube area, it will take me about six.

I settle in and get started.

****

True to my prediction, I finish the report at about three in the afternoon. And also as predicted, my mind is now mush.

I skipped lunch, which is fine because I need to lose a few pounds. Even though I don't consider myself obese, it's a constant struggle. And I have two sets of clothes—one for when I'm at my ideal weight and one for when I'm not. Today I'm wearing the *"not"* wardrobe. And the other set has been sitting in the dresser drawers for too damn long.

I'm ready for a break, but as soon as I stand up to go over to the snack bar for a coffee, Faith is in my cube, her face a foot from mine. Her skin is pale, and she's clearly agitated about something.

"Faith, what's up?"

"Oh June, he's dead!" she wails, grabbing my forearm.

"You mean Elvis? Yes, he is, but I thought you took solace in the fact that he still walks among us, and…"

"No, no, I mean Melvin!"

"Melvin? Melvin Hamm?"

She nods and gives me a look of despair. Melvin also works for me. I haven't seen him yet today.

"Faith, calm down. Let's go to a break room."

I don't know what this is about, but there's no point in agitating anyone else, and in the cube area nothing spoken remains private for long. Fortunately, it appears that no one was within earshot of Faith's alarming claim. I take her by the arm and lead her toward a small room adjoining the cubes. I intentionally take a short detour so that we walk past Melvin's cube, and I see no indication that he's in. There's no briefcase or coat, or anything else

13

that he might have brought to work.

After we enter the break room, I shut the door and we sit down. The place is just a glorified closet with two chairs and a ridiculously small table which holds only a telephone. Our chairs are backed up against opposing walls to prevent our noses from touching as we converse.

"Faith, take a deep breath and tell me slowly what's going on. Why do you think he's dead?" I ask.

Her eyes grow wide, and she gestures with both hands, using them to roughly frame a rectangular field of view about a foot in front of her eyes. "Ah had a vision, June, a vision, just a few minutes ago! As plain as if ah saw it on a TV screen!"

Uh, oh. A vision. Should I ask her if Melvin was in a white sequined jumpsuit, like Elvis? No. I need to show some respect for her beliefs. She thinks she saw *something.*

"Faith, what exactly do you mean by a vision?" I ask in a relaxed tone. I hope that my sense of calm will spread to Faith, but she remains panicky and agitated, like a squirrel on uppers.

Faith leans toward me as she tries to explain. "Ah mean, you know, ah didn't see his ghost walkin' around in a store or anything like that. Ah just had a *vision.* You know, ah just saw a *still* scene. Ah can't control these things, they just pop into my head sometimes when ah touch somethin' belonging to a person that ah have some connection with. Well, ah touched Melvin's chair just a minute ago when ah stopped at his cube so ah could ask him somethin' about the monthly reports. That's when ah got the vision."

I'm not sure what to say to her. I mean, I have scenes pop into my head all the time. My last one was on the way to work this morning, when I pictured my boss hanging upside down over a huge bonfire, by strings tied around his balls.

I take my usual methodical approach: First, get all the facts.

"Okay, can you describe this vision?" I ask.

Faith shakes her head and says, "Oh, June, ah saw his dead body. It's in the trunk of a car, and his eyes are open and he's dead. That's all ah saw. It was awful!"

"Okay, okay, just try to relax. Faith, when you see these things…uh, I know you're clairvoyant, but these things that you see, are they in the past, the present, or the future?"

"Sometimes the past. Could be the present. Might be the future, too. Definitely one of those three."

Hmmm, that helps a lot.

Melvin is a bit of an odd duck, for sure. I've known him only since he transferred into my group about eight months ago. He's okay at his job, but he's rather withdrawn, and he never struck me as being very likable or even sociable, so I'm a bit puzzled as to why Faith would psychically *connect* with him. And even though I don't like to speak ill of anyone (there are exceptions for sure, like Larry), I'd have to say that Melvin definitely got hit by the ugly truck. He's about twenty-five years old, short, and as skinny as a fishing rod, with a pointy and prematurely balding pate. He has a rather large, hooked nose, almost no chin at all, and oily skin scarred and cratered by severe acne that's still raging. The thing that most people seem to remember about him is that he's constantly getting nosebleeds, and at least once a day you can find him sitting in his cube with his head tilted back and a tissue shoved up one or both nostrils.

"Uhhh…so, why are you getting a vision of Melvin? I mean, he's no Elvis. I'm pretty sure Melvin can't even sing."

"Oh, June this is so *different* than seein' the King's ghost!" she admonishes. "My visions like this are usually about important things happenin' to some person, you know? As far as why ah got a vision of *Melvin*, well ah just don't know. Guess it's cause ah see him at work almost every day. It's not like he and ah are close, or anything like that. Ah've worked with him on a few projects, and he and Verne and ah went to that production accounting conference two months ago and well, he's shy and awkward, but he's all right, you know? He's kinda like the odd little pig in the litter, as my Momma would say, and as such, you can't but feel a little sorry for him. And bein' murdered an' all is an important thing that's happened in his life, wouldn't you agree?"

"Uh, yes, in my book getting murdered ranks up there as an important life event."

"Ah had better tell the police about the vision, June. Right now!"

Before or after the part about Elvis in the Piggly Wiggly?

"Listen, not that I doubt your…er, powers, but let's take this one step at a time. Let's go ask his cube neighbors if they've seen him today."

"Well, ah already did that. Ah asked Pog, Mary, and Gary, and they all said he never came in today."

Undaunted, I say, "Okay, then we'll call his cell."

She shakes her head and says, "Oh, June, ah already tried, it just goes straight to voicemail."

"Let's try again," I say, as I take out my cell and find

his name in my contact list. I punch the call button and sure enough, it goes immediately to voicemail. I disconnect without leaving a message.

"Okay, same result. No answer," I calmly concede.

"That's 'cause he's been murdered, and the killer took his phone!" cries Faith, dropping her face into her cupped hands.

"Probably his cell battery is dead, or he turned the phone off for some reason. Let's not panic. Let me do some checking."

I open my laptop and quickly find that I have no new e-mails from Melvin. I also log onto the company website and see he hasn't put his employee ID badge into any of the badge readers at the plant today.

"Nothing," I simply tell Faith. She raises her eyebrows and gives me the *I told you so* look. "But we'll call his wife next."

I peck at the keys of my laptop again and find that Melvin's wife is named Annuska, and her cell number is listed as his emergency contact. I've never met her or even talked to her, but the time is right to introduce myself. I tap her number into my phone, and then I put my finger to my lips and give Faith a warning look. I don't want her blurting out any comments, questions, or lamentations that Annuska might hear.

Someone picks up on the third ring.

"Yes?" It's a female voice.

"Hi, this is June Bloom. I'm Melvin's manager at Fleener Plastics. Am I speaking to Annuska?"

Another, "Yes?"

"Melvin didn't come to work today. I was just calling to make sure that everything is okay?" A few seconds of dead air ensue as Annuska apparently ponders her response.

An answer finally comes in a deep voice with a very thick eastern European accent, possibly Hungarian or Romanian. It reminds me of Natasha from *Rocky and Bullwinkle*. "My Melvin did not come to work today? He leaves at regular time this morning. I do not understand where he could be." I can detect traces of concern in her voice, despite the thick accent.

"Ummm…well, we just tried calling him and it went right to voicemail."

After a few seconds of silence, she says, "Perhaps cellphone is not working, for it is old and battery is not excellent. But…why is Melvin not at work?" The inflections of concern are morphing into worry.

"Is there anywhere he might have gone?" I ask. "Like…well, I don't know…anywhere?"

No response.

"Okay, well, then you should call the police," I say in a calm and commanding voice, even though I know they will probably wait at least twenty-four hours to start any kind of an active search. No point in telling Annuska that. And there is no point at all in scaring the shit out of her by telling her about Faith's so-called paranormal vision.

Annuska quickly agrees and we end the call after she says that she'll call me later. I tell Faith we can't do anything more until tomorrow and that she should go home.

An hour later, Annuska calls back and says that after trying Melvin's cell a few times herself with no success, she called the police. All they did so far is a check on traffic accidents in the area, and they quickly ruled out the possibility that Melvin was in an accident on the way to work. They told Annuska to call back tomorrow if Melvin is still missing.

I give Annuska a few lame assurances and tell her we'll talk again in the morning. Now she sounds a *lot* more worried than on our previous call.

If Melvin doesn't show up soon, she is going to have one very long night.

Chapter 2

As I enter my cube the next morning, Faith materializes, anxious to invade my personal space before I can even put down my satchel. I'm dragging even worse than usual because I didn't sleep well. I was thinking about Melvin for much of the night. Even though I've never considered him a friend, having an employee of mine missing is serious stuff. And I feel for Annuska.

Faith and I both open our mouths to speak, but before either of us can utter a word, my phone rings. I hold up my index finger to stifle Faith and push the answer button.

Annuska speaks in a weepy voice. Between her gasps and her thick accent, she's difficult to understand. "Oh, June, Melvin has not come home and still does his phone go to voicemail," she wails. "I have called police once more, some few minutes ago, but they say investigation must wait until tomorrow morning."

Even though I don't believe in Faith's visions, I can imagine the anguish that Annuska must be experiencing. I give her a few more pathetically insincere assurances and ask her to call me again later in the day.

I turn to Faith and say, "Well, Melvin hasn't come home yet."

"Oh, he won't be comin' home, June," she says in a no-nonsense manner. She leans towards me and states in a resolute tone, "June, ah'm goin' over to see Annuska on my lunch break, you know, to console her and whatnot. Ah'm thinkin' that maybe if ah'm near his house and his wife, ah'll get another vision that'll help us find the body real quick."

I hold up a hand and say, "Whoa, Faith, maybe that's not such a good idea. I mean, you seem to be convinced that Melvin's dead, and we shouldn't be even suggesting that to Annuska at this point, so…"

"Oh, June, don't worry, ah won't say nothin' to her 'till his dead body is found, ah promise," she says with a shrug and a wave of her hand, trivializing my concerns. "But sooner or later she's gonna find out he's dead, and until then she's gonna be worryin' like a barn rat at an alley cat hoedown."

"Faith, don't write him off yet. I think it's more likely that he skipped out for some reason."

"Ah saw what ah saw," she says with indignation, folding her arms against any further suggestions that she might be mistaken.

"Listen, if that's the way it works, instead of going to his house, can't you just go into his cube over there and…rub his pencil holder or something like that, and get another vision?"

She replies in a flustered tone, "Ah tried that early this mornin', but ah got nuthin', June, nuthin' at all! Ah touched everything on his desk. Ah even opened his bottom drawer, which was unlocked, and there was a pair of his shorts in there, so ah touched 'em, and still got nuthin'."

I snap my palm up and say, "Stop right there. I don't need to hear anything about Melvin's soiled shorts."

She admonishes me in her southern style with a

wave of one hand, and says, "Oh, c'mon, June, they were clean. That's maybe why ah didn't get a psychic signal, it mighta worked better if he'd worn 'em. They was just joggin' shorts anyway. He was scheduled to run in the lunchtime five mile last week, but he canceled 'cause he got one of his bleeds. One of those nostrils was runnin' like a hose at a hay fire. But you know, it's also possible that the first vision ah got yesterday, when ah touched his chair, sucked all the psychic juice right outta his cube. If that's right, then ah need to be in his house and maybe near his wife to get another vision." Faith leans a little closer to me, lowers her voice, and says, "There's always the possibility that Melvin's wife *did* somethin' to him...know what ah mean?" Her eyes widen again, and she raises her eyebrows as she stares at me, apparently encouraging me to consider the sinister possibilities. "Ah might get a vision of her smackin' him with a lead pipe or somethin' like that!"

"A lead pipe? That's a bit cliché, isn't it? This is real life, not a board game. I really think you shouldn't go over there."

She warns me in her colorful southern pouty voice, "June, you can't stop me, cause it's something ah'll be doin' on my lunchbreak. If you're so worried, well then, come with me."

I hesitate, but then quickly realize that if Faith is determined to go, I'd better be there to try and keep her under control. "All right, all right. I'll go with you, assuming Annuska is okay with having company. But let me do all the talking. Don't say anything...about *anything*! Just stand there silently and...*prognosticate,* or whatever you call it."

"Thanks, June!" She claps and smiles like a kid

who's just won a carnival prize.

I immediately call Annuska back and say, "Annuska, I was just wondering if there's some way I can help? I know this must be a very difficult time for you. May I come over to your house at around noon, maybe we can talk a while?"

"I do not mind this. Thank you, I would like company. I have no family here, neither does my Melvin."

After further lame assurances on my part, I end the call and manage to gently convince Faith to get out of my cube and back to work.

At eleven-thirty on the nose, Faith appears in my cube again, anxious to go on our mission. I stand up and search frantically for my car keys. They aren't in my purse, my briefcase, or in any of my pockets, and for one tiny, brain fart of a moment, I actually consider asking Faith if she can pull up a vision of where my keys are.

I must be losing my mind.

But then I spot the keys on the floor under my desk, and we are off. As we walk to my car, I mull over my mental *to-do* list for the day: *Take boys to soccer game, pick up ground meat for dinner, work on first-quarter consumable materials forecast*, and the newest item, just added: *Look for Melvin's dead body in car trunk.*

****

As we drive to meet with Annuska, Faith starts to chat about Melvin.

"Just so you know June, ah don't think that Melvin was all that happy in his marriage. After he had two drinks at the conference, he slipped and told me his wife was a witch."

"A witch, huh? Well, that's really none of our

business, is it? So, when you see Annuska, don't breathe a word about *anything* that Melvin said about her, okay? This is not the time to be bringing that up."

"Oh, June, don't worry. Of course, ah won't mention it," she says, swatting away my worries. "But Ah'm just sayin', if their marriage is bad, it increases the chances that she smacked him on the head with a lead pipe."

"There you go again with the lead pipe. Just forget about the pipe, okay? We're just going there today to comfort and console. I want you to look sad, not suspicious. Can you do sad for me?"

"Oh, June, come on, of course. Ah'll look sadder'n a tick on a rattler that's sheddin' his skin."

"Wonderful." I decide to change the subject. "So…how are things going with Ralph?"

Ralph is Faith's new boyfriend, a shy accountant whom I've never met. I'm a little curious about him because success with the opposite sex doesn't seem to be in Faith's destiny. I've heard through Mary that Faith, no big surprise, has had a rather "rocky" romantic life, although I think *train wreck* is a more fitting term. A couple of boyfriends supposedly croaked on her. It wasn't during sex. I think Mary said that one had been eaten by a shark, another one was hit by a meteorite and vaporized. And I think a third one croaked after eating some bad egg salad, or something like that. Sounds about right for Faith.

"Oh, Ralph's all right, June." She doesn't sound too enthused. "Fun to be with, but ah don't know if we're really well suited for one another. We're no Charles and Diana, that's for sure."

"Uh, they weren't really well suited for each other."

"Right, that's what I'm sayin', we're like them in some ways but not others."

"What ways?"

"Well, don't be silly. Neither of us is British, of course, for one thing. And ah don't have blonde hair, for a second thing."

I shake my head. "Uhhh…sure, why didn't I think of that?"

We pull up in front of Annuska and Melvin's house on the northern outskirts of New Haven. It's a tiny, run-down ranch in a treeless neighborhood of other run-down houses in a mishmash of awkward styles. There is no garage or even a driveway, so I park in the street, and we walk to the front door along an ancient walkway, a narrow strip of badly crumbled concrete that long ago surrendered to the weeds that now consume it. The tiny front lawn is an almost unbroken field of spring dandelions. The house's peeling paint is a garish canary yellow that reflects enough sunlight to burn your retinas. The crumbly brown remnants of two tall shrubs, long dead from neglect, flank the front doorstep like ancient sentries. I knock on a screen door that has no screen except for a few rusted bits of metal clinging to a rotting wooden frame.

I find myself wondering what Melvin must be doing with his money. He should be able to afford to live in a better place than this. Fleener certainly doesn't pay top dollar, but his wage is at least decent.

"June, that car parked out front at the curb, we gotta check it out," Faith whispers to me as we stand waiting. It's a banged up, red sedan at least twenty years old, puckered with rust spots.

"Faith, calm down, we can't just go poking around

their cars. Let's talk to Annuska before we do anything."

An elderly woman in a pink tattered bathrobe and matching slippers answers the door. She is perhaps seventy-five years old, and a little over five feet tall, with a thin, wiry frame. She has a crocodile complexion— deeply wrinkled and leathery. Her short grayish orange hair reminds me of a used scouring pad, misshapen and left rusting on the sink top. A few hair tufts are wound like baling twine around one enormous plastic curler in the front, just above the assortment of multi-hued liver spots on her brow. There's a cigarette dangling from her lips, a cheap plastic lighter in her hand, and a nasty scowl on her mug.

"I ain't buyin' it, whatever it is," she begins immediately. "Got no money. My asswipe of a tenant took off with it." The bright red tip of her cigarette bobs up and down as she speaks, and a bit of gray ash flutters to the floor as she finishes each sentence.

"Uh, we're not here to sell anything," I answer.

"You don't sound too sure about that, missy," she says to me.

"We're very sure," I say.

"Then whad'ya want? You preachin' some religion? You can forget that, 'cause I'm way beyond redemption."

"We're here to see Annuska Hamm. I'm June Bloom, Melvin's manager at Fleener Plastics. And this is his co-worker, Faith Gelner. Uh, are we at the right house? Is this Melvin and Annuska's house?"

The woman coughs for a few seconds, the deep, hoarse hacking of a lifelong smoker. It sounds like something is loose and rattling around inside her. She answers, "It's *my* house. Melvin and his wife rent this place from me. I live in the basement. But you're outta luck, she ain't home. Neither is Melvin."

"Annuska told me on the phone that Melvin was missing."

"Missing? Yeah, right, he's either run off or he's dead. Either way, yeah, I'd sure call that missing. He's nine days overdue on this month's rent, which I don't expect to see very soon, if at all. Whad'ya want with Melvin, honey?"

"Well, we're just concerned about him," I answer.

Faith interrupts, "And we're concerned about his cars, too. Is that Melvin's car out there parked by the curb? Ah know he doesn't drive that car to work, but is that their second car?" She points to the old red sedan.

The woman gives us a puzzled grimace. "Yeah, Annuska drives that one. It's a real clunker, isn't it? Guess you don't pay him enough to be able to have two decent cars." She looks at me as if it's my fault that Melvin is late with the rent.

"Well…do you know where Annuska went?" I ask.

"Nope. I try to mind my own business. Since her car's here, maybe she went to stretch her legs. She walks and hikes a lot, for exercise, and I guess to de-stress." With a sarcastic smirk she continues, "I guess she needed a de-stressing today, on account of her missing honey-pie."

"And are there any *other* cars?" Faith asks anxiously. "If that's Annuska's car, where's *your* car?"

"*My* car? So nice of you to be concerned about *my* car, sweetie. You see that used Japanese piece o' shit the size of a shoebox that's parked out in the street? Well, that's what I'm drivin' now, ever since I lost the beauty I had for twenty-six years. It was a big ass hunk of solid

Detroit iron. Built like a blast furnace, not like these foreign featherweight things that're made outta tinfoil and toilet paper. But the insurance company only gave me a couple hundred bucks to replace it. That was the full blue book value, they said. Can you believe that? The shoebox out there was all I could afford."

"Oh, my. You totaled your big car?" Faith asks.

"Not really. I drove it into Balmville Lake."

With an innocent expression, Faith asks, "On purpose?"

The old woman barks, "No, not on purpose, you little southern fried twit! Do I look like a moron? It was a *mechanical* failure! Even my Detroit beauty had an occasional problem here and there. But the insurance guy had some stupid ass idea that I hit the gas when I was tryin' to hit the brake, and they jacked up my insurance rates after they cut me the check. That's prejudice against senior citizens, *I* say, and—"

"I see, well this is all quite interesting," I say, interrupting the pointless conversation. "But do you have any idea when Annuska will return if she took a walk? I talked to her on the phone a little while ago, and I thought she'd be here…"

But then Faith cuts me off to ask the woman, "Well then, are there any *more* cars that are normally parked here?"

"Ooh, ya know, toots, sometimes I forget that I'm the official person in the neighborhood who's in charge of keeping track of all the cars. Yeah, and they even gave me a whistle and a cap when they appointed me to the job." She takes a long, deep drag on the cigarette, and adds, "It's a free country, any asshole can park in the street." She looks at me and says, "So you're Melvin's boss? You actually hired that wingnut?" She chuckles and shakes her head. "What's that say about *you*?"

Still facing the woman, I notice movement at the corner of my vision, and I turn to see Faith headed toward Annuska's car. She's walking fast, already halfway there.

"Faith, wait," I shout. "Wait!" My order doesn't even slow her. I turn to the woman and say, "Uh, please excuse Faith, she's a little, uh…upset…and…uh…I'll be right back."

I take off after Faith. By now she's already reached the car and stands behind it, her finger on the place where the trunk key is inserted, her eyes open wide in astonishment. I catch up to her as she raises her hand to her face and remarks in a startled tone, "June, oh my Lordy Lord, this surely looks like blood!"

I see the red spot on the keyhole and the matching stain on Faith's index finger. It sure looks like blood to me too, but even so, I say, "Okay, calm down Faith, maybe it's not blood, and even if it is…"

Faith quickly moves up to look inside the car windows, and my eyes follow hers. But there's nothing much to see. The interior is empty except for burn marks, coffee stains, a nice assortment of food crumbs, and some finger or toe-nail clippings on the dingy seats and carpets.

Despite my uneasiness about Faith finding what might be blood, I am determined to remain calm and in charge. "Okay, let's call the police," I say with authority. "We shouldn't touch anything else or try to open the trunk ourselves." I turn toward Melvin's house, thinking that we should tell the elderly woman that the police will be coming. Then I hear two clicks, and I spin around and see that it's too late, because Faith has opened the unlocked car door, and popped the trunk latch. The trunk lid is now open a few inches.

"We might as well look," Faith says innocently, as if the trunk had magically popped open by itself and invited us to peek inside. For all I know, this might be a crime scene, and Faith has already touched the trunk keyhole, the door handle, and the trunk release lever inside the car. Not good.

I say to her, "Faith, wait, don't touch…"

Too late again, because by the time I had gotten the *don't* out of my mouth, Faith has her hands on the trunk lid and is pulling it up. I see her eyes widen; her anxious stare is directed at the expanding trunk opening.

Then Faith lets out a nice healthy scream.

And of course, I scream too, just as a reaction to Faith screaming, and then Faith screams again when she hears *me* scream, and for a few seconds we have a good tag team screaming thing going. I'm still standing by the driver's side window, my feet frozen in place, when I finally shut my mouth and just stare at Faith, waiting for her to describe to me the horrible scene inside the trunk—what I assume must be Melvin's bloody, mangled, rotting, dirty, smelly body. My heart is thumping so hard I can see my bug brooch jumping off my chest with every beat, the ugly silver dragonfly with the red eyes that my youngest son gave me for Mother's Day and which I feel obligated to wear every few weeks.

Faith stares back at me, still wide-eyed, and asks, "June, what is it, why'd you scream?"

"Whad'ya mean, why'd I scream? I screamed because *you* screamed. You scared the crap outta me. Oh, dear God, is it…is Melvin in there?"

"No, no, it's empty, but ah sure expected him to be in there, because ah saw him in a car trunk in my vision, and ah'm never wrong, and this has gotta be his blood, right? So ah just kinda screamed in anticipation, ah was so sure. He *must* have been in here, June, at one time, and then they must've taken his body out and stashed it somewhere, that's gotta be it!"

A surge of relief hits me as I realize that I won't have to look at a dead body. I grab Faith's arm and walk her quickly back to the house. She wants to examine the car more closely and so she goes grudgingly, like a kid being dragged from a toy store window.

The old woman meets us at the door. She is casually lighting a new cigarette, using the butt of the one she had just finished down to the filter.

She looks up at us and says, "Seen a ghost, ladies?"

I reply in a slightly shaky voice, "There's blood. I mean, there's some red stuff on the outside of the trunk. It *might* be blood. Faith thinks that…well, maybe it's Melvin's blood. We need to call the police. I guess there's a chance…"

"Blood?" asks the old woman with surprise. "What are you gals sayin'? You looked in the trunk, so was his dead body in there or not? 'Cause if it was, don't sweat it, he had it comin'. And if he was in there, did you check his pockets for my rent money?"

"What?! No, no!" I bark. "There was no body, but we need to call the police to have them look at the blood. That car might be a crime scene. And what did you mean by, 'He had it coming?'"

"Oh, nuthin, nuthin, don't grow a hemorrhoid, toots. Probably nobody would want to kill that moron, anyway, 'cause he had pretty much nothin' going for him. I'm just sayin', survival of the fittest and all that. That dipshit was at the bottom of the evolutionary ladder. It was just a matter of time before life ate him up and shit him out like a turd on the sidewalk."

Faith looks appalled. "My Lord, how can you talk about Melvin like that?" she protests.

I raise my hands to separate the two of them, and say, "Look, we're talking about him like he's dead, and we don't know that for sure. Let's slow down and take this one step at a time."

"But ah *know* it, June, ah *saw* him!" Faith wails.

And then the old woman pipes in, "I thought you just said you didn't see his body in the trunk, sweetie. So, did ya or didn't ya?"

"Well, ah didn't see him in there just now," Faith explains. "But ah had a vision earlier today, so ah'm sure he was in there at one time, and then someone must have removed the body."

The old woman rolls her eyes and belches a stream of tobacco smoke from a single nostril like a factory smokestack. "Oh, I see, you got super-powers, honey, is that it? You can see things? Travel through time? Got x-ray vision too, maybe? Well, can you see where my rent money is?"

"We need to call the police," I say. "And then we need to wait here until Annuska comes home, to console her about her missing husband."

"Console her?" the old woman replies. "Yeah, right. That Romanian she-devil's probably the one that popped him."

Chapter 3

I dial the police on my cell and speak to the dispatcher, explaining the situation. I'm instructed to keep everyone in the house until an officer arrives.

The decor in the living room where we wait is a cross between trailer park chic and mid-century Salvation Army, but at least everything matches. The coffee spills on the grimy tan couch match the ones on the carpet. The two end tables have matching water ring stains. The coffee table is one of those naked lady things where she's on her hands and knees balancing an oval of plate glass on her back, with her Brobdingnagian bosom almost touching the floor, and her bare ass appropriately pointed at people entering the front door. Over the naked lady is some kind of hideous hanging light fixture, made from what look like deer feet or hooves or whatever you call them. The walls are covered with cheesy landscapes in garish colors painted on old hand saws and washboards.

Faith excuses herself to use the bathroom. I stand awkwardly in the middle of the living room, while the woman leans against a wall, eyeing me suspiciously while still puffing away.

"Well, you might as well take a load off, toots," she says with some wariness in her tone. "This is Melvin and Annuska's living room, but it's got all my treasures that I've collected over the years. Pretty sweet, huh?"

I nod and smile politely, wondering if I should sit on the lumpy furniture and trying to think of something nice to ask about the decor…like maybe whether she killed the deer for the ugly hanging lamp with her big-ass hunk of Detroit iron car. But thankfully, Faith emerges from the bathroom and starts jabbering. We soon learn that the woman's name is Florence Schmoo.

"Florence is such a beautiful name," says Faith with her southern charm. "Your Momma and Daddy named you after the town in Italy, is that right? Ah hear it's such a lovely place, have you been there?"

"There's a town in Italy called Florence? They named me after a pet."

"Ahh, that's so sweet," Faith replies. "A beloved dog, or was it a cat? In either case, man's best friend, surely. Pets can become so close to you, it's like they become part of you, don't you agree? Why, when ah was a little girl in Tennessee, ah had me a special golden retriever that—"

"It was a cockatoo," Florence interrupts. "God, I hated that damn bird. I ended up killin' and cookin' it one day. I guess you could say it became part of me."

"Why that's just awful!" Faith cringes.

"Nah, it wasn't bad," replies Florence with a wave of the hand that isn't occupied with the cigarette.

Faith abandons further attempts at small talk and gets back to the business of finding out what happened to Melvin. "So, you live in this house with Melvin and Annuska?" she asks.

"Yeah, I live downstairs, toots. In the basement, I got my own whole luxury suite down there. A combination palace and bomb shelter."

"Ah see, well that sounds real cozy," remarks Faith.

"Now, are you sure no one uses the car out there other than Annuska?"

Florence shakes her head with weariness. "Still obsessed with the cars, honey? All I know is that it's Annuska's car. Maybe she lends it sometimes. Like maybe to that guy out there."

"What guy?" I ask.

"That guy right there by the car now." Florence points with the cigarette. "That ugly guy who's by Annuska's car now."

"There's a guy…?"

I look out the same window and catch a glimpse of a thin elderly man with wild gray hair. The car is pointed toward the street, and he is leaning against the frame of the open driver's side window, trying to push it. In a few seconds the car starts to slowly roll down the driveway. His grimy jeans are hanging down in the back, and with every step he takes, they fall a little further, exposing the crack of his ass.

"Uhh…do you know him?" I ask with concern.

"Nope," says Florence, as she casually lights another cigarette. "Do you?"

"No, of course not. But don't you…I mean, aren't you going to do something? It looks like he's stealing Annuska's car!"

Florence shrugs her shoulders in a *who gives a shit* manner, and says, "Yeah, well this is a pretty lousy neighborhood, you know? Good thing I got the theft coverage on *my* little piece o' shit car."

Faith and I run outside just as the old man jumps into the driver's seat of the car and slams the door closed.

"C'mon, June, let's git him!" Faith screams, and she takes off after the guy like a bullet.

"Faith, wait, no!" I scream back, but it's too late, there is no stopping her, so I bolt after her. The engine starts with a belch and a few hard bangs. It slowly accelerates and we run after it like idiots. For what reason, I'm not sure, but there we are, in a chase scene like two cheesy television detectives.

And just like on TV, we both yell, "Hey, you, come back here!" Did I really expect the guy, who was stealing this car, to hit the brakes and say, *Who, me? Oh, okay, I'll stop and turn around, no problem.* I suppose not, but we were running like hell, and it seemed like a waste not to shout something, and *hey you, come back here* fit the bill just fine.

And so, we run and run, Faith and I, women on a mission, at full speed or pretty close to it. Faith has me on age, seeing as she's about fifteen years younger, but I'm quite surprised at how adrenaline can make up for the age thing, and I almost keep up with her. And even though I'm hauling around an excess ten pounds and I'm horribly out of shape, I think: *Hey, not too shabby, this is a sustained burst of speed, and I haven't stroked out yet.*

And then an amazing thing happens: The car stops. *Well, maybe I really do have a commanding voice...*

But then I quickly realize that the car stopped only because it came to the end of a cul-de-sac. It then makes a U-turn and comes barreling down the road right back at us, and of course we do a U-turn too and run like hell, even faster than before, faster than I would have imagined possible for me, but it's probably because in addition to the adrenaline, the *scared shitless* motivational factor has fully kicked in now, and it's truly amazing what that can do for your running abilities. Even so, my heart is racing like a fruit fly's and my calves are burning so badly I expect to blow out one of my varicose veins down there any second.

The terrain beside the road drops off quickly behind the guardrail, and I'm thinking about whether I could hop it or not, and whether the guy would seriously try to run us over or whether he just wants to scare the crap out of us. But now he's close behind us, or rather behind *me* because Faith is running ahead of me, and I'm not going to wait any longer to find out.

"Faith, jump!" I yell, and then she and I hop up onto the guardrail with our right feet and launch ourselves over it, our arms spread like two deranged flying squirrels as the car passes by in a cloud of gray dust. We both hit the ground hard and barrel-roll downhill, and the first casualties are my knee-high stockings, which I can feel being shredded around my ankles. And then something, maybe a plant root, catches my pants on the side, and I feel them tear as I cartwheel like a tumbleweed, alternately seeing blue sky and green grass. As I slow, I see one of my shoes fly by my face, doing its own strange pirouette as it spins down the hill beyond the point where I finally come to rest.

"Oh, my Lordy Lord, June, are you alright?" Faith asks, her young voice filled with fear and doubt that the brittle old bones of a forty-year-old woman can survive such an ordeal without snapping like dry twigs.

I actually don't know if I am alright. Still shaking with fear and exertion, I look down at my legs, expecting the worst, like maybe a broken bone sticking through my pants or a knee twisted at an impossible angle, and perhaps I'm not feeling the pain of it because I'm in shock, or maybe my spinal cord is fractured and the pain signals to my brain are now and forever disrupted. But after a few seconds of inspecting my body, I'm pleased to see that my legs are straight and my clothes are on, ripped at the seams, but nonetheless still on, and the rips are down the sides of my pants, exposing both legs, but fortunately not my butt. The fact that I'm not laying there bare-ass on this suburban lawn strangely gives me a tiny boost of self-confidence. I pick myself up and successfully move all of my extremities to verify that nothing is broken, so maybe those geriatric calcium pills I'm taking have somehow paid off. I begin brushing myself off, and Faith does the same.

"I'll live," I say. "How about you, anything broken?"

"No. Ah lost a bracelet, but other than that, ah'm fine."

The car is long gone, and the only evidence of its passage is the rapidly dispersing trail of billowy road dust.

We hobble back to the house, humbled and defeated. Florence greets us at the front door with a smug look on her face, and we all walk inside.

Florence asks, "So, did you catch the car? Did you catch it and hold onto it like Superman? Is that what you were trying to do there, ladies?"

I am still huffing a bit, and unfortunately a thick, soupy fog bank of grayish-blue cigarette smoke hangs near the ceiling of the small living room. Breathing in here is like sucking the tailpipe of an eighteen-wheeler.

A glum response comes from Faith, "No, we didn't catch it."

"Oh, well, then you must have got a real clear look at the guy's face, huh? Any identifying marks on it?"

It's my turn. I mutter, "Well, no, we didn't really see his face too well, there was a lot of dust, and…"

"We only saw him from the back, really," Faith adds. "Ah saw his gray hair, and…oh, his behind was exposed because his pants kinda slipped down."

"Oh, that's excellent, so you got a good look at his ass. Can you describe it?" Florence asks.

"Oh, yes, certainly," says Faith in a serious tone. "It was white and saggy. I might even go so far as to call it flaccid."

Florence claps her hands together and says, "Okay, fantastic ladies, so, assuming that you can pick his ass out of a police lineup, and that's assuming they can find five other old guys with saggy white asses to join the lineup, then it sounds like your chase was well worth it. Good job."

Florence puts her hand out to give a congratulatory shake to Faith, who actually begins to raise her hand to shake with Florence until I slap at Faith's hand and blurt out, "This is not helping!"

Florence says, "Awe, that car was beggin' to be boosted. It's an old piece o' shit with door locks that don't work no more, and the key's broken off in the ignition."

Just then I hear a car pull up to the curb in front of the house. I look out the window and catch a view of a woman with dark hair stepping out of the passenger door of a small black sedan. The driver is a man, also with dark hair, who remains in the car. As she walks toward the house, the car pulls away.

Florence is apparently looking too, because from behind me I hear her say, "Oh great. Here comes *Mrs. Freeloader*."

A woman who I assume must be Annuska opens the screen door and enters, eyeing each of us. She's about five foot three, probably in her mid-thirties, olive-skinned, with high cheekbones and plenty of dark eye makeup that compliments her shoulder-length black hair. She wears a simple, form-fitting, knee-length black dress. Annuska is shapely, and she obviously takes care of herself. She has piercing, black eyes that are also a bit reddish at the moment, possibly from crying. I'd call her face a beautiful one, but at the same time it's somehow a little scary if that's possible. I catch a whiff of perfume which seems to have both a flowery note, evoking the image of a sexy temptress, and a musky note which makes me think of an aggressive female animal, perhaps a wolverine or mink, cornered and ready to fight. Her fingernails are long and painted a glossy black. They're perfectly shaped for scratching out someone's eyes.

"I am Annuska," she announces solemnly in her husky and heavily accented voice. She examines Faith and me, and then gives Florence a special little sneer. I'm guessing that their relationship is not high on the warm and fuzzy scale. She continues, "And I see there is a gathering in my house."

"You mean there's a gathering in *my* house," corrects Florence.

"I'm June, and this is Faith Gelner, one of Melvin's co-workers. I'm so pleased to meet you, I just wish that it were under happier circumstances." I hesitate, unsure how to proceed. It appears that it will be my unpleasant task to first tell her about her stolen car before we get into Melvin's situation. I think I'd better completely skip the part about the blood on the trunk keyhole.

"Annuska…your car…it seems that it's been stolen.

We saw someone, an elderly man, drive it away. We're waiting for the police."

"Yes, I see that my car is not where I leave it. But I cannot think of my car now because my dear husband Melvin, he is gone. I am missing my husband and now I am missing my car. Too much sorrow for one short time." She raises her hands to her face and shakes her head slowly as if she cannot believe her bad fortune.

Florence pipes in between puffs, "Oh yeah, lots o' sorrow."

Out of the corner of my eye I see Faith begin to open her mouth to speak. I immediately shoot her a stern look, and her mouth mercifully closes.

I continue in a gentle tone. "Annuska…about Melvin…"

"Yes, I cry to think of my Melvin alone somewhere, maybe lost, maybe wounded, maybe hungry."

"Or maybe relieved that you're outta his hair," mumbles Florence. I'm not sure if Annuska heard the comment, but she didn't react.

"I fear for my Melvin," Annuska says. "I sense with my Wiccan powers that my Melvin is in such trouble."

"Huh? You have…uhhh…powers?" I ask her.

"Yes. I am a witch. But Wiccan is actually proper term. I am bonded with nature. I *see* things."

I think, *So now we have* two *people in here with powers? Lots of psychic energy shooting around the room, for sure.*

"Oh, my Lord," Faith says. "It's so warm in here, and the smoke. I *do* have to sit down." Faith fans herself with one hand and moves to the greasy couch. The thing looks like it was made before World War II. She sits down in the center of one of the cushions. The stuffing is completely shot because she sinks down about two feet, and the cushion makes a huge V around her ass, almost blocking her peripheral vision.

"You work with my Melvin?" Annuska asks Faith.

Faith answers, "Well, as a matter of fact…"

I burst in to change the subject, afraid that Faith might discuss her vision. "I'm so sorry that he's missing, Annuska. Melvin was, I mean *is*…a fine man."

"Oh yeah, such a *very* fine man," Florence says with her sarcastic grin. This time Annuska apparently *did* hear the remark because she directs a piercing glare in Florence's direction. Maybe the Romanian evil eye.

And then we all sit down and wait for the cops. And wait. And wait more. We don't have much to talk about since I very quickly use up all the good things I have to say about Melvin, which admittedly aren't many because I really don't know him all that well, and outside of work I don't know him at all. I don't want to heap too much praise on him, for fear of sounding like a complete faker, but I've probably already busted through that barrier. And I just don't feel right about giving any more assurances to Annuska that Melvin is fine when Faith is over there convinced he's dead.

While we wait, Annuska makes some kind of traditional Romanian herbal tea which she says is supposed to have a calming effect, and Faith and I sip it politely even though it tastes like dishwater spiked with Drano. Florence declines the tea, with some mumbled comment about how she doesn't need another case of the runs.

We talk a little about the weather, and we all happily agree that it's rather warm now, but it won't stay warm forever, and it probably won't cool down much before it gets warm again, but it will most definitely get warm again. Everyone joins in the weather talk except for Florence, who puffs away, and she seems all the time to be sizing up Faith and me.

It's stifling in the small, smoky living room. I feel like I'm trying to breathe with my head inside a plastic bag. We watch the sweat beads form on each other's noses. Florence eventually leaves the room, saying that it's time to take the waste basket-sized curler out of her hair, and then finally, mercifully, there's a rap on the living room door and an officer immediately opens it and enters.

He wears a gray uniform and a black tie. A silver badge is pinned onto the lapel of his shirt pocket, and around his waist is an impressive black leather belt with a gun in a holster and lots of leather pockets, like a superhero's utility belt. But unlike your typical masked crimefighter, this guy is pudgy. He has a face as round as a melon, a thin mustache, and his utility belt is way too tight. The man's spongy stomach spills over it like a waterfall of pudding. He looks to be in his mid-thirties, and he quickly introduces himself as Special Agent Filbert.

"I'm the one who called. We've been waiting for you," I say to the officer. "Unfortunately, he's long gone."

"*Who's* gone?" he asks.

"The guy who stole the car with the blood on it," I explain.

"What car? What blood?"

"Annuska's car." I point to her. "It was outside. Someone stole it. It had some blood on the trunk. Or at least, it *looked* like blood. We chased the car, Faith and

43

I."

"I'd better take notes," he says decisively, pulling out a small pad and a pen. Turning to Annuska, he asks her, "And Madam, your full name is…?"

"Annuska Hamm," she answers in her throaty timbre.

"And Ms. Hamm, where are you from?" he continues.

"I am originally from Transylvania, but I become American citizen from marrying my husband."

"Transylvania?" he asks. "That's where vampires come from, isn't it? I thought it was a fictional place."

"No, it is quite real, but sadly, it has become part of Romania. So now I am Romanian citizen. But also American citizen."

"I see, and…" Filbert stops to answer a ringing cellphone which he pulls out of his utility belt.

"Listen chief, I got my hands full," Filbert says. "We got a stolen car here. We got a possible murder, we got blood, and maybe vampires. I'll check in later, ten-four." He tucks the phone back into his belt.

I'm beginning to see why this guy is named after a tree nut. I say to Filbert, "There are no vampires here, officer. And…"

"Officer?" he interrupts. "I'm not a police officer, if that's what you mean. I'm an exterminator."

"Ohhhh, an *exterminator*," Faith ponders. "Is that some special elite branch of the police, like a highly trained SWAT team of some sort, so you don't really consider yourself a regular cop?"

"No, I go after bugs," he says.

Faith continues, "You mean those miniature electronic listening devices? You're specially trained in locating them?"

"No, I mean bugs. *Real* bugs," he says.

"But you have a gun in your utility belt," I say.

"It's a squirt gun. It has insecticide in it."

"But you were talking to the chief of police on the radio," I note.

"No, I was talking to the dispatcher at the company I work for, *Don't Bug Me.*"

"Your dispatcher? You said you were an *agent*. 'Special Agent Filbert,' you said."

"An *Extermination* Agent. It's my official title. My boss says I'm special."

"And why are you taking notes?" I ask.

"Well, ma'am, we see a lot of strange stuff in this business, and I hope to write my memoirs someday."

So, the world is full of waiters who want to be actors. Why not an exterminator who wants to be a writer?

"See, there's my van outside," Filbert says. He points toward the living room window. There's a white van parked out front with a huge red plastic ant on top. Its bulging eyes are flashing a menacing green. On the side of the van in large orange letters is the company's name and a toll-free phone number.

"Pretty cool, huh?" Filbert says proudly. "The big plastic ant, that cost quite a bit. But it really drums up business! Looks pretty menacing, an ant that size, huh? It totally turns heads!"

Filbert is grinning proudly. Maybe he thinks the van is a powerful chick magnet. I take a few steps toward him and peer at the shiny silver badge pinned to his lapel. Sure enough, in tiny letters it reads:

Filbert Crumm, Extermination Agent
Don't Bug Me

"Who called you?" I ask him.

Just then, Florence enters the room and says, "*I* did. I called him over to de-louse the whole place. Can't seem to get the little buggers completely out of the furniture." Florence turns toward Filbert and bellows, "This is your last chance, Crumm. I ain't payin' you anymore for shoddy work." She takes a long, hard drag on her cigarette, and it decreases in length by about an inch.

I stand up from the chair I'm sitting in and involuntarily begin to scratch at my torso.

Chapter 4

About two hours later, after the police have finished interviewing us, Faith and I are getting into my car for the drive back to work. I ask her, "So…what did you tell the cops about why we went to Melvin's house?"

"Ah did not tell them ah had a vision that he was dead, if that's what you mean. Ah find that most people don't have a positive reaction if ah reveal my clairvoyin' powers to them. So, ah just told 'em that ah tagged along with you for moral support and then we saw some blood on the car trunk lid and opened it, but saw nuthin' in there. What did *you* tell 'em, June?"

"That we went to console Annuska because her husband, my employee, was missing. I didn't tell them about the vision you had either. Somehow, I thought it would…well, you know…muddy the waters a bit?" I give Faith a tepid smile.

We buzz down interstate ninety-five in heavy traffic, the billboards and neon signs bombarding us with a deluge of words and pictures that I'm much too numb to absorb. My muscles are aching from the run and the somersault down the hill, and I'm dazed by jumbled thoughts of what might have been Melvin's blood on the trunk lid, the police interrogation, and also by the exhaust fumes that I'm now inhaling since we're boxed in between two eighteen-wheelers.

The questioning started as soon as the real police,

two uniformed officers, arrived at Melvin's house. We told our stories in detail several times, and they even split us up for the questioning, I suppose to be certain that we wouldn't be influenced by each other's recounting of the details. Even though we might have screwed around with evidence as far as the blood on the trunk, we weren't charged with anything yet except aggravated stupidity, probably because the evidence had disappeared. Our whole story was certainly bizarre by any standard. Judging by the expressions on their faces as we answered their questions, the officers probably thought we were just a couple of morons.

They couldn't deny the fact, however, that someone had stolen Annuska's car. Faith and I could give only an extremely vague description of the guy who took it. Neither of us would be able to pick him out of a lineup if they eventually caught him, even if they *were* able to find five other saggy ass volunteers to stand next to him. And neither of us had the presence of mind to take pictures or video of anything with our phones—not the blood or the car thief. The only surviving pieces of evidence of the wild chase were my torn stockings, ripped pants, and a few scratches on our legs. But the police took from Faith's hand a sample of the blood from the car trunk lid, since she had the sense not to wash it off, and they were going to submit it for DNA analysis. For reference, they also took a tissue scraping from the inside of Faith's cheek, and some hair follicles belonging to Melvin which they found on a comb in his bathroom. The cops also questioned Florence, Annuska, and even Filbert the exterminator. The only one who looked enthused by the whole police ordeal was Filbert, who promptly volunteered to discretely cruise the streets of Melvin's neighborhood in his inconspicuous exterminator van with the enormous red ant on top, looking for Annuska's car. But the cops explicitly warned him to put that idea out of his head.

The cops also suggested we not leave the country for the time being. Not a problem, I told them. Darryl and I don't have the money to be zipping around the globe, and Fleener Plastics has never sent me on business travel farther than Scranton, Pennsylvania. And now the company is on an austerity budget with no end in sight, which means that pretty much all travel and perks are cut out, except for executive bonuses of course. At the moment I don't have enough money in our department budget to buy a friggin' box of donuts for a meeting.

I feel bad about leaving Annuska in her current state of grief, without even a car to get around in. Before we left, I asked her if her insurance would cover the cost of a rental for a while, but she shook her head and said she'd manage. Then a few minutes later, when we were out of Annuska's earshot, Florence mumbled to me with a smirk on her face that the guy who dropped her off was her boss, and he'd be her personal chauffeur for the time being, and would probably meet all her other personal needs as well.

I say to Faith, "So, that technician guy who took your DNA, I saw he was flirting with you. Didn't see how you responded though. Your back was toward me."

She sighs and says, "Yes, he wanted my phone number. Goodness, you'd think they'd be more professional."

"You'd think."

"Ah didn't give it to him, of course, because Ah'm seeing Ralph."

"Of course. I guess men hit on you a lot, huh?"

"Yes, unfortunately. It can be so annoying, you know? Ah envy you in that regard, June."

"You do?" I ask with zero enthusiasm. "Gee, I guess I'm just so…lucky."

She raises her hands, looks at me with alarm, and blurts out, "Oh my goodness, June, ah surely didn't mean that the way it sounded! Ah meant that you're wearin' that wedding ring all the time, so men know you're taken. If you didn't have that ring, why they'd be buzzin' around you like flies on a pile o' pig shit. You're attractive, smart, and you are in *darn* good shape. Why, you went glidin' over that guardrail like a buzzard over a dead heifer."

"Uh…I don't remember much about the gliding like a buzzard part. But I do recall the dropping like a sack o' sand part."

"Well, you should give yourself more credit. And you did a very fine tuck and roll when you hit the grass."

"I didn't die or even break my neck, so I guess life is good. So, Faith, can I ask you…how long have you had visions?"

"Oh, all my life," she wails. "The earliest ah can remember was when ah was a little girl, maybe six years old. My sister lost her favorite doll, and ah could see in my mind where the doll was layin' on the ground out behind the house. Then when ah was twelve, a neighborhood kid was lost. When ah touched his baseball glove, ah could see him in the woods. He'd wandered into a nature preserve. So, ah told my parents. They were skeptical of course, but there were a lot of people lookin' for this kid. My parents went where ah told 'em, and they found the kid."

"Did it get you any public attention?"

"No, what it got me was a whole lotta trouble. The cops thought ah must have brought the little boy in there and left him, maybe so ah could find him and be a hero, or somethin' like that. My parents went through a lot to get me out of that trouble. They seemed to believe ah had some special ability, but it made them very scared. After that, they told me not to talk about any visions to anyone, ever again. But overall, the visions are more troublesome than they are useful. Why, ah remember in college my roommate's computer was stolen, and ah got a vision of where it was, in another dorm room. So, my roommate marched over there and got in one hell of a cat fight with some other students. She had to get herself stitched up and never did get her computer back. After that, ah swore ah'd just try to ignore all my visions. But ah just couldn't ignore this one of poor Melvin."

"Hmmm…did you ever get tested? I mean, some kind of testing by a scientist who studies extra-sensory perception. I'm sure there are university programs that dabble in that stuff."

"Oh, my goodness, no. My parents would never have allowed it when ah was young. And when ah got older, ah never even considered gettin' tested anyway, 'cause ah knew it would be pointless. If somebody held up a playin' card with the back facin' me and asked me what card it was, why that'd *never* work, and they'd just say ah was a fraud. Ah can't *control* what ah see. Stuff sometimes just pops into my head when ah touch things. Visions that have something to do with someone ah know."

We barrel along the bumpy interstate highway. After a few more minutes of silence, Faith turns to me and asks, "June, when you were a child, did you aspire to be a manager at a company like Fleener where they make extruded and injection molded vinyl and plastic products? Was it your *dream*?"

I look at Faith like she's out of her mind. Who could possibly say that they're living their dream by working at Fleener Plastics? But instead of giving her a *you gotta be kidding* line filled with contempt for the crappy company we work for, I decide to skip the commentary on my current job and describe my aspirations to her.

"I wanted to be a reporter," I say. "Do you remember Brenda Starr, ace reporter?"

She gives me a blank look at first, and then says, "Is she the one that used to do the financial news on cable?"

"No. You're too young to remember, I guess. She was a comic strip character, a newspaper reporter. She got into all kinds of scrapes and faced all kinds of dangers and bad guys, and in the end, she always escaped and helped capture the bad guys, and everything turned out all right. Oh, and she loved some dude with an eyepatch. I can't remember his name."

"Well, that sounds like somethin' you'd surely be good at, June. Did you ever try it? Ah mean the reporter part, not the lovin' the dude with the eyepatch part."

"I did. It was my very first job after college. I was a reporter for the Buxton City Sentinel."

"Wow, how exciting! So, you became an ace reporter?"

"No, far from it. I was the youngest reporter, and the only female one. I did a lot of fluff stories, the same stupid things over and over. The night before a big snowstorm was coming, I'd interview the guys who drive the salt trucks and plows. On the hottest day of the summer, they'd send me out with a cameraman to see if I could fry an egg on the sidewalk. I'd go to Buxton City Hospital on January first to interview the parents of the first baby born in the new year. I'd interview the teenage girl that was crowned Queen Butternut at the annual squash festival. And when it was time to change the clocks, I'd ask dim-witted people on the street if they thought they were losing or gaining an hour."

"And you eventually quit because…?"

"Well, I suppose that I just came to the realization that it wasn't the glamorous job I'd hoped for. You worked long hours. You had to meet strict deadlines. And it wasn't all that rewarding, because the day after your story came out, people usually forgot all about it, especially when it came to the kinds of silly stories *I* did."

"Ah see what you mean, June, ah surely do. And so, you came to Fleener Plastics looking for the glamour?"

"Well…not exactly." I don't want to tell her that my job at Fleener was supposed to be an interim position, something I would do only until I found a career I really liked. I've been in this so-called transitional job now for about fifteen years.

Faith lets out a gloomy sigh and says, "Oh, June, ah just sometimes think that maybe plastic is not my destiny."

Ya think?

But I know that I shouldn't badmouth the company to young employees like Faith, even though I'm sure she's on a dead-end path at Fleener unless she gets into upper management, and Faith is just too nice a person to be a success at that. You have to be willing to step on people, to crush their heads to a bloody pulp, in order to become an executive at our company. Faith just doesn't have it in her. For the same reason, I know that I won't go any higher than first-level management. And for Faith, there's the psychic thing, too; Definitely not typical of your starched shirt, upper-level exec.

So, Faith's fate, if she stays in her current position, will be to plug along for a few years, getting pathetic or non-existent raises, until the day comes when she'll quietly be told to train her replacement, who will very likely be stationed overseas in India or Croatia or wherever, and who will do Faith's job for a small fraction of what she's earning. And then she'll be unceremoniously laid off before she gets too many years of service in and accrues too many seniority benefits.

I'm about to give her my standard career counseling spiel. The charts on this subject that Fleener recently distributed to first-level managers like me are deplorable; They're a barely disguised attempt to placate young employees into thinking that the majority of them have a bright, prosperous future at Fleener, the best company in the world to work for. The usual waves of guilt start to sweep over me.

"Faith, you've only been with Fleener for about five months. Maybe you'll grow to like it more than you do now."

Unlikely. Immediately I feel like a heel for saying that. So, I switch gears and ask, "Well, what do you think you would *really* like to do with your life?"

"Oh, ah just don't know, ah surely don't. Ah guess ah'll just…see what happens." With a sad expression on her face, she looks down and shakes her head as if she's resigning her fate to chance.

Faith becomes silent again. I don't press the subject.

I'm not in the mood for mentoring right now anyway.

We pull into Fleener's parking lot. It's almost three o'clock. I tell Faith that I'm going home to change my ripped clothes. She waves goodbye and quickly walks to the building entrance.

I turn the engine off and sit in the car for a minute to gather my thoughts and re-run today's weird events in my head. I consider my options regarding what I should tell the rest of my employees about Melvin, and I decide that all I should reveal to them is that he's missing. So, no details at all about what transpired today. I've already sworn Faith to secrecy. I don't know what to think about Faith's vision, but I surely am not convinced that Melvin is dead.

Since I missed a good chunk of the workday, I reconsider taking a trip home. I really have to finish that report, so I should get back to my desk immediately. My busted pants seams will be noticed, and of course there's always a slim chance that the last few remaining seam threads might spontaneously rupture, leaving me bare-assed. But then again, I have a long raincoat in the back seat of the car, which should provide adequate cover.

I step out of the car and reach for the raincoat when my cell rings. Caller ID indicates that the number is private. I press the accept button.

"Ms. Bloom?" A mature male voice asks.

"Yes?"

In a wary tone, he says, "I can't tell you my name, but I have some information that you might be interested in. Are you the June Bloom, the manager of Melvin Hamm'?"

I cautiously answer, "Why do you ask?"

"Because I have some information regarding Mr.

Hamm, but I don't want to talk to him directly. I'm not at all sure how he'd react to the information I have."

I don't like the sound of this, so I answer in a business-like way, "I'm June Bloom, but I think you'd better first tell me who you are, and what this is about, or I'm going to hang up."

"Mr. Hamm may be at risk of being conned. Of having all his money taken from him."

"Why do you say that?"

"About a year ago, I…got involved with a woman, and I ended up giving her a sizable amount of money. I really can't go into details, but let's just say I made some bad personal decisions there. I believe she was some kind of con woman and maybe she does this kind of thing over and over. And now I think she's involved with Mr. Hamm."

"But why are you telling *me* this? And how did you get my personal cell number?"

"I'm telling you because you know him, but you're not emotionally attached, or at least I assume you're not, being his boss. I felt that I had to tell *someone*. Getting your name was easy since you're listed as the manager of his department in your company's public directory. I tried calling you at work a few times, but you weren't at your desk, and I didn't want to leave a voicemail. So, I called a few other people in your department and asked about another way to get in touch with you. One of them gave me your cell number."

"Well, I really don't think it's appropriate for me to be involved in this. You should call the police. And how do you know this woman is involved with Melvin?"

"I saw her with him in public, just by chance. And I'm not talking to the police, I don't want to get involved in any police investigation," the man insists. "This woman might take revenge on me if she found out. I've suffered enough at her hands. I've already said too much. I just…well, I thought that somehow, he should be warned, and…"

I decide that I've heard enough. "Call the police, sir. I'm ending this call!" I tap my screen to break the connection.

And then I immediately think that maybe ending the call abruptly was a really stupid thing to do, because if the caller is right about Melvin being involved with a con woman, then I should have somehow pumped the guy for information. I don't have any record of the phone number because it was blocked, so I can't call him back now even if I want to. I don't even know if the cops can now figure out where that call came from.

Wonderful. I really don't want to get involved in this mess. Now I have another dilemma to struggle with. I have to decide whether or not to tell the cops about this call.

Chapter 5

I walk into the plant wearing my raincoat. Several people stare at me and one of them even asks me if it's raining. Very few folks have windows at Fleener Plastics. Part of the conspiracy, I suppose, to keep the worker bees penned in and toiling without distraction. Analogous to putting blinders on a plough horse.

Could Annuska be a con woman? Florence had called her a she-devil. It's hard to believe that Annuska is evil, though. She's just too weird. I don't want to make a shitload of trouble for her by suggesting to the cops that she might be a con woman if she's truly innocent of any wrongdoing, because of the anguish she must be going through right now if she really loves her husband.

I walk towards Pog's cube, holding my breath. My first hurdle in the morning is usually getting past Pog's cube on the way to the snack bar without losing consciousness from the cooking odors.

Pog works for me, and that's his first name. His last name is unpronounceable, at least by me. And for that matter, Pog is a nickname for an unpronounceable first name. He's a young fellow, in his twenties, an engineer who orders chemicals and decides on their quality control specifications and how they should be tested when they arrive. He's brilliant and very likable, and probably should be in academia. I haven't a clue why he's hanging around here, working this dead-end job.

I'm not even sure what far away country he's from, and it doesn't matter a bit to me because I'm not prejudiced in the least. But if you walk by his cube without holding your breath, you can pass out from the fumes. Some people have coffee machines on top of their desks, but not Pog. He always has a hot pot going. He seems to be continually making soup stock, and at about eight o'clock every morning he starts to boil his fish heads. In a cube area, the effect can be deadly. I've seen people who happen to be walking down his cube aisle for the very first time, and they're totally unprepared for it. They catch the scent and suddenly their faces contort and sometimes their knees buckle, and they almost go down.

When I reach his cube, Pog is there, toiling away. The guy works like a machine, almost never breaking concentration. Fleener is so lucky to have him. I'm relieved to see that he has consumed the last of his fish head stew and the stench has abated for now.

Even without the fish smells, the walls of his cube always make me slightly dizzy and nauseous. Instead of having a few calming pictures of oceans or beaches or forests like most people have, Pog's walls are plastered, top to bottom, with every scientific reference chart you can think of. I'm vaguely familiar with the periodic table of elements from my required college course in basic chemistry which I barely passed. But Pog has tables of polyatomic ions, radii of atoms, equilibrium constants, acid-base indicators, and other things so far over my head that I'm embarrassed to even ask him why he needs them. And I actually see him now and then at lunchtime, as he's eating his fish stew, browsing through scientific reference books, apparently for pure pleasure.

So, I never have to worry about Pog looking at

internet porn at work during lunch, which, by the way, my department set a recent record for, since it started being tracked and reported by the IT department; The record is for most pornography views within a one-week period. That's right, my department has the gold medal in that category right now. I'm not sure who's largely responsible for the record because it isn't broken down by person, but I apparently have at least one very frustrated person working for me whose hormones are in overdrive.

Pog looks up at me and a big smile forms quickly. He's one of those people who looks perpetually happy. He's got a mop of unruly, jet-black hair, and generous ears which stick out, I suppose to better suck up all available audio data in the air.

"Hi, Pog."

"Oh, hello there, Miss Juney!" he replies, his grin growing from large to colossal. "Very nice day, yes? But perhaps it is raining because you have raincoat?"

"Oh no, it's not raining. I'm just a little cold right now. It's a very nice day, yes, it is indeed. Uh, can I ask you something about Melvin? You know him better than I do. How long has he been married?"

"Married? Not long. About one year. I went to wedding. We dance the alley cat and the hoochie-coochie."

"Uh, yeah, I think you mean the hokey pokey. That's nice. So, how well do you know his wife, Annuska?"

His face scrunches up, as if he's considering a difficult scientific problem, and he answers, "Not too well, Miss Juney. I meet her for first time at wedding. And then I go to Melvin's house for dinner twice since wedding. She seem nice. I have some trouble understanding her speech."

In my mind I picture the two of them trying to converse: Annuska with her Romanian accent, Pog with his unidentifiable accent. Tower of Babel.

"Do you know how they met?"

"Ahhh, how they met? Internet. Some site like sexy girly cutie brides from Eastern Europe dot com, or some such thing as that."

"Ahh, on the internet. I see. And then they dated for a while?"

"For very short time, I think, Miss Juney. Melvin so much in love with Annuska."

"He is? How do you know?"

"Melvin tell me so."

"I see. Do you know anything about her background?"

"From Romania."

"Right. But I mean, did she come to this area straight from Romania, or did she move here when she started dating Melvin?"

"Don't know that, Miss Juney."

"Okay, thanks. Uh, listen I need to tell you something about Melvin. He's missing."

"Missing? Missing what?" he asks with a puzzled look.

"Just missing. Meaning that we don't know where he is…uhhh, well, I mean, he didn't come to work yesterday or today, and his wife doesn't know where he is."

"Ahh, missing? I see. Don't worry, Miss Juney. Melvin be fine." The happy face comes back. Pog is the perpetual optimist. I smile politely at him as I think:

Melvin might not be fine. He might be dead.
****

A few hours later I'm barreling home in my junker car. As I'm pulling into my driveway, I spot an enormous red ant with green eyes careening up behind me. Beneath the ant is the white *Don't Bug Me* van.

I stop my car in front of the garage as usual, since we have one of those garages that's overstuffed with all manner of extremely valuable crap. It's mostly the assorted detritus of Darryl's homegrown engineering projects, but I too share some guilt as a hoarder-in-training. So, it's impossible to get even one car into our two-car garage, and cleaning out that space is at the absolute bottom of the to-do list.

Since I can't go any farther, I just sit there for a few seconds, watching those big green bug eyes in the rear-view mirror grow ever bigger, waiting to get rear-ended, expecting my head to violently snap back in a moment from the impact. And if it has to happen, well maybe a good whiplash will somehow miraculously end my headaches, the way a chiropractor cures your ailments by snapping a wayward spine back into shape.

But the van slams to a stop just inches behind my bumper, its brakes squealing, and Filbert Crumm jumps out, in all his battle regalia—the uniform, utility belt, insecticide gun—pretty much everything except body armor and night-vision goggles. He's ready to rumble with hordes of cockroaches, locusts, termites, or whatever vermin are foolish enough to tangle with him.

With a cheery smile on his pudgy face, he walks over to me as I get out of my car. I give him a slightly pissed off look as I point at the tiny space between the two vehicles and say, "A little close, don't ya think?"

He looks surprised at my concern. "Huh? Oh, don't worry. There was never any danger of a collision. I'm a highly trained professional. It's nice to see you again, Ms. Bloom. I'm Filbert Crumm. Do you remember me? We met at the murder scene earlier. I protected you and the other women."

"Protected?"

"Well, you know, I waited while the cops were on their way. I *would* have protected you if the murderer had re-appeared. I had the weapons and the will. I couldn't help but overhear you give your address to those policemen. So here I am, to offer my protective services again."

"Yes, of course I remember you, Agent Crumm. All of that stuff happened just a few hours ago. I may look old to you, but my memory isn't completely shot yet. And you want to offer me your protective services? Well, thanks so much for saving our skins earlier, but I don't need protection now. No murderer has appeared, and Melvin Hamm may have just left town willingly, anyway."

"That may be true, but even so, I believe that I can be of great help to the police. I can keep an eye out for Mr. Hamm. I know exactly what he looks like, how he walks, how he smells even."

"You smelled him? That's gross."

"Well, not on purpose or anything. I just have a good sense of smell. Excellent, really. I developed it from sniffing out termites. I just want to ask you a little about his social habits so that I can find his dead body more quickly."

"He's probably *not* dead."

"Okay. Well, his *alive* body then. I'm just trying to

break the case wide open."

"What case? There is no case. He probably just left."

Filbert leans in towards me and whispers, sharing a secret about himself, "Ms. Bloom, please, I need a break here. I'm trying to become a private investigator. I need to sort of solve a case before I can get my license. You would not believe the stuff that the state licensing board wants you to go through, to become an investigator. If you're not a former police officer, they actually want you to demonstrate some level of intelligence and competence before they'll give you a license."

I give him a puzzled look and say, "I thought you wanted to be a writer, Filbert. You were going to document all the weird stuff you encounter in the extermination business."

"Well, yeah, there's that. It *would* make for an interesting book. For instance, you would not believe the things I find in people's houses." He raised his hands and chopped at the air to emphasize his point. "For instance, I was in the house of a town councilwoman yesterday and I found a pair of nipple clamps on the floor when I was looking for silverfish. Do you know what they are?"

"Yes, I've got some."

"Nipple clamps or silverfish?" he asks.

"Silverfish."

"That's awesome!" His eyes light up with excitement.

"It's awesome that I'm infested with silverfish?"

"Yes, it's awesome because this week we're offering a special on house inspections. It's completely free."

"Free, huh? Free is a good price, but this is not a good time. I have to go in and make dinner. How long is the free offer good for?"

"Until Monday. It might get extended. The home office tells us every Monday if it's extended for another week or not."

"I see. And how many weeks in a row has the offer been extended for, so far?"

"I'm not certain the exact number, but about three hundred weeks."

"Hmmm. That's about six years. So, it sounds like it's *always* free."

"Well, that's one way to look at it."

"So, I'd say, no big hurry in agreeing to get the free inspection done."

"Why don't you want it done now?"

"I'm having a little party soon. Don't want anyone gassed out from insecticide fumes."

"Oh, I *love* parties. Anyway, if you want, I can do the inspection now and if I find something, I can gas you out at some future date."

"That's really a tempting offer, Filbert. But I don't think this is the best time for even an inspection. If you fall down the stairs and break your leg, I'll have to call the meat wagon to come and pull you out of my basement and that would delay my getting dinner on the table. Let's just make it some other time, okay?"

He looks so sad. The guy is obviously lonely, bored, whatever. I actually feel bad for giving him the brush. So, I say, "Listen, Filbert, seriously, I'll have you do the inspection, but not right now, okay? Dinnertime on a weeknight is not a good time. How about sometime on a weekend?"

His sad response is, "Okay, if you say so. Oh boy, it's just so slow right now. There's nothing to do. I'll probably get laid off soon. It's a good thing we've got a few houses like Florence Shmoo's, that are totally infested. Thank God for lice and bedbugs, they're really hard for me to get rid of."

"Okay, now you're definitely *not* inspiring confidence."

"Oh, sorry. Don't worry, I can get rid of anything I find in your house, as long as you allow me to apply limitless amounts of poison chemicals."

"Okay, that sounds wonderful. I'll call you soon."

I switch to a sterner tone and say, "And listen, just forget about Melvin missing, okay? Don't get involved. I saw that the police already warned you off, so you're just asking for trouble." He looks dejected at my insistence, like a kid whose had his lollipop swiped by a bully.

Filbert says a solemn goodbye and waddles back to his van. His overflowing belly jiggles up and down as he takes the big step up into the driver's seat. He waves tepidly out the window before he does a three-point turn and heads down the driveway.

I watch the big ant's crimson ass fade into the pinkish setting sun.

****

The next morning, I'm sitting in the cubical of a personal trainer at the local gym, at an obscenely early hour. After the physical activities of the previous day left me nearly paralyzed with muscle pain, I've decided I can't put it off any longer. It's time to get into shape.

I arranged for my husband to get the kids on the bus this morning so I could come here before work to go through an initial evaluation test and fill out a questionnaire. The trainer, a twenty-something super muscular kid named Billy with slicked-back hair and a superior attitude, is looking at my paperwork now. He frowns and shakes his head as he eyes my test results and stats, while I sit across the desk from him.

I'm anxious to get this over with and get out of here. The florescent lights above the desk are singeing my corneas. I have a four-alarm headache and a nasty buzz in my ears that I'm praying will abate as soon as I get my morning caffeine fix. I'm also slightly nauseous from the perky purple and pink wall colors in this place, and despondent from the super-oversized pictures on the wall of twenty-somethings, with bodies like Hercules or Wonder Woman, happily exercising, so happily in fact that they appear to be on the point of achieving orgasm right on the floor mat or the stationary bicycle. The implication is that *you, too, can be just like them,* if you agree to pay the seventy-nine dollars per month fee to join this gym. And if you spring for the ninety-nine-dollar package, then I suppose multiple orgasms are a possibility.

Billy finally speaks, "Uh…Ms. Bloom…so here, where it asks, *How often do you drink alcohol?*—it gave you choices, like one drink per week, three per week, and so on. You didn't check any of the boxes, you just penciled in *as needed*. What does that mean?"

"Just trying to be honest."

"I see. And, uhhh…you answered *yes* to sometimes having *all* these things: shortness of breath at rest or with mild exertion, excessive buildup of fluid in tissues, sudden rapid heartbeat, occasional lameness, fatigue, shortness of breath with usual activities, and so on. Was that a mistake? I mean, answering yes to *all* of them?"

"No mistake."

"Hmmm. So, we measured your body fat percentage as…"

"Okay, let's not go there, shall we?"

"Right."

Billy looks up at me, taps his pencil continuously against the papers and declares, "Okay, so I can see we have some work to do. Can you start coming in every other day for personal training sessions starting tomorrow and going on until…well, let's just call it an indefinite period of time?"

"Every other day…in perpetuity?" I ask, jerking my head back with surprise. "I don't even get weekends off? Holy cow, how much is this gonna cost?"

"Lots. But I think you'll agree that when it comes to whipping you back into shape, price is no object. We'll design a weightlifting routine specifically for you."

"Lifting weights? Isn't there some easier way to accomplish my fitness goals?"

"Well…how about water aerobics?"

"Oh. Do I have to wear a bathing suit? And get wet?"

"I'm afraid there's no way around getting wet when you do water aerobics. You could wear your sweats in the pool, I suppose."

"I'll think about it. Listen, I have to go, I'll call you."

I leave the place and trudge out to my car, completely discouraged. No way can I afford to drop fifty to a hundred bucks every other day on an open-ended quest to tone up my sorry and probably un-tone-able ass. I'll have to try it without the trainer. But with or without the trainer, I figure my chances of ever looking even half as good as my neighborhood nemesis, Abbey, are nil. I have to admit to myself that looking like

Abbey is my goal. My almost certainly *unachievable* goal.

When I arrive at work, I gather everyone in my department together in a meeting room and fumble through a three-minute announcement about Melvin being missing. There are twelve people present. I include a nice crock o' shit about how the police are actively searching for him, which I know isn't true yet because he's only been missing for two days, but at least it sounds upbeat. I get a few questions thrown in my direction that I basically brush off because I have so little information, including one from our own flaming conspiracy theorist named Harold, who wants to know if Melvin has ever in the past, to my knowledge, been abducted by aliens, and I swear to God he is dead serious. Harold is a young guy, the jittery type, eyes constantly darting around the room scanning for threats both earthly and extraterrestrial, and always afraid he'll be the next one to get sucked up by the tractor beam. Spends all of his free time watching X-files reruns. He really needs to get out more and socialize with some earthlings.

I try to treat his inquiry with respect, and so I ask for some clarification, "You mean…abducted in the past…and then presumably returned…like, sent back from the mother ship?"

"Well, yes, of course," Harold answers without the slightest trace of a smile. "They would have sent back either him or some type of body double."

I nod in careful consideration, then I make some lame-ass comment about how I'll definitely make sure the police and NASA look into that angle.

I dismiss the group, asking that they stay hopeful. Faith remains in the back of the room after the others have left, a sad look on her face, apparently a result of the burden of knowing that Melvin has recently departed this world. And since she doesn't look happy, I have to assume she hasn't yet had visions of him singing any duets with the Elvis.

I walk over to her and thank her again for not blurting anything out about yesterday's activities during the meeting. She nods solemnly and walks out. I don't know what I can or should do to console her, but I have to hustle to my next appointment, which is a visit with a police detective from New Haven who has been assigned to the case. She's meeting me in the building lobby.

Chapter 6

It takes me a good seven minutes to get through the labyrinth of hallways and down to the lobby. I find the detective waiting patiently for me in one of the faux leather chairs that are available for the honored guests of Fleener Plastics. As she stands to face me, she smiles, and I'm shocked to see a familiar face.

"Louise? Louise Turner?" I sputter in surprise.

She breaks out in a huge grin. "Hi, June. It's great to see you again. It's been…wow, about twenty-two years since our high school graduation."

"Right, a long, long time, but I recognized you immediately. You look great!" And I'm not just being polite. Louise *does* look great.

"So do you, June," she replies. "Anyone who knew you in high school would spot you immediately."

We stand about five feet apart. I'm wondering if we should embrace, and I guess she's wondering the same. After a few seconds of smiling, we move toward each other at the same time and give each other a polite hug. Just the right level of affection to suit the casual level of friendship we had in high school.

Stepping back but still grinning, Louise says, "Sorry, June, I should have told you when I asked you for the interview. I knew of course, even though you changed your name when you married. I always do a quick bit of research in public databases on anyone I'm about to interview."

I look at Louise with admiration. She wears no makeup or jewelry, and she doesn't really need it because she's attractive in a tough, no-nonsense sort of way. Her auburn hair is done in a short and stylish cut that gives her an air of intelligence and authority. At about five foot eight, she cuts a trim figure in a black pantsuit and she obviously keeps herself fit. I remember her as being very intelligent and hard-working, and I'm not at all surprised that she's made detective, perhaps the only female detective on the New Haven force.

"I always liked you, June. Lots of the girls in our class were rather mean, but not you. You were nice to me and everyone else."

"Think so? Maybe I was yearning for affection and approval."

"No, I'd say you're just a good person. Remember when Lisa what's her face and I got in a spat in tenth grade, and she grabbed my little beaded purse and scattered the contents all over the parking lot? You helped me pick everything up. I never forgot that."

I raise both eyebrows in genuine amazement that she remembers me helping her, and say, "Really? It was such a small kindness, Louise."

"But Lisa was one of the cool girls, and helping me could have alienated you from them. You helped me anyway."

"I see what you mean. But maybe at that point I was already a shunned outcast."

"Even so, it meant a lot to me."

"I'm really touched to know you felt that way…and glad…that I made a *difference* to someone." I pause as I think about our interactions in high school for a few seconds, then ask her straight out, "Why do you think we weren't closer friends in high school, Louise?"

"I honestly don't know, June. We were fairly compatible, I think."

"Well, in eleventh grade you *did* start dating that short guy with the acne and the crew cut, you know, the one who pestered you all the time until you finally agreed to go out with him. And then you started spending a lot of your free time with him, so I certainly couldn't fault you for not spending more time with female friends. I forget, what was his name?"

Louise nods her head and says, "Oh yeah, *that* guy. The pest. I know who you mean. His name was Henry Freemont. I married him." She grins.

Even though I'm not near a mirror, I'm sure my face turned the color of cabernet. "Oh, dear God, Louise, forgive me," I grimace. "Good thing you're in great physical shape because I may need your help pulling my foot out of my mouth. It's wedged in there super tight."

Louise chuckles and gives a swoosh of her hand. "No worries at all, June," she assures me. "You didn't really know him at the time. He's a wonderful person. And much better looking now that the acne's gone and he's grown out his hair. And he's a great father."

"Ah, how many?" I ask.

"Two boys. And you?"

"Same, two boys, seven and nine." We both pull up pictures on our phones, show them to each other, and simultaneously give nods of approval and admiration.

Louise says, "Mine are a little older than yours, fifteen and thirteen now. Henry and I married as soon as we finished college. And how about you, did you also marry a high school sweetheart?"

"That would have been difficult. In fact, let's call it a clear impossibility since I didn't really date in high school. Unless you count going to the prom with my cousin, Homer."

"Well, all those guys who didn't ask you out at the time really missed out. Because like I already said, you're a good person. That's why I'm guessing you must be pretty distressed about your missing employee."

"Well…yes, of course. But I'm hoping this whole thing is just a fluke and Melvin will show up soon. Anything new on his whereabouts?"

"No. Still missing, and calls to his cell are still going to voicemail."

"What exactly does that mean?"

"Well, the phone might be powered off. Or maybe the battery ran down. It hasn't been pinging cell towers since the middle of the night before he didn't show up at work. But Mrs. Hamm said it was an old phone with a weak battery and it was always running out of power."

I nod and say, "But yesterday we were interviewed by uniformed officers, and now a detective has been assigned. Why? Did the tests on that blood spot turn up something?"

"Yes. It's definitely blood, first of all."

"Okay. But I'm not sure why you're telling *me* about this. I'm just his manager. Did you talk to his wife about it?"

"Well…June, is there somewhere we could go to talk privately?"

I'm hit with a brief flash of trepidation at that request, but I manage to keep my outward cool and say in a calm tone, "Sure."

She follows me into one of the building's hallways

and within a minute I find an empty break area, a tiny room that's essentially a converted closet. It contains a few stained chairs and a microscopic table holding a twenty-year-old coffee maker that reeks of burned brew. We both sit down and settle in.

Louise seems unfazed by the dingy and claustrophobic surroundings. She eyes me as if considering whether or not to reveal something. If there's an internal struggle, I guess I come out on top because after five seconds of slightly awkward silence she says, "June, I'm going to tell you some things which I shouldn't, but it's because I know your character and I trust you, even after all these years. I feel that if I confide in you, it might help us to locate Mr. Hamm, which is what we all want. I'll ask that you not give this information to anyone else. Could I have your word on that?"

"Yes, of course. Thanks for your trust."

She takes a deep breath and says, "The blood from the trunk, which we got from Faith Gelner's finger…it *is* Melvin Hamm's blood. We can do DNA analyses very quickly these days, and we reached that conclusion by comparing it to DNA from hair follicles on a brush that was in the bathroom. But something else popped up. When we do these analyses, we always run them through the national DNA record database, which includes the profiles of many convicted felons, some from missing people, and some samples that were gathered at crime scenes. There was no entry in the database for a Melvin Hamm, but we got a match to someone else. That's why I'm here."

"A match to whom?"

"Six years ago, a young man, nineteen years of age

and living in Seattle, was reported missing by his father. As part of the investigation, a DNA sample from the young man was obtained from the house where he lived with his father. At first it was thought he might have been abducted, but eventually the police came to think he probably left willingly. Interviews with the father and some acquaintances revealed the father and son didn't really get along. The young man was never found. Until now."

My body stiffens and I stare intently at Louise. "You mean…Melvin?"

"That's right. Melvin's real name is Maximilian Tremayne. Known as Max to his father."

"Melvin is not Melvin…wow." I shake my head in amazement.

"Did you have any knowledge at all of the fact that he'd changed identities?"

"Not a clue. I mean he really never talked about his past, and I didn't ask him about it, and there was nothing I recall that looked weird in his personnel file. When did he start using the new identity?"

"We don't know for sure, but at least beginning two years ago. We looked for evidence of Melvin Hamm's existence—records of financial activity, tax payments, voting records, licenses, social media activity, whatever. The earliest things we found are a bank account opened two years ago, and a Connecticut driver's license obtained at about the same time."

I say, "He's worked for Fleener for about the same time, two years. I believe this is his first real job, after college. His prior employment was just unskilled stuff, so I'm sure we would not have even called those places for references."

"Were you the one who hired him?"

"No, he transferred into my department about eight months ago."

"And what exactly does he do here?"

"He makes decisions about how much chemicals and other raw production materials are to be ordered and *when* they should be ordered, based on current production usage, and future contracts. The idea is of course to keep material costs at a minimum, by purchasing quantities as large as possible, but without keeping excessive inventory on hand, or having any of the raw materials reach their expiration dates." *And yes, it's one of the most boring jobs ever.* I almost dozed off trying to explain it to her. The only job more boring might be managing a whole group of people who do this sort of stuff. And that's *my* job.

"So, *how* did he make a new identity for himself?" I ask.

"We traced his social security number. It belongs to a male who was born at about the same time as Max, but who died shortly after birth and was buried in Alabama. For whatever reason, the federal government has a record of birth for this person, but not death. People do this kind of thing all the time, use someone else's social to change identities. They can file their taxes with it and everything. It's illegal, of course."

"But why would Melvin do this?"

She shrugs her shoulders. "Well, like I said, he had a falling out with his father, and he apparently didn't want his dad to ever find him. According to the case file I read, his father can be rather overbearing. Max Tremayne was born quite late in his father's life, and maybe that complicated their relationship somehow. I don't have any information on the specifics of their rift, but it happens."

"Is the father still alive?"

"Yes, but probably not for long. He's eighty-two and currently living in a hospice in Seattle with advanced pancreatic cancer, and they expect he'll live maybe another month at most. His mind is still clear. We talked to him this morning and explained we had information about his son. He was very excited and wants us to keep him informed. He appears to bear no ill will toward Max. Perhaps the cancer has mellowed him. He'd like very much to reunite and reconcile with his son before he dies. The father's wife, Max's mother, is dead and the father has no living relatives except for his son."

"So…does the father have a will?"

She pauses, tilts her head a bit, and gives me a slight smile. Perhaps it's a subtle compliment. Maybe she's acknowledging my perceptiveness.

"Why do you ask? Does Mr. Hamm have financial problems that you're aware of?"

Louise obviously wants to know what I know about Melvin, which isn't much. "Well…no," I answer cautiously. "I only know what he's paid by Fleener, and I know his wife has a job in a funeral home since her place of employment is listed in Melvin's personnel information. Beyond that, I have no idea about his finances." *Other than the fact he lives in a shitty neighborhood and doesn't always pay his rent on time.*

"Well, the father has a rather unusual will which was done about half a year ago, after he was diagnosed. Except for a small amount of money to be spent on the care of his beloved cat, the will bequeaths everything to his son, who is his only child, if he comes forward. The will stipulates that the executor is to keep the estate in escrow for up to ten years after the father's death, waiting to see if the son surfaces to claim everything. The father apparently suspected all along that his son was in hiding and is hoping that if Max hears of his father's death, he might eventually come out of hiding and claim the money. In the event that Max doesn't claim the estate, but the executor becomes aware of Max's death, meaning that a death certificate is issued before the escrow period is over, then the estate would be divided equally between Max's children. If there are no children, then the estate goes to a charity, an organization that trains Seeing Eye Dogs for people who can't afford them. And if nothing happens within ten years of the father's death, then it goes to the same charity."

Louise pauses again and looks carefully at me, I suppose to see if I have any reaction to what she's said.

"So…I'm guessing that the amount of money involved is not insignificant?" I ask.

She gives me another half-smile. "You're correct. The father, Peter Tremayne, is quite wealthy. Does his name ring a bell?"

I shake my head. "No. Should it?"

"Probably not, unless you follow the fossil fuel industry. He's worth about fifty million bucks. His fortune was made in the fracking boom after Max left him. The fact that there's a lot of money involved makes this missing person case more…interesting. The money could potentially go to Max."

"Holy crap. So, Melvin…I mean Max…is rich?"

"He *will* be rich, but only if he shows up and claims the money once his father dies. He's also a lawbreaker for using a stolen social security number. It's a crime,

S.E. Greco

and so is getting that bank account and driver's license under a false name. But he probably wouldn't serve any prison time for it, assuming he hasn't used the false identity to do anything bad. We ran a check on the financial activity associated with the social he's using, and there's no evidence of anything shady. It appears that he's been living as far under the radar as possible. He has no credit cards or loans. And fortunately, he didn't vote or get a passport using the false name either, both of which carry heavy penalties. We couldn't even find any record of him flying on a commercial airline under his new identity. If he comes forward, he'd be arrested for the bank account and driver's license fraud, and assuming there's nothing worse, he'd probably be convicted and given probation."

"And would the DNA match be sufficient to allow him to inherit the father's money?"

"Yes, there's precedent. It's held up in court in many prior cases."

"What about his wife, Annuska? Will *she* get the money if Melvin is dead?"

"Dead? Why do you think Mr. Hamm is dead?" she asks, as if my use of the *dead* word is a surprise to her.

"I don't. I mean, there's the blood smear on the trunk lid, right? I certainly *hope* he's alive, but in the unlikely event that he's dead…would she get the money?"

"She can't inherit it directly from Max's father when he dies. It could only go to Max or his children, and Max doesn't have any children. Apparently, Peter Tremayne was taken to the cleaners when he divorced Max's mother, so he only wants his money going to a blood relative. Max's wife could get it quickly enough if Max inherited it and then he died with a will that passed it to her. I interviewed Mrs. Hamm this morning.

"Without being indelicate, and without bringing up her husband's true identity, we discussed the possibility of her husband being deceased. She said that to her knowledge, he has no will. However, according to Connecticut inheritance laws, Max's full estate would go to his spouse if there is no will. It would take longer without a will, as it has to go through the courts of course, and there would be some investigation mandated to determine if it was some kind of a sham marriage."

"A sham marriage? What do you mean?"

She smiles. "Well, what do you know about a website called *Sexy Girly Cutie Eastern European Brides dot com*?"

I sit back in my chair and say, "Sounds like you've been talking to Pog?"

"Yes. I ran into him in the parking lot. By the way, how do you pronounce his last name? I wrote it down, but…" She pulls a small notepad with a leather cover from her inside pocket and flips it open to apparently look at the name she recorded. I like that she still uses pen and paper. Old school, like me.

I answer, "Well, to be honest, my pronunciation of it is really bad, so let's just refer to him as Pog."

She gives a knowing smile. "I flashed him my shield and he got me past the badge lock door and into the building. He asked if he could show me to where I was going, and I said I was meeting you in the lobby, and he said he works for you and is a friend of Melvin Hamm. So, he told me how Mr. and Mrs. Hamm met. I didn't get a chance to take a look at this *Sexy Girl* website yet, and I suspect Pog may have gotten the name scrambled a bit, but I'll find it and take a look. Mrs. Hamm simply told me they met through internet dating."

"So, if Melvin...I mean Max, found Annuska on this website, does it automatically mean that it's a sham marriage? And that she wouldn't inherit anything if Max got the money and then died?"

"No, not at all. It may be a perfectly legitimate marriage, and they may be madly in love. Lots of legitimate marriages result from these types of websites. It's not that much different in concept from dating websites, except that the women are usually not American citizens. But they become citizens as soon as they marry an American. The marriage must be a real marriage, of course. The man and woman must live together as husband and wife for a certain period of time. Mr. and Mrs. Hamm have been married for a year, and according to Mrs. Hamm, they've lived together the whole time. I'll dig a little more, of course. There's also the complicating factor that the marriage may not be legal because of Mr. Hamm's identity change. We'll check it all out." She shifts her weight in the chair and I notice the slight bulge under her left arm, probably a handgun in a shoulder holster. She continues, "So, are you close to him? Do you consider him a friend?"

"No, we aren't close at all. We have just a cordial manager-employee relationship."

"Is he good at his job?"

"He does well enough. His ratings are always adequate or a notch above that. No problems at work."

"You folks are going through a layoff here. Will he be getting laid off?"

I raise my eyebrows in surprise at the mention of this supposedly confidential piece of information, but then I remember that as soon as it hits one person's e-mail, it spreads like a hayfield fire, so of course the police would know about it.

"Well, I actually don't know yet," I answer truthfully. "I'll probably be informed today of the people getting laid off." The list is confidential, but not for long. The layoff will happen tomorrow morning, and everyone being shit-canned will be told then, all at about the same time. But even if Melvin isn't on the list, if someone killed him or if he just left and never comes back, he'd still be counted as one more employee gotten rid of toward whatever the headcount reduction target is. Laid off, quit, shot, stabbed, squashed by a falling grand piano, or hit by a manure truck—it doesn't matter to Fleener's bean counters. Downsized or dead, it's all the same to them.

Louise asks, "Do you know anything about his relationship with his wife? Do they get along?"

"I really have no idea. Yesterday was the first time I ever spoke to her, and Melvin never talked about her, at least not to me. Oh, sorry I called him Melvin again. Just can't get used to the fact that his real name is Max."

She gives me a slight smile and assures me, "Oh, that's okay. To avoid confusion, let's both refer to him as Melvin. So, can you infer anything about their marital relationship, perhaps by how often you may have noticed him calling her, or by things you may have heard from third parties?"

I shake my head. "I don't remember him ever calling her in my presence or even talking about *any* aspect of his home life. We just talk business and exchange normal pleasantries. He's quite a private and withdrawn person, at least in front of me. And I have no third-party information either."

Louise seems satisfied at that and says, "Okay. Well, can you tell me who his friends are at work?"

"I only know of Pog and Faith, and maybe Mary. I'm really not sure how close any of them are to him. Like I said, he's not very sociable. Maybe Melvin goes out to lunch with them occasionally, for a birthday celebration or something like that. And Pog went to Melvin's wedding, but Faith didn't. I don't know about Mary."

"Okay. I'll be talking to Faith today. And by the way, June, I haven't told Mrs. Hamm about her husband's true identity and the inheritance yet. It might compromise the investigation. I'll tell her at the proper time."

"I understand. Uh, so, are you thinking that maybe Annuska may have...*murdered* him?" I ask gingerly, not wanting to accuse anyone of anything, but I guess that Louise has already considered it. And in a meeting room this small, it's hard to ignore the elephant sitting on the tiny table right between us.

"At this point, June, I'm just gathering information."

"Are you going to declare Melvin dead?"

She looks surprised at the question. "Based on a blood smear on a trunk latch? Not a chance. We need a body."

"Maybe the body was in that trunk."

"Or maybe he just had a cut on his finger when he opened the trunk. Mrs. Hamm said he drove her car sometimes, even in the past week, and it hasn't rained recently. It's very easy to get DNA on a car that you drive or ride in. Heck, when I drive my kids to and from school sports, I guarantee you their blood and snot gets all over the car, inside and out."

I like her down-to-earth way of talking. "Louise, I'd like to be helpful, but I just don't think I have any useful information that could help in locating him."

"That's okay, June. I'm sorry to hit you with all these questions, but sometimes a little detail that you think is inconsequential may turn out to be important."

Louise asks me to go over some of the events of yesterday one more time, and I go through what I already told the uniformed police officers. She stops me now and then with a few questions, but I really don't have any more detail to add. When I finish, she stands up and smiles.

"Thanks, June. That's all for now. If Melvin doesn't turn up soon, it's very likely that I'll be in touch with you again about this case. I really do appreciate you giving me some time from your busy workday. And even if I don't need to discuss the case again, let's get together for coffee and chat about old times."

I nod. "Sure, I'd like that, Louise."

We exchange our personal cell numbers. I escort her out of the building, and we say our goodbyes.

Fifty million bucks? Holy shit!

If Melvin does re-surface, he'd be an idiot *not* to claim that money. The alternative would be to work at his lame, dead-end job at Fleener Plastics until it kills him; to slave away like an anonymous worker bee until he has a heart attack or an aneurysm in his cube and his stiffening body, the flies buzzing around it, is eventually noticed by the guy who empties the wastebaskets; to give his all in the name of making better and cheaper (but mostly just cheaper) injection molded and extruded vinyl and plastic products.

Chapter 7

As I leave the lobby area and begin the walk back to my cube, I pass the framed poster that I see every day, the one with the big picture of a group of smiling employees above the caption: *Let's Pull Together for Fleener Plastics.* As expected at a large company, great pains were taken to make the group in the picture as diverse as possible, and I think they have every racial /ethnic /cultural /religious /socioeconomic group represented in that shot except maybe for one-armed albinos.

Fleener Plastics makes things like that tacky looking vinyl trim that you see at the bottom of the walls in industrial buildings. Or the equally tacky vinyl strip that goes along the wall about waist high to prevent chairs or rolling carts or whatever from scraping the paint off the walls. If it's tacky looking and made of vinyl or plastic, it's a fairly sure bet that Fleener Plastics had a hand in it.

And me, I'm a first-level manager in the area where all the action is: Procurement and Requisition. Yes indeed, excitement is a way of life in my group. We buy everything the company needs to keep the production gears turning, from chemicals to production line equipment to brooms for sweeping the factory floors. And all the while we must assure that everything we buy meets quality standards at the lowest possible cost to the company, so we're encouraged to badger our suppliers into giving us the goods at lower prices, by basically threatening to shop elsewhere if they don't. That's capitalism, I suppose.

It's a damn old factory building that I work in, almost crumbling in fact, but at least the lobby at Fleener, where I met Louise, is reasonably presentable. That's because guests of the company, some of whom are potential customers, have to enter the building through the lobby. Then they're quickly herded to a plush executive conference room a very short walk away, where they get hammered with a sales pitch while being plied with cappuccino and chocolate croissants.

But me and the other grunts, we head in the opposite direction from the conference room, and soon enter what I call the industrial swampland. How can I accurately describe the windowless hallways at Fleener that I walk through every day on my way to the cubicles? Ever been in the New York City subways? And I don't mean the platforms where you wait for the subway, which are leaps and bounds above the quality of Fleener's hallways. I mean the subway tunnels themselves. That's right. Bad lighting, trash, and rats. Fleener's hallways definitely have the first two, and as for the rats, although I haven't actually seen them scurrying around in the hallways here, I have no doubt that they come out at night to feast on the leftover nachos, pizza crusts, and apple cores spilling from the overstuffed waste cans. In these times of extreme austerity, Fleener laid off seventy percent of the cleaning staff. They also seem to be turning down the hallway lighting a little more every week, so it really *is* getting close to the dingy light level of a subway tunnel. At least it makes the puke green color of the walls less obvious.

I get back to my cube, sit down, and open my laptop.

"HI JUNE!" bellows Verne, and my butt jumps ten inches out of my chair the way it always does when he greets me as he walks by. I should be used to it by now.

Verne works for me. They call him High Volume Verne for obvious reasons, and so I put him in a cube way over on the other side of this floor. It's a new cube area and the only people over there so far are Verne and my boss, Larry. They're both loud, and they don't seem to mind being seated next to each other.

Even so, Verne comes over here several times a day to talk to me and some of his co-workers. Verne is a young guy, kind of a joker with a cheerful face, some extra pounds around the middle, and one damn powerful set of pipes. His stadium loudspeaker voice is just one of the many sounds and distractions in the cube area which make it difficult to get any real work done.

"Yeah, morning Verne, turn it down a little for me today, will ya? The little guy in my skull with the sledgehammer is working overtime this morning."

"Oh, sure, June, sorry about that," he replies as he walks on by.

I read through all the notes again that I received about the *Human Resource Initiative* (remember, happy euphemism for layoff). All bullshit aside, it usually means that some upper-level executive screwed up a project and we fell short on a big delivery, and the only thing that can now save his pension, his stock options, and his ass is cutting costs by canning some of the lower-level people's asses. It's happened before. This will be the third time we've been through a layoff since I became a manager. The lovely job of bearing the bad news is always left to the first level manager grunts like me. And

I stink at it.

Last time I had to do it, about a year ago, I told an elderly gentleman who had been with the company more than thirty-five years that he had to go, and of course, I'd received Fleener's useless management training on how to do this in a so-called *sensitive and professional* manner. Believe me, there is no sensitive way to tell someone their ass is being shit-canned. When I gave him the news, he promptly stood up from his chair, then stepped up on top of my desk, pulled out his wang and urinated on my phone as I watched. Not too bad a reaction, I guess. At least it was nonviolent.

The time before that was worse, although fortunately still without bloodshed. I had to give the axe to a woman in her mid-twenties, a pretty redhead with a bombshell of a body, but she didn't do any work around here. Somehow, she'd been able to get the male members of our group to do all of her job for her, go figure. When I told her, she calmly leaned toward me and said she'd get even with me by breaking up my marriage. She said that she was going to sleep with my husband, and I was kidding myself if I thought that he could resist her. Well, my Darryl, even with his erectile dysfunction, has a healthy enough sex drive and if she approached him, he'd be so clueless that he probably wouldn't realize what was happening until she had her hand down his pants. So, I told Darryl about the whole thing, and even though he laughed it off and told me he'd be on constant guard against aggressive redheads, and even though I haven't seen the woman since then, I'm still a bit worried that she might re-surface. I sometimes find myself doing a double take at some woman in a crowd, thinking it's her. But by now she's probably not doing her work at some other big company far from here.

I quickly read the rest of the note and see that I will also have to tell everyone in my group who's *not* getting laid off that their medical benefits are being cut again. Our company's medical plan, as pathetic as it is, is underfunded.

The note gives the standard line about how the plan was formulated fifty years ago and was never meant to take care of people who live into their nineties. So, the company's genius fix for this is to cut back on medical benefits for retirees so that they croak sooner. And while they're at it, they might as well cut medical benefits for the current workforce as well.

And so I'm supposed to have a meeting with my people to tell them, with a straight face, how these benefit cuts are actually doing a *greater good* for employees, because the long-term health of our wonderful company will be improved, and their job security will increase, and so their sacrifice will have meaning. And I kid you not, the note also said that I'm supposed to stress the words *sacrifice* and *greater good*. In the meantime, my employees are checking insider trading websites every day and seeing our upper execs raking in obscene profits from selling stock options. My people have every right to be pissed.

I search my inbox again for the e-mail which will tell me if I'll have to lay off anyone in my group this time. Sometimes my group is spared, sometimes not.

Found it.

And unfortunately, it states in the first paragraph at the top of the note that someone in my group, one person, is getting the axe tomorrow, and that I should reference a different note to find out who it will be. It also explains that it would have been *two* people if not for the fact that Melvin is now on some kind of a hold status because I reported him missing.

I go back to my inbox and look for the other note, the one that contains the infamous list, which is simply a ranking of all the people in my group based supposedly on performance ratings and skill set evaluations, and some other secret criteria. The list gets formulated at management levels above me, and it's revised about every two months since layoffs are a continual thing around here—a long, slow, steady bleed. The person at the top of the list is the most desirable to get rid of, and then you go down in order and the one at the bottom of the list will be the last one to go. At layoff time, the bean counters decide how many people in your group need to get shit-canned, and then you have to take as many as needed, in order from the top. I just get to see the list when the time comes, because I get to do the dirty work. I guess I should be grateful that it's only one person this time.

I find the note and look to see who's due to get the pink slip tomorrow (an anachronism because of course these operations are paperless now), and…

Oh, shit.

It's crazy Wally.

Wally is the guy who everyone knows is mentally unstable, but for the most part, the truth goes unspoken. He's about sixty and has been around for as long as I can remember. Wally's the scary silent type, with a face that's always nearly expressionless. You just can't read the guy, and when he looks you in the eye, you don't know if he's about to say something or just shove his ball-point pen into one of your major arteries. I've never seen him smile or talk to people about anything other than work. When you ask him a question, and of course it's a work question because nobody would dare raise anything personal with him, you usually get five seconds of chilling silence (which you can use to ponder whether you're about to die) while he stares at you with those crazy, empty eyes.

As far as his appearance goes, the thing that jumps out at you is that he's shaved bald. And by that, I mean you can tell from his five o'clock shadow he has a full and potentially very thick head of hair, but he shaves everything off, down to the skin, every day. Go figure. Most men who do this probably start when they think they're losing their hair, but not Wally. I'm guessing he's been doing this since he was in the Marines, so he must have started about forty years ago. His top end up there is all shiny and smooth. It doesn't give him a friendly appearance, like a giant dildo. More of a deadly one, like a ballistic missile. Maybe he does it for the fright factor.

Other than the baldness and the heavy-duty steel rim glasses (military-grade, no doubt, because they look like they could survive a hit from a hunting rifle), his image is unassuming. He's of medium height and lean, with wiry muscle, the kind you might expect a prisoner in solitary for ten years to get from doing push-ups and sit-ups for twelve hours a day. He's not handsome, not homely, just scary, and it's mostly because of those blank psycho eyes. I heard that the Marines let him go after about five years. They gave him some kind of a general discharge, not a dishonorable one since that would have been highlighted in his personnel file. I'm not sure about the details of the discharge, but it was probably one that implied: *Hey fella, sorry, but you gotta go. You didn't really do anything wrong, but you're just too damn scary for the Marines.*

Apparently, he used to be married, a very long time ago. His house caught fire, and there's another rumor that Wally once said he'd burn the damn house down before he'd let his wife get it in the divorce settlement, but at least she wasn't in it at the time.

He's been in my group for less than a year, and I haven't even had to give him a performance review yet, which I've been dreading. Wally's been bounced around between departments like a turd that nobody wants to touch because all the managers realize that with these never-ending waves of layoffs, he's bound to be targeted sometime soon, and God forbid you're his manager when it happens because you'll have to tell him. He's competent enough at his job, except in the *plays well with others* department. Can't check that box.

Without a wife and kids, Wally must have lots of free time, and who the hell knows what he does with it, but I'm hoping it's nothing more serious than pulling the legs off spiders or maybe biting the heads off live chickens. I have no idea, and I don't really want to know. But now I've got to lay him off.

Ho-leeee-shit.

So, as far as the layoff thing goes, the company's procedure is to have all the first-level managers like me do them all on the same day and at the same time, which is usually ten o'clock in the morning. We're literally supposed to drop everything and do it at the designated time. Why? Well, I suppose if a person thinks he might get laid off and he knows it's coming, they don't want to give him time to run out to his car and get his handgun out of the glove compartment. Seriously. But if three

S.E. Greco

hundred people are getting laid off throughout the whole company, they can't possibly all be given the axe precisely when the clock strikes ten. Moments after the very first one is done, word gets out within twenty seconds.

Oh, and then there's the security thing. Lots of managers like me might have a little wariness about telling an employee that he's getting laid off, even if the employee isn't as crazy as Wally. So, they ask for a security guard to be discretely present outside the room where you give the bad word. When there's a massive layoff planned, like tomorrow's, they have only one guard covering a huge area, and hopefully the poor guard won't have to face the pitchforks and torches of an enraged mob.

And on top of that, security has had manpower cutbacks too, so they're stretched extra thin, and you take what you can get. For the last layoff I did, I got a security guard named Horace, who I think must be about ninety years old. He's a nice guy, and I can appreciate the wisdom that comes with years of experience, but I find myself wondering why this guy is still around in a security role.

Thank God they don't carry firearms because Horace can't see very well, and if it came down to a firefight, I'd be the one who got shot in the ass. Maybe they give Horace some non-lethal weapons, like rubber-band guns and such. Come to think of it, Horace might be using a cane or a walker by now, and he could probably beat someone with that if he had to.

****

The next morning, I stand in a small meeting room waiting for Wally, clutching my coffee, the cup shaking

94

and the brew spilling on my shoes. I bought decaf this morning, to try and keep myself calm, and I *never* buy decaf.

Damn, I wish there was a shot of liquor in it. Irish whiskey, rubbing alcohol, lighter fluid, whatever.

I can feel the sweat dripping down my upper chest and back, soaking my bra.

Cripes, it's as hot as a bread oven in here…

I look around for a thermostat to adjust, but there is none, and then I remember that they removed all of them last month in favor of a central environmental control system as part of a "workplace efficiency" upgrade. God forbid someone should try to turn the temperature in a meeting room lower than eighty-three in the summer or higher than sixty-three in the winter.

Wally walks in right on time, with his usual deadpan, unreadable expression. My pulse doubles and my chest feels as tight as a piano wire. *He must know, just by virtue of having been summoned at the zero hour.*

"Hi, Wally, have a seat," I say.

Amazing that I can even speak, and…did I make that sound too cheery?

He responds in a monotone, "I'd prefer to stand if this is going to be brief."

I close the windowless door behind Wally. It's just him and me now, no witnesses. I try to clear my throat, but the action is useless. It feels like I'm gagging on a two-pound hairball. I sit down and begin my rehearsed spiel, my crock of corporate bullshit.

"Well, no doubt you know that we have a resource action going and, well, there's no easy way to say this, Wally, but I'm afraid we have to let you go…" *Please don't kill me immediately,* "And it's really got nothing to do with your performance..." *Because I'd like to say goodbye to my family first*, "It's just that Fleener is cutting back production in some areas and these layoffs are being done by skill set and we...uh...I mean the company...is looking to retain employees with a lot of computer skills these days." This was the standard Fleener line to try and absolve the company of liability because almost all of the people being shit-canned have ratings that indicate their performances are adequate, some even *better* than adequate. I continue, "As per company policy, you'll have to give me your badge and leave the plant immediately, and then we'll send you your personal belongings from your cube. I'm so sorry, Wally. But let me explain to you Fleener's generous severance package."

Generous? I'd laugh if I wasn't scared shitless. I can't believe I'm saying this, spewing out the exact lines written on the company charts. If this guy can't land another position in production accounting, which is unlikely given his age and the state of the business economy right now in southern Connecticut, he'll be lucky to find a job scraping gum off the sidewalk. But I suppose this particular guy could always get work as a hired assassin.

"And I'll write you a nice reference letter, of course, to help you land a good position at another company." *Of course I will. What company wouldn't want a crazy Wally on their team?*

He immediately unclips the ID badge from his shirt, raises it to his eye level, and then throws it down onto the table, snapping his arm like a baseball pitcher. It hits with an alarming CRACK and then keeps going, whizzing past me and landing on the floor. So I guess he isn't planning to stay and hear about the severance package. Just as well, since it sucks.

Wally turns abruptly, walks to the door, and opens it. I think he's just going to leave without saying anything at all, which is probably the best outcome I could have hoped for. *Yup, just head straight out to your car to get the pipe bomb or the assault rifle or whatever it is you have ready...*

And just as I'm thinking it's over, Wally turns around. He stares at me for a few seconds, that expressionless, un-nerving zombie stare again, and then says in a cool, even tone, "We'll see each other again, June, I'm sure. It could be tomorrow, or it could be five years from now. You might be walking down the beach and you'll turn around and I'll be there, walking ten steps behind you. Or you might be sitting on a park bench and look over and I'll be on the next bench. And I'll wave to you."

Yikes!

And then he smiles, and it's probably the first time I've ever seen him smile, and it's also probably the damn creepiest smile I have ever seen, first of all because it takes a full five seconds for the corners of his mouth to slowly turn up enough so that I even realize it's a smile, and second because it's the kind of psycho smile you might see on a juvenile delinquent's face when he's torturing a stray kitten with a cigarette.

I unconsciously sink a few inches down into my chair, shrinking from the malice that drips from Wally. In a robotic voice, he says one more thing without breaking that scary clown grin: "You just be sure to take care of yourself, June. I mean, *really* good care." He turns and leaves.

What the hell was THAT supposed to mean?

Considering the tone, it doesn't exactly come off as friendly advice. I'm sure it was a threat, but I find myself wishing that it was a *clear* threat, something more specific that I can tell the cops about. Why didn't he just say, *I'm gonna kill you*, or maybe something more graphic like, *I'm gonna gouge your eyes out, bitch?* Or even a simple, *I'm gonna get you,* would have been good enough. But an *implied* threat? What the hell good is *that* for, other than destroying my chances of ever getting a good night's sleep again?

Maybe that's the whole damn point.

I get up and walk to the doorway and see that there are four people—Pog, Faith, Verne, and Mary—standing outside, holding their coffee cups. Two seconds ago, before they knew what was going on in this little room, they were probably chatting happily about the weather or some new restaurant in the area, but now they look shocked and terrified—except for Pog, who sports his usual happy guy face.

"Oh, dear God, June, ah heard that!" Faith exclaims, her eyes wide with alarm. "Ah'll bet you just told him he's laid off, right? Well, he's a crazy person, June, just crazy, and oh my Lordy Lord, you must be shittin' seashells right now, June, ah don't blame you, and—"

I shush Faith with a raised hand and we all look at Wally as he walks out of the cube area, and I'm just hoping he'll quickly leave the building and not talk to anyone else or even stop. But then I see Horace, the oldest working security guard in the world, step almost in front of Wally. I suppose that Horace has his hearing aid cranked up to max and he'd caught some or all of Wally's implied threat. Horace apparently takes his job seriously, and I guess what he has in mind is escorting Wally out of the building.

Wally stops and stares down Horace for about ten seconds. Wally doesn't speak, he just gives Horace that stare. No words needed.

Horace melts into a blob on the floor, and then Wally starts walking toward the exit again.

Faith wails, "Oh, sweet Jesus on a hayride!"

She and I race toward Horace. I fumble in my pocket for my cell but then realize that I left it in my cube.

I bark, "Faith, call the emergency response number, Horace might be having a heart attack!"

And someone please get me a Xanax.

Chapter 8

By early afternoon I'm relieved to hear that Horace's heart is as fine as any century-old organ could be, he simply had a low blood pressure episode. He'd soon be back at work in his security role, saving our vulnerable asses from all kinds of terrorist threats and various assorted mortal dangers.

And as for me, I'm finally starting to get over the anxiety brought on by the Wally debacle. Except for a little residual chest pressure, dizziness, numbness in my left arm, tremors in both hands, and blurry vision, I'm feeling just fine.

I scan through all the e-mails that flooded my inbox in the last few hours, and I'm in disbelief as I read one from upper management announcing that they're going to hold Diversity Jubilation Day next week.

Diversity Jubilation Day is the company's feel-good lip service farce of an event dedicated to equal opportunity and inclusiveness, and obviously they decided to schedule it soon after the layoff as a way of distracting the surviving employees from today's downsizing misery. You're supposed to dress up in the clothing of your ancestors, and at a certain time of day you go into the largest public area, which is the cafeteria, and parade your sorry ass around, show off your native garb, and dance your native dances. You're also supposed to bring in a dish to pass around, a specialty from your native land.

Like we don't have enough to do? Endless meetings, reports, employee appraisals, production line crises, and miscellaneous catastrophes. And now they want us to be dancing fools, as well. And of course, my asshole of a manager Larry sent me a note saying that he expects all of the managers under him to set an example by fully participating in Diversity Jubilation Day, even though the idiot says that he regretfully will not be able to take part in the wonderful festivities due to having planned some "urgent personal business" for that time, which means either an afternoon on the golf course or a four-hour bowel movement.

As far as my ethnic background, I'm kind of a mutt, I suppose. I've got some French, English, German, Spanish, and even some Norwegian in me. And if you're not sure what your ethnic background is, that's not a problem because the company has offered to test your DNA. No way in hell am I giving them *my* genetic code. They'd probably test it for the genes that trigger early onset dementia and any number of other incurable diseases to get a better idea of when my health care costs will spiral out of control.

I think I may go with the Norwegian theme this year because I have a Norwegian folk dress that I wore for a Halloween party some years back. Except I was maybe ten pounds thinner then. So, if I don't split any of the seams while I'm dancing like a moron, it'll work out fine.

And as far as bringing in my favorite native dish, well, I have absolutely no time to be cooking extra food when I can barely get dinner on the table for my family every night. So, I think I'll throw together some week-

S.E. Greco

old mac and cheese with whatever other leftover slop I have in the fridge, add lots of mayo, send it through a food processor just long enough so that the elbow macaroni is unrecognizable, and serve it with a purchased bag of some ancient grain chips that look really cool and rustic, and I'll call it an ethnic dip. It'll taste okay because who doesn't like cheese and pasta and mayo? And it won't kill anybody.

****

A short time later, I'm stirring my coffee as I wait for Louise, who sits across from me, to tell me why she needed to see me again so soon. We're in the relative comfort of my favorite coffee house, a little place that's just a few blocks from Fleener. I'm grateful to get away from work for a few minutes.

"Thanks for buying," I say. I sip the steaming drink, grateful for the caffeine boost that I forfeited this morning. Louise has her arms folded casually on the table, a large cup of hot tea in front of her.

"No problem," she answers. "Thanks for seeing me again on such short notice. I didn't mean to inconvenience you. I could have met you at work."

"Oh, it's good to get out of that place for a few minutes. So, you have more questions for me?"

She nods. "I spoke to Faith yesterday. And I wanted to chat with you about what I learned and get your take on it. Because you seem to be close to her."

"Oh, she told you that?"

"Yes. She spoke fondly of you. She looks up to you, certainly. Does that surprise you?"

"That she looks up to me? I suppose not, because I'm her manager and I'm also about fifteen years older than she is."

102

"Well, the first thing I have to say is that I had a hard time believing, when I read the notes of the first interview done by the uniformed officer, that she just happened to notice that blood spot on the trunk lid as she was walking by the car. Mostly because the car is red. The paint is not exactly *blood* red, but it's close enough to it so the blood would not have stood out very well. So, I suspected there was some other reason that she went over to the car. And then her friend Mary explained to me that Faith is clairvoyant. Mary seemed completely serious and totally convinced that Faith has this talent, although when I asked Mary for some evidence, she couldn't give me anything concrete. So, after I talked to Mary, I interviewed Faith and asked her about it. She admitted to being clairvoyant, said she has visions. And she told me that she had a vision of Melvin's body in the trunk of a car."

Louise's skepticism is obvious. She raises her eyebrows in a *whad'ya think?* expression and gives me a very slight smile, waiting to see how I'll respond. I don't want to badmouth Faith. I remain silent, expecting a question to come eventually.

She continues, "So, do you know about Faith's alleged abilities? And did she tell you she'd had this vision?"

I nod. "I guess *she* believes she has this ability, but it's just too crazy, you know? I'm a skeptic."

"Then we have that in common. I've had a bad experience with a self-proclaimed psychic."

"What kind of bad experience?"

"I worked with one on a case because my boss is apparently a believer. It was a homicide case, and it was going nowhere, our leads had dried up. Department policy is that we don't officially consult psychics, but my boss bends the rules, and he justified it under our mandate to run down all credible leads because this psychic came to us saying he had information about the crime." She points her eyes towards the floor and shakes her head slowly back and forth, as if remembering a quite unpleasant experience, like a tooth extraction.

"This guy called himself *The Amazing Wojtek* and he spoke with a Slavic accent. My boss said, 'Oh yeah, this guy's the real thing for sure, a bona fide spoon bender.' So, I poked into the guy's background, and it turned out his real name was Phil Mudd, and he was born in Brooklyn. That didn't faze my boss at all when I told him. He ordered me to work with the guy anyway. So, *The Amazing Wojtek* had us running all over the city, chasing dead ends. Sometimes he would say that it was imperative that we follow him into empty fields, or into the woods, or wherever, while he tried to sense electromagnetic energy fields. And he would come out with these extremely vague statements, like, 'The body is buried in a very isolated area, and there are trees visible from the area.' Well, if you're going to bury a body, the chances are good you'd put it in an isolated area, and how many places are there that *don't* have a view of at least a few trees? When he failed to help us locate the body, he turned his attention to the murder weapon and gave us about a dozen possible places to look for it. He said he was sure it was hidden in one of them. Needless to say, he struck out there, too. Finally, he blamed me personally. He said I was a nonbeliever, and I was dimming his visions. My brain was emitting too many negative energy waves or something."

I chuckle and ask, "So, did you ever solve the case?"

"No, we didn't. But if it's ever solved and the body is found, believe me, *The Amazing Wojtek* will go over every single statement, every prediction he made to us about the case, to find something that vaguely agrees with what happened, and he'll ignore the other ninety-nine-point nine percent that doesn't agree. At the end he was throwing so much shit at the wall, I'm sure he figured that *something* would eventually stick. Then he'll probably take it to the press, and they'll print something about how Wojtek had solved the crime, but the police were too stupid to realize it."

She sips her coffee. "Sorry for the rant, June. All that being said, let me add that the CIA recently declassified a report on some very well controlled tests that they conducted on the famous psychic, Yuri Gellar, in the seventies. They unambiguously concluded that his powers were genuine. And there are a number of credible reports in the United States and abroad of psychics helping police solve crimes. It's very rare, but it *has* happened. So, I *do believe* that some people have genuine psychic abilities. I'm just quite certain that the fakers far outnumber the genuine psychics. So anyway, I'd like to know what you think about Faith's alleged…*abilities,*" she says.

"But why do you want *my* opinion?"

"Because you see Faith every workday. And you're the one normal person in a case with a rather bizarre cast of characters. We have a clairvoyant, an Eastern European internet bride, a chain-smoking elderly woman with a severe attitude, and an exterminator who thinks he's a superhero and wants to join forces with us to solve the crime, and we don't even know yet if any crime has been committed. Some of Faith's co-workers are rather eccentric, too. I talked to a few more yesterday. One of them urged me to investigate the alien abduction angle."

"Oh, yeah, that would be Harold. He pretty much sees the alien hand in everything. I think at home he sleeps in a tinfoil tent. Right, a weird cast, I know. And the additional fact that Annuska is from Transylvania…"

"Transylvania? She told me Romania."

"Right, it's part of Romania."

"I see. And now you're going to tell me she's a vampire? Which seems to somehow fit strangely with her job in a funeral home. I assume she has to suck the blood out of dead people. But with a syringe, hopefully."

"She's not a vampire. She's a witch."

"A witch? You're kidding, right? She didn't tell me that either."

"Did you ask?"

"It's not usually on my list of standard interview questions."

"Actually, I shouldn't have used the term witch, it's not right. She's a Wiccan. As I understand it, Wicca is kind of a nature-based religion. Anyway, she has special powers, too. We didn't really get into the details. But I wonder…Melvin is gainfully employed, and Annuska has a good job as an embalming technician, so it's sort of strange that they aren't living in a nicer place. Unless they really spend a lot."

Louise remarked, "Actually she does more than just embalming. She was certified as an embalmer in Romania, but couldn't get work in it over there, so she got involved in that sexy bride business to pay the bills. But here she landed a job at a funeral home right after she got married, and now she pretty much runs the whole place for her boss, the owner. So, she's apparently quite intelligent and capable. And she also has a temper."

"How do you know that? From Florence Shmoo?"

Louise smiles. "No, from a more objective source, a police report from about a year ago. Someone cut her off in traffic. She got out of the car and tried to scratch the man's eyes out, but no charges were filed. Sounds like she totally lost her temper but then somehow talked the officer out of arresting her."

"She must be quite persuasive too."

Louise nods and says, "Apparently so. And as far as what they spend...well, she certainly does dress nicely. I noticed she was wearing a pair of nine-hundred-dollar Italian boots when I talked to her. Not something I'd buy on a detective's salary. Anyway, let's go back and talk about Faith, if you don't mind. Can you think of any reason why she might pretend to have a vision about seeing Melvin dead?"

"Pretend? Why, no. What possible reason could she have?"

"Well, the most common one is to achieve fame. And then possibly the financial gain that could come with it."

I'm sure my expression of utter skepticism reveals that I think the whole idea is ridiculous, even before I say, "Faith? Not a chance. She told me this whole thing of her getting visions has been a pain in the ass. Not that I even believe she's getting real visions, mind you. But you're wasting your time considering this angle. Faith is a scatterbrain. She's naïve about life and about relationships. She thinks dead people walk around stores and buy stuff in the housewares aisle. Believe me, there is absolutely no way she would make this up, to become famous or for some other weird purpose. She noticed that

Melvin wasn't at his desk, and for some reason she imagined that harm had come to him, that's all. It's clear that she's got an overactive imagination."

"Maybe you're right, but I hope you understand that when a self-proclaimed psychic gives details about a crime, we have to consider that the psychic might be…intentionally deceitful."

I nod my head in agreement. I know it's a detective's job to consider every possibility. But her next question catches me off guard.

"By the way, did you know that Faith was arrested when she was very young?"

"Arrested? No, I didn't know. There's nothing about it in her personnel file. Arrested for what?"

"Shoplifting. In a discount department store, with her mother and father. It was kind of a coordinated operation, where the little girl would take something, then pretend to bump into one of the adults and pass it off."

"Faith told me that her family was quite poor when they were young. Maybe they were just desperate. Her parents are both dead now. So, what came of the arrest?"

"Nothing at all. She was a juvenile, only eleven, and it was her first offense. They didn't even send her to a detention center."

"How'd you find out? Aren't juvenile records from long ago expunged or sealed or something like that?"

"Yes, sometimes they are. But not an adult's records. The parents were arrested too, and their records of the incident have details of their child's involvement. So anyway, Faith said that she's been working at Fleener for about five months?"

"That's correct. But why are you telling me all

this?"

"Because I want to know what you think of her...abilities. You've already told me that you're skeptical about her being a true psychic. Then what do *you* think drew her to the car?"

I shrug my shoulders and say, "I think that she's one of these people that *thinks* she gets psychic visions. Maybe when she saw that Melvin hadn't shown up for work, she felt worried enough about him to imagine that he was...well, dead. And she fooled herself into thinking that it looked like his body was in the trunk of a car. I mean, it's not like the inside of a car trunk has a very distinctive look to it. It's usually just, you know, gray or black felt. She didn't say she saw a tire jack next to his head or a pair of jumper cables or a spare tire. I think the car trunk idea may have come about as a result of her searching for more answers in what she *thought* was a psychic vision. And even if she *did* see something in her mind which evoked the inside of a car trunk, it still doesn't mean she's clairvoyant. If I say to you, *Quick, tell me where Jimmy Hoffa is buried,* and the first thing that pops into your head for whatever reason is a baseball field, does that mean you had a psychic vision? I don't think so, but maybe Faith would think so. So maybe that's why she went for the car. And as far as the blood on the trunk lid is concerned, it's probably just a coincidence. Melvin probably cut himself and touched the car, like you said."

Louise smiles and takes a sip of her tea.

"You and I are pretty much on the same page on this. In any case, I also wanted to let you know that as of today, we're keeping an eye out for Melvin. If he just took off in his car and keeps using it, we'll eventually

S.E. Greco

locate him. A flag will be raised if his car is stopped by the police anywhere in the country. If he goes through a camera tollbooth somewhere we'll get a read on his plate. Also, if he withdraws money from an ATM, I'll be notified. That's about the extent of our monitoring at this point. Of course, if he took off and really doesn't want to be found, he could be careful enough such that none of these measures will be useful."

"Is that what you think, that he just took off?"

Louise shrugs and says, "Could be. He did it once before. Successfully, in fact. The police never located him until this fluke with the blood spot on the trunk. So maybe he decided to abandon his life again. Annuska said that Melvin was home on Monday night and left for work on Tuesday morning, as usual. Said she didn't notice anything out of the ordinary. Florence Shmoo was out on Monday evening and said that when she got home, Melvin's car was there. On Tuesday morning Florence slept very late, but a neighbor said that he saw Melvin's car from down the street leaving the house at the normal time. So, if he never showed up at work, it's possible that he just drove away on Tuesday morning."

"So, you're not thinking that Annuska might have...*done* something to him?"

"You mean murdered him? It's okay, June. You don't need to use euphemisms with me. Even if she knew his true identity, killing her husband would not get her the inheritance. It's more likely that he just took off because they had a bad relationship and he wanted out. Florence Shmoo said they argued a lot. If he filed for divorce and got involved with lawyers, maybe he was worried that his real identity might come out. As for Annuska, she came to the States with a valid Romanian

110

passport for a vacation, met Melvin, and got married. She has no arrest record here, just a bunch of traffic tickets. The only thing she's guilty of is being a lousy driver, like fifty million other people in this country. However, she may have something else to worry about now. If the marriage wasn't legal, then she's not an American citizen, and she might be subject to deportation. That could be a huge mess for her. Fortunately, it's not a mess that I need to be involved in. The immigration department will eventually sort it out, but I wouldn't be surprised if it takes a very long time."

Since Louise is being open with me, I make a snap decision to share another piece of information with her. I don't see how it can hurt.

"There's something else I forgot to tell you when we spoke yesterday…" *Okay, so I didn't really forget, I decided not to tell you until just now…*"I got a very strange phone call the same day that I went over to Melvin's house after I got back to work. It was from a man who wouldn't identify himself. He said that he'd been taken in by some kind of con artist, a woman. She apparently cleaned him out. And he said that he happened to see Melvin with this woman in public. He didn't say the woman's name or even his own name. He made it clear that he didn't want to get involved, but he felt Melvin should be warned about this woman."

"So how did he know it was Melvin? Could this man have been a friend or acquaintance of Melvin's?"

"Don't know. Our conversation didn't get that far."

"Did he describe the woman?"

With a sheepish grin, I say, "No. I sort of cut him off, told him that he had no business calling me and that he should talk to the cops."

"Did you tell him *anything*?"

"No. I mean, really, what business is it of mine?"

She pauses for a few seconds as if to make me consider the answer to my own question, and that makes me feel even a little more guilty.

"Do you have the phone number, June?" she asks hopefully.

"No. On my phone it appeared as private."

"Well, it might help if you could tell me exactly what time you got the phone call."

I take out my phone, look at the call log, and say, "Two fifty-eight."

"Okay. Please let me know if he contacts you again, and if he does, try to convince him to give you his name."

I'm pretty sure I'll fail at *that* mission. So, why do I say, "Uh, sure, I'll do my best."

Chapter 9

I sneak out of work early since it's Friday and I have to get ready for a little party I'm throwing this evening.

I don't do much entertaining. After all, I have a job that sucks the life-force out of me, and constant pangs of guilt at not spending enough time with my kids and husband. But various neighbors have had Darryl and I over for dinner or small parties, and my reciprocation is way overdue. Tonight, I'll take care of them all in one shot.

The hors d'oeuvres will be purchased stuff, like little frozen meatballs and ready to eat shrimp cocktail, dressed up and re-plated to look like I've been slaving all day in the kitchen. And then I'll have a little buffet with simple home-made stuff on it: chicken marsala, a pasta dish, and a green salad. After that, I'll serve a few desserts, which will be obviously and unashamedly purchased at the local bakery. I've always found that by dessert time, if I keep the wine, beer, and booze flowing freely, no one gives a damn that they're not eating homemade desserts. The men are usually too stoned by that time to discriminate, and most of the women barely pick at the desserts anyway.

By five o'clock I'm back from dropping off my nine-year-old Ricky and my seven-year-old Vince at their friend's house where they will happily spend the night. I'm sweeping some leaves and assorted debris off the front steps, tidying up the entrance in preparation for my guests' arrival, when I hear my next-door neighbor Murray start to play his alto saxophone from his back patio.

Murray is about seventy-five years old and long retired with lots of time on his hands, so he took up the saxophone at a very late age, and by late, I mean only two months ago. And he also decided that he would bestow upon us, his valued neighbors, the gift of music.

The problem is, Murray can only play one song, *The Girl from Ipanema*. He plays slow, medium, and fast versions. All three of them sound like shit. You would think he might play the slow version a little better than the others because the fingering might be easier to deal with—but nope, it sucks just as bad as the fast version. Every other note is a screech, like he's stepping on an alley cat's tail.

Sometimes I daydream about walking right over there, ripping that shiny silver horn out of his hands, and shoving it up his ass, wide end first. I would never really do it, of course. I can't even bring myself to go over there and simply tell him to give us a break from it. But fantasizing about it makes it a little easier to endure the torture of his playing.

Other than being completely inconsiderate about the noise pollution, Murray is a nice enough guy, and so I invited him and his wife to my little party tonight. It will give me a few hours that I don't have to listen to *Girl from Ipanema*. And I'll be including an appetizer of fried calamari with cherry peppers, very hot and spicy. I'll try and push it on him. If I can raise a blister on his upper lip, he might skip practice tomorrow.

I finish with the porch sweeping and go inside. The

noise level drops a few decibels, but I can still make out every squeal from Murray's horn. I find my cell and call my brother.

His name is Paul and he's thirty-six years old, and he's a professional fast talker. You've heard it, on radio commercials where they might say something about a sale or a special promotion, and then at the end they have someone make a disclaimer to absolve the company of some liability. It's all legal mumbo jumbo. Nobody listens to it, and they say it at breakneck speed, so it doesn't use too much costly commercial time. Well, my brother's one of those guys that does the fast talking, and that's *all* he does. You would think that his vocation would be obsolete by now because they'd have computer programs to speed up the talking without making the voice sound like a chipmunk's, right? Well, they do, but the fast talkers have a strong union that actually lobbies against the use of this software, and they even have conventions and everything, where they get together and give speeches on how to take legal action against anybody trying to use fast talker software. And my pathetic brother is one of them.

He considers himself some kind of a celebrity by virtue of his ability to spew out a few blazingly fast sentences at the end of ads for liposuction, hair transplants, condoms, junk bonds, or whatever. Being a fast talker is what he lives for and all that he aspires to be. He's never been married or even had a long-term girlfriend that I know of. He's been trying the internet dating thing for years, but not hard enough I think, because he's had zero success. So, he needs a push. When I have people over to our house for little parties, I try to invite whatever single women I can scrounge up, and usually I do okay, snagging at least one or two for him to meet. I'm not sure why I feel it's my duty to try and fix him up. Protective older sister thing, I suppose, since our parents aren't around anymore. Anyway, halfway through the evening I usually find that dork sitting in the corner of the room, demonstrating his fast-talking prowess to one of the single women, as if he thinks this is the greatest way to impress the ladies. And I glance at the woman's face as she listens to the fast talking, and she usually looks trapped and gives me a look back as if to say, *Who is this babbling imbecile?*

His phone rings eight times before I hear a sleepy, "Hello?"

"Are you kidding me, Paul?" I yell. "You're asleep at this hour in the afternoon? Well, get your rear end out of bed, or wherever it's parked. Remember, you're coming over here tonight at six-thirty for a little party. There'll be a few single women, so you'd better get here on time. And Barbara's one of them. You met her at my last party. You never told me what you thought of her, so I asked her over again. Did you want to see her again, you think?" There's a pause, and I envision him trying to shake off his stupor.

"Uh, hi Juney," he replies slowly. "She's very nice, but I just don't think there's any chemistry there...between us, I mean...you know."

"Whad'ya mean, no chemistry?" I rail. "You two were talking at the last party for quite a while." *Or rather, you were talking AT her, two thousand words a minute.* "You seemed to hit it off just fine."

"Juney, she's nice, but I'm just...she deserves someone different...better than me. I'm just not good enough for her."

"C'mon now, first you say no chemistry? And now you're not good enough for her? That sounds to me like a crock o' shit. I know you too well, there's something about her that doesn't appeal to you. *Tell* me, Paul."

"Juney…thanks for trying to fix me up with her, but I…I…"

It's obvious that he's flustered and looking for a way out. I raise my voice a notch and press on.

"Okay, I accept the fact that you don't want to see her again, but Paul, how can I help you find a woman who's right for you if you won't tell me what you *don't* like about her?"

"Juney, I can't, I…I…"

"What? Spit it out, Paul. What is it you don't like about her?"

And then there is silence for about five seconds, before he finally says, in a barely audible monotone, "Her breasts aren't big enough."

I pause. "I'm sorry, *what* did you say?" I reply softly, trying for the moment to remain calm, thinking that perhaps there's a small possibility I didn't hear him correctly.

"Her, uh, breasts. They're not quite…*big* enough," he repeats sheepishly.

"YOU PIG!" I scream. "I can't *believe* what you just said!"

"But Juney, I…I…didn't want to tell you, I…"

"ALL RIGHT THEN! If *that's* what you want, if *that's* what's so important to you, FINE! I'll find you some cow with HUGE UDDERS! I'll just look in the phone directory under DAIRY!"

One thing I don't like about cell phones is that you can't slam the handset down when you're angry. So, I just give him a parting threat in a menacing tone, "Get over here on time, and don't you *dare* do any demonstrations of your fast talking to try and impress anyone!" I end the call.

Some men are swine, and my brother is apparently one of the king pigs. A fast-talking pinhead and a swine rolled into one. It's like those stupid reality shows where they have a dozen women competing to marry some rich and handsome bachelor guy, and for eight weeks they try to impress him, and they go through all kinds of humiliating trials and contests, and in the end, he picks the one with the biggest boobs. What the hell is the point?

I take a few deep breaths to calm myself down and walk into the kitchen where Darryl is working on a tray of ziti, spreading sauce and cheese.

"How we doing, hon?" I ask him.

"Fantastic, hon," he answers, never breaking his concentration. "Everything's under control." He steps back for a moment to evaluate his work, staring at it through the thick lenses of his geeky eyeglasses. I've been begging him to get a more fashionable frame. These look like industrial safety glasses.

Darryl is pretty good looking, but besides the glasses I find myself wishing that he didn't wear his sandy hair in such a short crew cut. When I last asked him to let it grow out a little, he said that the increased effort needed in taking care of longer hair would not be offset by the admittedly nebulous benefit of wearing it longer. Pretty much every decision comes down to a cost versus reward analysis. That's my Darryl.

Darryl's a mechanical engineer and he cooks like one, too. As I fuss with the meatballs, I watch him as he measures out every ingredient, even the amount of cheese and oregano he sprinkles on top. When he measures out a tablespoon of oregano, he dips the measuring spoon into the oregano bottle, then scrapes the contents flat with the back edge of a butter knife.

Next, I see him contemplating something, probably whether he should try to compress the oregano slightly to squeeze out some of the airspace because these oregano flakes are maybe slightly larger than your average oregano flakes. At the high end of the standard deviation, or whatever.

When he's cooking, he always wears an apron with many pockets, like a carpenter's tool belt. In the pockets he always keeps a spatula, a set of measuring spoons, and a ruler, of all things. What the hell do you need a ruler for when you cook? I asked him once, and he looked at me like I was a dull student, and said in a no-nonsense manner, "Why, to check the size of a pan, of course. For instance, if a recipe calls for a nine-inch pan, I need to make sure I'm not grabbing a nine and a half inch one, because then the contents would be thinner, and would cook faster, correct?"

Of course, how silly of me.

If I had to pick one word to describe my husband, it would probably be *oblivious*. A second choice might be *dull*, but even so, I love him. He's a real stick in the mud, my Darryl. He can concentrate like a demon on whatever the task at hand is, in this case making ziti, but he's unaware of about eighty percent of what goes on in the world around him.

He designs commercial refrigeration equipment for a living. He spent two years working on a certain refrigerant metering valve, a revolutionary new design, and he would tell me all about how they couldn't decide whether to make the flapper valve or the fleugel stem or whatever out of stainless steel or titanium. I heard every night for two months that the titanium was stronger and lighter and would probably last longer but it was more expensive than the stainless steel and there was a massive task force at work to make this decision, and this was Darryl's idea of drama and excitement. You don't see a lot of emotion on Darryl's face, unless he's discussing compressors and heat pump efficiency ratios.

I worry sometimes that Darryl is aging faster than I am. It's not just the erectile dysfunction thing. There are unmistakable signs, first of all the stuff you might expect, like setting the thermostat to eighty-five degrees in the winter. But lately, he's even mentioned putting a monthly payment down to reserve a condo for us at the local retirement community, *Old Fart Village* or whatever it's called. And for his birthday he asked me for, get this: a metal detector. I can picture him on our next vacation, spending his time wandering the beach in striped shorts, black shoes, and black socks, slowly moving the metal detector back and forth, a grown man judging the success of his day by how many nickels he finds in the sand.

"Less than two hours to go, hon," I say, as we near the time our guests will arrive.

"Great, hon, almost done. They're gonna love my ziti. Abbey says she hardly ever makes Italian food for herself because she watches her figure so diligently. This will be a real treat for her."

Abbey?

ABBEY?!

I can feel my irritable bowel starting to seize up.

Okay, stay calm. Don't get mad at Darryl. After all, he's friggin' clueless.

In a controlled and pleasantly conversational tone, I ask, "Uhhh…hon? You invited Abbey?"

"Yes, sure did, hon," he replies, as if inviting my nemesis into our house is the most natural thing in the world. "She was out there jogging when I went to get the mail, so when I asked all five of the guys to come, I asked her, too. I said she could bring a date if she wanted to, but she said she wasn't seeing anyone right now. Said she's currently available."

"Available, oh? That's great, hon. Just great." I don't think Darryl catches my sarcastic tone. Sarcasm usually sails ten feet over his head. It's part of the whole *oblivious* thing he's got going. Available? The guys out there probably spewed a cloud of pheromones when they heard her say that word.

Abbey. Coming to my party. Wonderful.

And, goddammit, I'm not even serving a sit-down dinner so I won't be able to spit in her soup.

****

"June, listen to me," whispers Faith. "Ah got a bead on the murder weapon!"

"A what on the what?" I ask. Faith just arrived for the party, and she immediately follows me into the kitchen as I'm getting the first of the hot hors d'oeuvres out of the oven.

I invited her because I've been concerned about her being depressed over Melvin, but now I'm having regrets. Her boyfriend Ralph wasn't able to come with her, so she came alone, and now she's on me like superglue. We're out of earshot of the others at the moment. Darryl and the rest of the guests are in the living room.

"You know, ah got a vision, just a little while ago, when ah touched a printed report ah had in my desk that Melvin had written and scribbled on, of all things. It was a vision of where the murder weapon is hidden. The one used to kill Melvin."

She looks at me as if of course I should understand what she's talking about because it all makes perfect sense. But I don't have time for this nonsense right now.

"Faith, please. We don't even know that he's dead."

She shrugs and says, "Ah can't help it, June. When it comes, it just comes. The visions, ah can't stop 'em."

"Yes, you can. Please stop them. Concentrate, you can do it, I *know* you can."

"No, ah can't," she implores.

"Can you at least delay the vision until after I serve dessert?" I plead.

"June, ah already *got* the vision." She moves closer to me and says in a hushed tone, as if we are secret conspirators, "It's a handgun, June! And it's—"

I snap my palm up in front of her face. "Stop right there," I command. But, of course, she doesn't stop.

"June, it's in a pond. Somebody threw it in a pond," she says in a whisper, her hand cupped against her mouth to ward off eavesdroppers.

"What? *Who* threw it?"

Oh Jeez, did I just say that? I can't believe I'm asking for details. It's a tacit admission that I think there's something legitimate about what she's saying.

"Well, ah don't know. All ah know is that's it's in a pond, sittin' on the bottom. And ah can see where the pond is—Balmer Park. That pond over by the dog walkin' area. You gotta tell the cops."

"What? Me? Why me?"

With a swat of her hand, Faith says, "Oh, they won't believe *me*. That Detective Freemont thinks ah'm a ditz. But I'll bet she likes you. So, y*ou* gotta tell her."

"But I'll have to tell her where I got the information, and that's from you."

"Yeah, but you tell her that you believe me. It'll make all the difference, and then she'll go after the gun."

"But there's one little problem. I *don't* believe you."

"What? June! Ah thought you were convinced about my powers!" Faith looks hurt and horrified, as if the only person on her side has abandoned her.

"Faith, listen, I…I don't know what to believe. I mean, I believe that you *think* you see something, but I just don't think it's a psychic vision."

"June, how can you doubt me? Tell her, *please*!" Faith pleads. "The pond in Balmer park. The gun is lying on the bottom. You gotta call her right now!"

"Faith, for God's sake, it's seven o'clock on a Friday night. It can wait until tomorrow. If the gun's there, it's not going anywhere."

"If you call tonight, maybe they can look for it tomorrow. But if you call tomorrow then they probably won't look 'till Sunday."

"Okay, Sunday, that's fine. If the gun's lying on the bottom, it'll be safe there till Sunday."

Faith waves her hands in a show of anxiety and says, "But it's probably rustin' down there. Or some forensic evidence is dissolvin' or somethin' like that. Ah just know we gotta get it as soon as we can." She looks at me, wide-eyed, hopeful.

"Oh, dear God," I murmur, as I think about Louise's likely reaction to this bizarre request. I shake my head and take the tray of meatballs out to the living room. Faith follows me like a puppy dog dutifully trailing its mother.

The doorbell rings. I open the door and there she is. Abbey.

Fashionably late so she can make an entrance, no doubt. She's wearing a little yellow sundress that's too light and shear for this time of year. Neckline too low and hemline too high. And the dress is super form-fitting of course, fits her like a condom in fact, to flaunt her trim figure. I could probably get only one leg into it. And a push-up bra. I think of the reaction of all the men. After the party, I'll have to find my bucket and mop to clean up the drool.

"Oh, June, so good of you to invite me!" Abbey is all smiles. She's either absolutely, overwhelmingly delighted to be here, or she's a damn good actress. I suspect the latter.

"Oh, Abbey, great of you to come." I feign exuberance. I'm not a bad actress either, when I need to be.

She steps inside. Luckily, she's holding a casserole dish with both hands, so we can't hug or touch or anything like that, because I've heard she does some weird shit to you as a life and personal wellness coach where she waves her hands over your body and re-shapes your electromagnetic aura. No way am I going to let her screw with *my* aura.

"What a lovely home you have."

"Oh, thank you. Darryl and I have been working on it for years. We're getting it into shape, slowly, adding our little personal touches here and there." *(Translation:We can't afford an interior decorator so it's taking forever)*.

Faith is right behind me, relentlessly stalking me, her shoe tips scraping my heels. I can feel her breath on the back of my neck. I turn slightly to bring her into the conversation.

"Abbey, this is Faith. We work together."

"Oh, how nice. Great to meet you, Faith," Abbey responds, with more smiles. Certainly, *I'm* no threat to Abbey's position in the pack as the preeminent bitch that all the males who want to be the alpha will fight over, but Faith is very young and quite attractive, and I think I've just detected a little something ever so slightly standoffish in Abbey's tone.

"Nice to meet you, too," says Faith, temporarily suspending her desperation to gain my attention again. But she's obviously not interested in an extended chat with Abbey, who holds out the dish towards me.

"I made some artichoke dip," Abbey bubbles.

"Fantastic. Smells great, Abbey," I say as I take the dish. "What's in it?" I feign as much enthusiasm for her culinary skills as I possibly can.

"It's my own recipe—artichoke hearts, spinach, diced mushrooms, cheese, sour cream, and homemade mayonnaise."

"Sounds scrumptious!" *But of course, HOMEMADE mayonnaise. Who the hell doesn't have time to make their own mayonnaise? And I'll bet she grew the mushrooms herself, fertilized with waste from her own septic tank.*

Abbey continues, "Darryl wouldn't tell me what to bring, so I just decided on this. Hope you like it. Your Darryl, he is just *sooo* sweet."

"Oh yes, he's a sweetie all right. Sweet as sugar. So

why don't you go right on into the living room and say hi to the others and help yourself to some hors d'oeuvres." I give her my absolute best fake smile as I take the casserole dish from her and point her in the right direction.

She goes in and every man in the room immediately turns to face her, with struck stupid grins on their faces. Even so, all the wives are here, so the men will have to restrain themselves. Well, except for Paul, who's the only single guy. When Abbey made her grand entrance, Paul was talking to Barbara, who's good looking enough, but let's face it, to most men Abbey is filet mignon and Barbara is brisket. Paul's jaw drops when Abbey walks in, and he practically bowls over Barbara to reach Abbey and introduce himself.

Paul glances at me, and I see a, *Thanks, sister!,* look on his face.

Crap! No way do I want Paul to get involved with Abbey. She'll suck the juice out of him like a black widow spider and leave him a dried up, empty carcass. Now I have *this* situation to deal with, along with everything else.

I watch as Abbey bends over in front of Paul, ostensibly to take a meatball, and she purposely exposes enough cleavage to drive a truck through. He salivates like an old hound dog, the slob.

When I spin around to go back to the kitchen, Faith is right on top of me, our faces inches apart.

"Faith, please, I need some breathing room."

"June, are you gonna make the call?" she begs again with those pleading, puppy dog eyes.

I know that Faith will be my personal flypaper all night unless I surrender. So, I decide to do it, to just get it over with. What the hell. Then I can get back to my party and back to dealing with Abbey and Paul. But I don't want Faith listening in, so I'm firm with her.

"Faith, I'll call if you go into the living room and wait," I say.

"Oh, thank you, June, thank you!" Faith clasps her hands together and smiles like a kid who's been promised a cupcake. She goes into the living room and joins the others. Everyone has arrived by now, and they are milling about the room. The wine and liquor are flowing, and people appear to be having a good time.

I sneak into the kitchen to make the call.

Chapter 10

I certainly don't like the idea of disturbing Louise on a Friday night. I assume all the detectives work first shift, except for emergencies.

I find her personal cell number in my contact list. She answers on the third ring, "Hello, this is Louise."

"Hi, Louise, this is June. I'm really sorry to bother you but I have some new information. Faith seems to think she knows where the murder weapon is." I pause, wondering if Louise is rolling her eyes right now.

A very calm and cool response, "Murder weapon? What murder?"

"Well, you know, if we assume that Melvin was murdered."

"I see. And how does she know the location of the weapon?"

I let out a long, hard sigh. Here we go, I have to say it, no matter how much it makes me sound like an imbecile. "Clairvoyance. She had another vision."

A pause. And then I hear a skeptical, "Really?"

"Well, she seems very convinced. It's a gun, by the way."

"A gun. What kind of gun?"

"Not sure. She just said a handgun. I don't have any more details than that."

"Uh-huh. And where does she see this gun?"

"Sitting on the bottom of the pond in Balmer Park."

After another thoughtful pause, Louise says, "My first question is this: If she can see it close enough to know it's a handgun, then I suppose her vision is a close-up picture of the gun. So then how does she know it's in the pond at Balmer Park?"

"Uhhh, well I don't really understand that part of it. Maybe she had two visions. Kind of like a high magnification one where she sees the gun, and then a lower mag one where she sees the whole scene. Or maybe she can just zoom in and out at will." *Oh yeah, I definitely sound like an idiot.*

Silence for a few seconds. I can just picture Louise shaking her head in disbelief. And maybe trying to hold back an outright laugh. Finally, she speaks in a deadpan, "I see, that explains it, then. She can adjust the magnification of the vision."

"Apparently."

"And why didn't she call me herself?"

"Because she has the impression you think she's a flake. Or something like that. So, she asked me to go to bat for her."

"And what do *you* think, June?"

"Well, I think she's kind of a flake. Guess I already told you that in so many words."

"Yes, you pretty much did."

"But, like I explained to you before, I believe she's sincere, meaning that she *thinks* she's having a psychic vision of some sort."

"So, what do you think I should do, June?"

"Well, why don't you search the bottom of the pond. I mean, what could it hurt?"

"June, I'm afraid I can't do that based on just a psychic vision. Do you know what that would cost the department? We're talking scuba divers, metal detection equipment, and lots of overtime. It'll blow a hole in the department's budget. There's absolutely no way I can justify it."

"But I thought you said your boss is a believer in psychic stuff."

"The boss that sent me off working with that idiot of a fake psychic is no longer my boss. He left involuntarily. Do you know why? It's because when cases got tough and leads dried up, he had his officers running around listening to phony psychics. I'm sorry, I just can't do it."

I'm not about to grovel. I did my duty. I gave it a fair shot for Faith.

"Okay, I understand, Louise. Thanks for your time, and my apologies again for calling you on a Friday night."

"No problem, June. I was going to call you anyway to tell you that I gave your phone number to Peter Tremayne. I hope you don't mind. He said that he wanted to talk to you."

I let out a huge sigh which Louise probably hears. I'm getting sucked in further. "Talk to *me*? Why *me*?" I ask.

"He apparently wants to learn about his son, to find out what he's like. In case they never get the chance to see each other again."

"But why doesn't he just call Annuska? She obviously knows Melvin much better than I do."

"I've explained the whole situation to him, and he doesn't want to talk to her. At best he's got her pegged for someone who married his son just to get citizenship. At worst, he thinks she may be involved in his son's recent disappearance. He wants nothing to do with her, at least for now. But he wanted someone else to talk to and, well, you're the logical choice, June. I mean, you said that Melvin doesn't really have any close friends that you know of. But if Tremayne calls, maybe you'd like to refer him to another person."

One of the last wishes of a dying man. To learn more about the son that he lost long ago. How can I refuse?

I let out another sigh, one of resignation this time. "Umm, that's fine, Louise. There's no problem with him calling me. Of *course,* I'll talk to him."

So, to soothe a dying man's spirit, I'll probably have to make up some load of horse shit about what a great guy Melvin is, even though I really don't know him well at all. But what the hell, I can handle that.

"Great. And June, sorry again that we can't search the pond, I hope you understand. I *do* admire you for trying to help out Faith, in any case."

We say our goodbyes and end the call. So that's that. I know Faith will be disappointed, but I have to tell her right away. She'll be on me anyway the second I step back into the living room.

I walk toward the crowd and Faith notices me before I've even entered the room. She pounces, gliding the five steps between us.

"June, what did she say?"

I shush her and motion for her to follow me back into the kitchen. No way am I going to stay within earshot of anyone.

The instant we make it to the kitchen threshold, she blurts out, "Are they going to look for the gun?"

"No. I tried. I talked to Detective Freemont directly. She wouldn't go for it."

"What? Why not?" She looks crushed, like I've burst her birthday balloon with a pin.

"Faith, you sound so surprised. Has it occurred to you that the *majority* of people in the world *don't* believe in psychic visions?"

She takes on an air of resolve and puts her hands on her hips. In a determined voice, she says, "Then we gotta go after it ourselves, June. We gotta find the gun that Annuska used to kill Melvin."

"What? No way! I've seen that pond. It's covered with scum. I'm not diving in there. And it's right near the dog walking park. All that dog poo probably drains into the pond when it rains. Besides, I can't scuba dive and I can't hold my breath."

"Oh June, don't worry about that," she assures me. "We won't have to dive underwater. The whole pond is probably shallow, and the water must be clear by now cause ah think they just loaded the pond up with an herbicide like they do every year."

"Oh great, now we'll get a mouthful of agent orange too."

"No, we'll just look around, in the shallow parts. And maybe we'll feel around a little bit with our hands and feet."

"No way." I stand my ground.

"June, please, you gotta help me do this," she wails. "Poor Melvin has been murdered, ah just know it. And they won't take it seriously until we get some evidence, ah'm tellin' ya." And then she starts to cry.

I can't stand the crying. I'm flooded with distant memories of my little brother, Paul. He was seven and I was eleven, and I walked him up to the corner convenience store to get an ice cream cone. On the way home he dropped his ice cream ball right onto the sidewalk where it stuck in a pile of gravel and bird droppings. He stood there with an empty cone, and then the wailing started and I didn't have any more money, and I couldn't stand to hear and see him cry, so I gave him my ice cream just to shut him up.

"Okay, okay, please stop crying, Faith," I beg. "We'll just go over there and take a look. But I'm not going into the water."

That's enough to immediately perk Faith up. She says, "Oh, June, you're the absolute best, thank you so much! We're gonna see this thing through now." She smiles, wipes her tears away, and gives a little hop for joy. "Okay, so we'll do it tonight right after the party. Ah got a flashlight right in my car."

"Are you nuts? At night? Not a chance."

"Well, ah just thought it would be best, since it's illegal to go in the water. There's a sign right there sayin' so. Subject to fine and arrest, and all that usual stuff."

"No problem there, because we won't be going into the water, remember? We're just going to look where it's shallow, and if we see anything that looks like a gun, which I have to tell you I seriously doubt we'll see, then we'll call the cops again. But I'm still not going to a park at night. Let's do it…on Wednesday at lunchtime. Oh, wait, Darryl's driving to Boston that morning, it'll be too hectic. Okay, I can fit it in Tuesday at lunchtime. Monday I've just got too much to do at work."

She raises both hands in protest and blurts out, "Tuesday! June, c'mon! If not tonight, then tomorrow morning, pleeease!"

"But tomorrow's Saturday, and my weekend is for family, and…the boys have baseball, and…"

"Oh, pleeeeease," she grovels.

I can see that Faith isn't going to give up, and I have to get back to my party, so I surrender to another flash of *just get it over with.*

Shaking my head in defeat, I say, "All right, all right, tomorrow. I'll meet you there at about one." I turn immediately, I suppose because I don't want to see her happy victory face, and I skedaddle into the living room.

"Oh, June, where have you been?" asks my neighbor Mona. "Your meatballs are scrumptious."

"Oh…uh…thanks. Old family recipe." *Why the hell did I say that? And did I leave the empty frozen meatball bag on the countertop, or did I throw it in the trash? Get your shit together, June. And did all the meatballs look too uniformly round, like they were stamped out by a machine? Damn, I should have squished a few of them. I'm slipping.*

Mona snags me, and she's now chatting excitedly so I can't dart back to the kitchen to check on the meatball bag, but I'm pretty sure that I've safely disposed of it. After a few minutes of small talk with Mona and her husband, I decide that things are under control for the moment. People are eating, drinking, talking. So, I figure I deserve a glass of wine while I mull over my options on what to do about Paul and Abbey.

I look at the bottles over on the dining room server. Where the hell is the Sancerre I'd bought? That's my favorite, and I saw Darryl put the bottle back there after he poured Abbey a glass, but it's gone now. Did that lush suck the whole thing down, an entire bottle before I even got a sniff of it? Did she think that bringing her crappy dip with the friggin' homemade mayo entitled her to scarf an entire twenty-two-dollar bottle of wine?

I look over and spot Abbey in the corner of the living room but there's no wine glass in her hand. She would have needed *three* hands to be drinking right now because her left one is occupied dipping a shrimp into cocktail sauce and feeding it to Paul, and *oh for God's sake, things have gotten so out of control* because then with her right hand she actually wipes his mouth with her napkin! She has him totally under her spell, and there's pretty much no sign of intelligent life left in his face. He has the goo-goo eyes for her. It looks like he's taking a long ride on the stupid train and will stay on all the way to the last stop.

I ponder how to best interrupt the social intercourse taking place between the two of them when I see her whisper something to him, and I'm not the best lip reader, but I swear to God it looked like she said, "Picture me naked." *Not much imagination required, honey, because in that dress you're practically there.*

Disgusted, I walk back over to Mona and happen to glance out the front window. There's a car parked by the curb, illuminated under the streetlight…and…

Holy shit, I'll be damned if it doesn't look like crazy Wally's car…

I move to the window and put my nose right against the glass, and I cup my hands around my eyes to cut off the glare of the room lights, not caring what my guests will think. It sure looks like Wally's car. He drives an unusual one to work every day, a funky looking little SUV with a weird sporty shape, in a rusty orange color. I don't know what the make or model of his car is because I suck when it comes to knowing anything about cars, but the one out there is way too familiar. I strain to see if there's someone sitting in the driver's seat, which

135

is facing me, and…sure as shit there is, but I can just barely see the outline of a person, and because of the distance I can't make out any details. I can't even tell if the person is bald.

And then the car takes off in a spurt, leaving nothing but a tiny puff of white dust.

Am I seeing things? Maybe. Yes, probably. Almost certainly.

I'm still spooked and jittery over the layoff meeting I had with Wally, and obviously my mind is playing tricks on me, and surely that isn't even an SUV, and yeah, it *looked* rusty orange, but it isn't, because that streetlight surely distorts colors, and I'll bet it's really white or maybe silver, and the pinkish streetlight just fooled me into thinking it's orange.

So…JUST CALM DOWN, June.

Before I can even pull my face back from the window, Faith comes up behind me and says, "June! Ah saw what you were lookin' at. That was Wally. He's a psycho, and now he's stalkin' you, and ah'll bet he's madder'n a wet hen! Oh, my Lord, you are so screwed!"

****

The next day, I shut the car door and lumber through the park along a crushed stone path toward the place by the pond where I'm supposed to meet Faith. A slow walk is all I can manage.

The air is deliciously cool, and the May sun is an enormous yellow beach ball, shouting promises of a warm Connecticut summer to come soon. But with my migraine raging, I squint against its majesty. Facing the glare directly is like shoving a knitting needle into my eye.

Okay, so I'm slightly hung over from the party last

night. I didn't get any of the Sancerre, but after I spotted that car outside under the streetlight, I sure as hell needed something, so I ended up drinking from a bottle of white wine that my neighbor Murray brought, and it was probably cheap stuff because this morning I woke up with a ripping headache. I think I had three glasses of it, and now I'm munching on ibuprofen like popcorn. This is not the usual little guy in my skull with a sledgehammer. More like a giant swinging a wrecking ball.

With the runaway nuclear reaction erupting in my head, I dragged my carcass out of bed this morning and took the boys to their baseball games, where I had to shrug off my suffering, suck it up, and put on my cheery face because I was the snack mom today. I brought carrots, celery sticks, raisins, and clementines. Healthy stuff.

Last time I'd brought potato chips and chocolate-covered donut balls, and I'd gotten snack-shamed by the other moms, who said in so many words that I was poisoning their kids. Well, maybe poisoning is too strong a word. It was a slightly more polite dressing down, as I recall. The phrase *encouraging bad habits* was used.

Anyway, this time I got it from the other side, from the kids who whine when they see the healthy fare. I guess to them I'm the junk food queen. They were all set for their fix of salt, sugar, and trans-fat.

Can't win.

And on top of that, I'm still annoyed at the fact that Paul left the party early with Abbey. He told me on the way out that she had some authentic piece of Mayan art in her house that she said he just *had* to see, and it couldn't wait, and who the hell knew that Paul had this previously undiscovered, yet now burning love of Mayan art? Not even Paul, apparently, until last night.

As I near the pond, I catch sight of Faith waiting at the bank. She looks anxious and is supporting a field rake in one hand. It's an enormous thing, standing taller than her. The head with its metal times looks to be at least thirty inches wide. The geese congregating around the pond scatter as I approach, leaving a dust storm of dander in their wake as they gaggle in protest. I kick at the goose turds as I walk. I'm wearing my sneakers, which will probably get wet and muddy, but what does one wear when searching a pond for a gun?

"June, where have you been?" asks Faith, her impatience erupting. "You were supposed to be here fifteen minutes ago!"

I give her my politely pissed off look and say in a calm but firm tone, "Faith, I have a *life*, you know. My kids come first, and I *did* tell you I had to take them to their games. And I didn't say I'd be here fifteen minutes ago, I said I'd be here at *about* one. It's one fifteen now, so in my book that qualifies as about one."

Her mood instantly turns apologetic, and she says, "Oh, no problem, June, ah didn't mean to sound ungrateful. Ah surely do appreciate your helpin' here. Listen, about that crazy Wally. He's stalking you now, June. Ah've been givin' it some thought. Let me go over to his house and talk to him."

I answer in a stern tone, "No, absolutely not! You're not to go near him."

"But you and ah are friends, June. You're helping me now and ah wanna help you. Ah don't think you should show your face to him right now, but ah'll go over there and see if ah can calm him down, or at least ah can maybe find out just how mad he is at you. And if he's packin' any loaded weapons."

"No way, you're not to get involved. It's *my* problem. And it's probably not even a problem. I'm sure it'll blow over."

Out of the corner of my eye I see a swan paddling toward us and damn, the thing looks huge. I don't know if they eat swans anywhere in the world, maybe in Africa or somewhere in Asia, but this thing could make a holiday feast for a tribe. Maybe this is a mother swan? It *is* a beautiful, graceful creature but I've heard that they can get nasty when their babies are about. I look around for the little swanlings or swan kiddies or whatever you call them, but I don't see any.

Faith and I are standing about three feet from the pond's edge and Faith doesn't seem concerned at all. She says, "You know, when ah was about seventeen, there was a guy stalkin' *me*, a sometime boyfriend. So, my daddy hired a couple of the local rodeo cowboys to go beat the livin' bejeezus out of him. Tennessee justice, my daddy called it."

I glower at Faith and say, "Nobody is going to beat the anything out of anybody. This thing with Wally will probably all die down quickly."

"Well, are you gonna tell the cops? Maybe the long arm of the law can do somethin'."

"No, I'm sure they couldn't do a thing. Wally hasn't committed any crime. He didn't threaten me, not specifically anyway. And even if it *was* him out there last night, there's no law against him parking in the street. And it probably *wasn't* him anyway."

"Oh, it was him all right, and he's loco," she assures me. "And ah'll bet he wants to string you up and bleed you like a pig before a Juu-lah the fourth bar-b-que."

"Okay, Faith, for a person wanting to assist, you're really not making me feel any better, you know?"

"Well, will you at least tell Fleener upper management?"

I just shake my head. What the hell will they do? Send Horace the oldest working security guard over to my house to protect me, now that he's out of the hospital? I can picture him taking a watchful position on my front porch, rough and ready with a water pistol or a cap gun, keeping an unwavering eye out for Wally. His ass will be glued to one of the rocking chairs. He'll never have to get up, I suppose, because I'm pretty sure he wears adult diapers, but I'll surely end up having to feed him and dust him off every four hours.

Faith shrugs and says, "Well, searchin' this pond will take your mind off Wally for the moment." We both turn to look at the pond, and I immediately realize what the rake is for. "Oh, God, June, you know ah didn't think it would be this scummy. Ah really can't see the bottom at all. Good thing ah brought this rake."

A thick and greasy-looking slime covers most of the pond, which is maybe half a football field in size. The slime is dark green in some areas and there are twisted ribbons of light fluorescent green in others. We watch as three beer cans bob in the oily ooze, drifting by in a lethargic current. Reeds stick up out of the water here and there along the bank, giving cover, I assume, to various water critters because I hear the occasional mating croak of a fat frog. A few foam hamburger boxes also amble by, chasing after the cans. And several half-submerged items, including an old truck tire and a rusted barbecue propane tank, attest to the fact that the place does double duty as a nature preserve and a shitpile dumping ground.

"This place is disgusting," I say. "You told me they sprayed algicide in here?"

"Well, ah *thought* they sprayed at least once this season. Perhaps it takes several applications to kill algae that's this...hardy."

"Oh, well then, so much for finding anything in here. Looks like we'll have to give up."

Faith's pleading expression returns. "Oh, June we *can't* give up before even startin'! It's here, ah just know it. You gotta wade in and feel around with your feet and use this rake ah brought. You can use it to push the slime aside so you can look, and then you drag the rake along the bottom and feel for the gun."

"Faith, why do you keep saying, *you, you, you*?"

"Please June, *you* gotta go in."

"Me? Why me? I didn't bring my wet suit and snorkel."

"Oh, come on June, you got a pair of spandex pants on so the leaches can't get to your skin. Take your sneakers off, pull your socks up high over your pant legs and just go in up to your knees. It'll be easy as slidin' off a greasy log backwards. And probably the whole pond is shallow cause it's man-made."

"Excuse me...leaches? Did I hear you say *leaches*?"

"Oh, they're nothin' at all. People used to put 'em on their skin for medical purposes, you know. They can't hurt you. Why hell, ah knew a poor family back in Tennessee that used to collect 'em and toast 'em and eat 'em up. Pure protein, they said."

"I don't *care* if they're edible. Don't care if they taste like chicken, lobster, or even caviar. I don't want them on me. And why am *I* going in and not you? You're younger and stronger."

"Sorry, ah can't, June. Unfortunately, ah have a yeast infection."

I turn toward her in disbelief. "What? You conveniently get a yeast infection the day we have to go diving in pond scum? And now you're implying that I'm to go in over my crotch."

"No, no, just to your thighs probably, but ah can't go in myself, just in case ah trip and fall."

I shake my head with resignation, as I slip into my *just get it over with* frame of mind. I don't expect to find a damn thing, but feel that I have to do it for Faith, and if I don't, then I expect to see the river of tears start to flow again. Faith is so like a little kid, and why the hell do I always slip into the mothering role?

We look around for people who might be close enough to notice me casually breaking the law. There are only a few folks with their pets in the dog park, which is a fenced-in area a few hundred feet away. The fence is high, and it obscures their vision enough so that I think they probably won't see me behind all the water reeds, and anyway I'll try to stay as low as possible.

Faith says, "Ah come here to walk sometimes, there are never many people here, except at night. There's a make-out spot over there at the far edge of the pond. The teenagers park their cars there after dark."

"Yeah, I can tell from all the condom wrappers floating around. Glad to see they're at least practicing safe sex. By the way, that swan looks like it might have a mean streak. I could get attacked if there are babies around. I don't see any, but…"

With a casual wave of her hand, Faith swats away

my apparently silly fear of gigantic waterfowl. "Oh, hell, June, you don't need to worry about that ole momma swan, she ain't gonna hurt you. It's the snappin' turtles you gotta watch out for."

"What? The snapping what?"

Faith hesitates, perhaps thinking that it's somewhat counterproductive to scare the crap out of me. She gives me an encouraging little grin and says, "Nah, on second thought, ah'm pretty sure there are no turtles 'cause the pollution in here would surely kill 'em dead in a day or less."

"Well, that's a relief."

I keep my sneakers on and wade in against my better judgment. The sneakers will be ruined after this farce of a search mission is over, but I'll sacrifice them gladly to prevent my feet from getting sliced open like a piece of baloney on some shard of glass sitting on the bottom.

I expected the water to be cold, but it's rather temperate. Probably from all the warm street sewer runoff and steaming dog poo that washes in here. I walk very slowly because I can't see the bottom, swinging the rake back and forth, swishing the scum aside and trying my best to see below the surface, but it's pretty hopeless because even as the swinging action of the rake clears the scum, it also stirs up mud.

"Go deeper, June, deeper," Faith says.

"I think this is far enough." I'm about fifty feet out from the bank and the water is just above my knees.

"No, go farther. If you're gonna throw a gun in, you'd have to be an imbecile to throw it this close to the edge. Go in farther. And drag the rake on the bottom."

I glance back at Faith. She's enthusiastically giving me hand signals like an airport runway traffic controller, making swinging and pulling motions with her arms.

I cautiously walk into deeper water. I'm in slime up to my upper thighs now and getting dangerously close to a body zone that I definitely do not want exposed to this bacterial bouillabaisse.

"Farther, June!" Faith implores.

"No way! If it's not here, we're giving up."

"And more to the left."

"What? To the left? How do you know?"

"I don't know how, I just know. You gotta try more to the left. And feel around more with the rake!"

I plunk the rake down and drag it, repositioning it a little after each pull. I do it three times, pause to consider my technique, and then three more times with my arm stretched to the max. I feel what I think are small rocks that move easily. I wander to the left, not daring to let the water reach my crotch, and continue to scour the bottom with the rake as best I can. I feel nothing but the rocks and maybe some underwater weeds which offer some resistance until they break.

My arms are aching now. Nearing my quitting point, I give what I think will probably be my last few tries.

And then…CLUNK.

Somehow, I can tell from the feel that it's metal on metal.

"I found something," I yell.

Faith bubbles with excitement. "Oh, June, you gotta reach right in there and grab it before you lose it!"

"You can forget that, my head'll be under. No way am I sucking a mouth full of this green swill. I'm going to try to drag it into shallower water."

I keep the rake down and walk backwards, with one eye on the mamma swan who has apparently decided to confront me because she's now swimming toward me, and she looks royally pissed off. Babies or not, I'm trespassing on her turf. I can feel the metal thing rolling in the tines of the rake, and then I feel it stop rolling, but I know that I still have it because I can feel its weight, so maybe I've hooked it somehow.

I'm back to knee-deep water, and the sun is hitting at just the right angle so that I can pick up a metallic glint from whatever it is I've hooked, even though I can't see its outline. Still dragging the rake, I turn around and walk forward to get away from the swan as quickly as possible, and I'm trying to recall if they can run fast on dry land—*but hey, they can fly, right? So, if that bird is really determined to get me, to peck me into submission, then I'm a goner, and gee, wouldn't that make one stupid ass sounding obituary: June Bloom Pecked to Death by Waterfowl.*

If I have to be killed by an animal, I'm hoping for something a little nobler, like maybe getting mauled by a lion on a safari. Getting snuffed by anything with feathers would be pathetic. So, I pick up the pace. I pull along with me what is surely just an old, busted bathroom faucet, or a piece of a table lamp, or…

I'm in ankle-deep water now, and with a quick glance backwards, I'm relieved to see that the swan has stopped swimming towards me, apparently having decided that I'm no longer a threat. And then when I face forward again, I'm startled by that *Oh my Lordy Lord* look on Faith's face, as she stares down in awe at whatever I'm pulling, which is only a few inches underwater now.

I reach in and pull it up out of the muck, and…
Holy shit.
It's a gun.

Chapter 11

After Louise questions Faith and me together, Faith leaves for a dental appointment and Louise asks me to stay behind. She and I now stand next to her car in the parking lot near the pond.

I say with an apologetic grin, "Gee, we're seeing a lot of each other lately. Really sorry I'm wrecking your weekend."

She smiles. "Oh, that's okay, June. Being on call is part of the job."

Louise places three clear plastic evidence bags on the hood of her car. One contains the gun. It's kind of silvery black and mean looking. The second holds what she calls the ammunition clip which she's removed from the handle of the gun, and the last bag contains a lone bullet.

"Where'd the bullet come from?" I ask her.

"It was in the chamber. I took it out it, standard procedure. For safety reasons."

"Wow, there was a bullet in the chamber? That's significant. What's the chamber?"

"It's the place in the gun where the bullet is fired from. In other words, the bullet was in the ready position."

"You mean...the gun was ready to fire?" I ask.

"Yes."

"Would it have fired if the trigger was pulled, I

mean, like accidentally, while I was pulling it with the rake, or after I got it out of the water?"

"Yes, probably."

"Okay, I just wanted to verify that I could have shot myself in the ass so that I won't be up at night wondering about that particular point."

"Right. You could have shot yourself. That's why it's not recommended that civilians try to retrieve lost guns from ponds."

I quip, "Well, no offense, but I *did* ask *you* to do it."

"I know, June. Let's just say I'm glad you found it and I'm doubly glad that you didn't get shot, but you shouldn't try anything like this again."

"No problem there. I'm pretty sure that my chances of diving in pond scum to look for a gun seen in a psychic vision twice in one lifetime are nil."

"You're awfully brave, you know. That pond has snapping turtles in it. The big ones can bite through a sneaker and take a toe off. Or a finger if you had your hands in the water."

"Good thing I was too ignorant to be scared." I look down at my pants, just to do another quick leech check. I've already done a thorough search, but of course I still have the creepy crawlies. And it's quite uncomfortable standing in these sneakers, with all that pond puke between my toes. My footwear is definitely destined for the trashcan. Even if I get the sneakers dried out, they'll forever smell like two dead sewer rats.

Louise continues, "But I can understand why you went looking for the gun. I'm sure Faith can be very persuasive, and you seem to feel protective of her. And let's face it, this case is rather unusual. Let's go over it again, if you don't mind. I mean, how you found the gun."

"There's not much to tell, Louise. It took less than ten minutes of feeling along the bottom with the rake, in the area where Faith told me to look. Oh, and when I was out there searching, she directed me, told me to go farther out, and once she told me to move to the left."

"And how far out did you find it?"

"I'm not very good at judging distances, but I'd say I was about seventy-five feet out."

"Pretty amazing. I mean, it's a big pond. But you two zero'd right in on it, and found it with only ten minutes of searching?"

"Yes."

"With just a rake?" she marvels.

"That's right." I spread my hands and shrug my shoulders. "No metal detectors, sonar, scuba divers, or anything. Just one rusty old rake and two production accountants. Guess I saved your department a lot of money."

"And how did Faith know exactly where to search?"

I look at her. We both know what I'm about to say. So, I don't have to say it.

"Right, she had a vision," Louise acknowledges with a nod, but there's a look of complete skepticism on her face. "Did she walk around the pond first before she chose this area to search?"

"All I know is that she was standing on the bank, right at the area she wanted to search when I pulled into the parking lot. I just walked over to where she was, and she asked me to dive in. I guess she somehow saw this particular area of the pond in her vision."

"Really? So, you seem to be coming around to believing that she's a genuine psychic?"

I shrug and make my confusion very evident. "I honestly don't know what to think, now. I told you that I'm a skeptic when it comes to this psychic stuff."

"Same here. But this is quite different than her getting that vision of Melvin in a car trunk. Your probable explanation of that was an overactive imagination, and I tend to agree. But here she knew there was a gun in a particular area of a pond. It's not like handguns are scattered all over the bottom of your average pond, so....what are the odds you ladies stumbled on a gun by sheer coincidence?"

"Quite low, I'd say. About one in a zillion, maybe? Louise, can I ask—what can you tell so far about this Austrian made Glock 17 that I found?"

"Oh, so you've identified the make and model?"

"I deduced it from the fact that Glock 17 and made in Austria were stamped on the side."

She gives me a good-natured smile. "I see. And what else did you deduce, June?"

"Well, let's see. The water and the mud will make it impossible to determine if the gun was fired recently. And unfortunately, we won't be able to get fingerprints from the gun or the bullets since water quickly removes skin oils. But we should be able to make a guess at how long it's been in the water from the level of corrosion on some parts of the gun. I assume you'll be taking a water sample from the pond to run a corrosion rate test."

Louise looks at me with surprise. "June, for someone who doesn't know what a gun's chamber is, you have a pretty good knowledge of police procedures."

"Not really. But I do have a cellphone, a data plan, and two working thumbs. I googled some things while we were waiting for you. It's amazing what you can learn from Wikipedia. But you can tell that my knowledge is very spotty, and in fact before today I knew squat about guns. Never owned one, never shot one, never had the urge to, either. I knew that if you pulled the trigger, the bullet comes out that hole in the end, and that's about it."

"I see. Well, I guess we're done for now, June. I can take it from here."

"Will you be able to find out who owns the gun?" I ask.

"Yes, we'll determine who it's currently registered to from the serial number. It's still possible that this gun has nothing to do with the fact that Melvin Hamm is missing."

"Are you going to talk to Faith again?"

"Yes, I'd like to delve a little more into the whole *vision* thing."

"You're thinking she's a fake psychic, like *The Amazing Wojtek*, huh? Another publicity hound?" I ask her.

She pauses and then answers my question with a question. "How well do you really know her, June?"

I pause, perhaps because I want to choose my words carefully. "I mean, I consider her a friend, but it's not like we hang out together. But…uh, I guess I need to take that back, though, because I had her over to my house last night. I had a little dinner party. I invited her to try and cheer her up since she's upset about Melvin. That's when she told me about the gun."

Louise's phone rings. She listens intently, says almost nothing during the very brief call, and then she quickly slips the phone back into her pocket.

"Well June, I suppose that you have enough skin in this case now that I need to tell you this. The gun is registered to Melvin's father, Peter Tremayne. So, I'd say...*holy shit* to that, wouldn't you?"

"Ho-lee shit. My thoughts exactly."

****

When I get back to the house, my cell rings just as I get out of the car. It's a number I don't recognize. I push the accept button and wait for the caller to speak.

"Hello?" A male voice, but not the mysterious guy again who'd been the victim of the con woman. This voice is older, weaker.

He continues, "This is Peter Tremayne. May I speak to Ms. June Bloom please?"

Oh, Geez. I have to talk to him. But I'll let him lead the conversation. No point in just gushing out a torrent of phony praise for his lost son.

My tone is solemn and respectful. "Hello, Mr. Tremayne. This is June speaking."

"Ah, Ms. Bloom. I assume that Detective Freemont has informed you fully of my son's case. Might I have a few minutes of your time?" Each word comes slowly, with measured effort as if he's being careful to preserve enough energy to get through the whole conversation.

He continues, "I...I...it's difficult to explain how I feel, having my son located after so many years. I'm an old man now, nearing death. I have no one here, other than my cat, Mister Tabby. A silly name for a grown man's pet, isn't it? My son named the cat when we got him as a newborn kitten and now in some ways, I feel that this cat is the only bond left between my son and me."

A long pause. I'm not sure if he's stopping to catch his breath, or if I'm supposed to say something.

I fill the dead air with some meaningless drivel:

"Well, pets can certainly be a comfort." Like I would know. I never had a pet except for one lone goldfish when I was a kid, which certainly never gave me any affection, and I managed to kill him from neglect after just a few weeks.

I hear wheezing for about five seconds, then he starts talking again: "My wish is to be reunited with my son, Ms. Bloom. If that's not possible, due to Max's unwillingness, or due to other circumstances, then I would at least like to know *of* him. I'd like to know what he's like as a man. Can you help me?"

I hesitate, then say, "Well, I…I…don't know him all that well, but…he's a fine man…a good worker."

That sounds pathetic. Cmon', June, you can do better than that.

I continue, "And he's very…reliable. And trustworthy. And very clean." *Clean? Oh, dear God, that's worse than pathetic. I need something else.* "And very devoted to Fleener Plastics." *Okay, so that last one's hardly a compliment, in fact it's more like a testament to stupidity considering how the company treats employees, but Melvin's father doesn't know that, and it sounds nice.*

"And…what does he look like?" Mr. Tremayne asks.

"He's very…ahhh…"

I'm just about to lie and say how handsome he is, but I stop myself when I realize that I have at least one picture of him, the portrait on his employee ID badge. He isn't smiling in it, but maybe Annuska can come up with a few better pictures if I ask her. Maybe there are even some nice wedding pictures? But I'll have to crop Annuska out, since Melvin's father apparently wants nothing to do with her. Whatever. Beauty is subjective anyway, so let Melvin's father make his own judgment.

My obliging response is, "I'll send you his picture if you give me your e-mail."

"Oh, thank you. That would be wonderful," he says in a grateful tone.

He recites the e-mail and I scribble it down. I hear more coughing and wheezing, then a female voice in the background, possibly a nurse, and it sounds like she's expressing some objections.

The coughing stops for the moment, and he says in an even weaker voice than before, "If he comes back, can you tell him to contact me at this number? It's my room at The Seattle Serenity Center." He then recites the number and I dutifully listen even though I have it stored in my phone log.

He continues, "The detective gave me Max's cell number, but my calls go right to his voicemail. I've left many messages. I asked the detective to contact me as soon as she hears anything, but she hasn't called in two days. Have you had any recent contact with Max, Ms. Bloom?"

"Uh, no, he hasn't returned my calls either. I guess he's…uh…busy." *Or dead.*

"Could I have his e-mail address?"

"Yes, sure." *Oh cripes, am I violating employee privacy laws or something by giving him the e-mail address? But…at this point, who cares?*

"It's possible that my son may not open an e-mail if he knows it's from me. I'll get a new e-mail address with a username that's not obvious. But I'd still like to have a backup. And I think a handwritten letter would be best. If I mailed the letter to you, could you hand it to him if he comes back? Maybe you could personally persuade him to take it. I mean, you could tell him that we spoke, and you're convinced of my sincerity and…am I asking too much of you?"

Yes, you actually ARE because this is really not my business to try and patch up your relationship with your son, and I don't even know you…

"Uhhh, no, no, you're not asking too much, Mr. Tremayne. Of course, I'll…try."

I am such a softy.

I hear coughing again, this time much worse than before. The nurse comes on the line and says, "Mr. Tremayne can't talk right now. He shouldn't have called you, he's getting intravenous medication and he's supposed to be lying very still."

"I understand. Tell him I said goodbye and he can call me later if he wishes. But he wanted his son's e-mail address and my mailing address. Can I give them to you?"

After I give her the information, we end the call.

Melvin's father doesn't sound good at all. But he does sound sincere. And I feel very sorry for him.

And then I have a weird thought—that maybe, for some reason I can't fathom, Melvin is headed back to see his dying father one last time.

Wouldn't that be nice?

After talking to Melvin's father for just a few minutes, I find myself hoping that they will be reunited.

But is Melvin dead or did he just take off?

All we know for sure is that, one way or the other, he's clearly departed.

****

On Monday morning I'm back in cubeland, and in

complete disbelief that the weekend evaporated so quickly. Darryl and I used the remainder of Saturday afternoon and early evening to bleach and scrub the backyard deck, one of our exhausting spring rituals.

Fortunately, Sunday was a little more relaxing. Darryl first suggested that we use the day to go on one of the educational adventures for the boys that he often pushes. This time he wanted to drive three hours to Podunk, Pennsylvania to go to the *Museum of Civil War Era Twine and Lint*, or something like that. Well, I vetoed that one quickly. We ended up taking the boys to the beach for a few hours because it turned out to be an incredibly warm and sunny day for this time of year. I didn't let them swim because the water was way too cold. They were content enough playing whiffle ball and badminton on the sand.

As for me, ocean swimming in Connecticut is pretty much always out of the question because the water has to be at least eighty-eight degrees, or my body seizes up like a car engine with no oil. So, I didn't miss anything yesterday. After I greased and basted myself with sunblock, I just sat in the sun for a while, enjoying the spring warmth and cooking like a Sunday roaster chicken. That's my idea of a good time after dealing with bullshit at work all week. Relaxing and doing nothing.

But now, my Monday morning work headache is really ripping, those blue-hot lightning bolts of excruciating pain shooting up through my neck and stabbing at my temples, forehead, sinuses, and frontal lobe. I've already taken three extra-strength pain relievers, downed with a large black coffee spiked with a double shot of espresso. The headache laughs at my pitiful attempts to quell it.

It's nine-thirty already and I haven't accomplished a thing yet, but I definitely need another coffee. I get up and start my walk through the rat maze of cubicles towards the snack bar, glancing at all the people, some of whom actually remind me of caged rats, staring at their computer screens. A lot of them keep their cubicle lights turned off, and their screens cast a ghostly bluish glow on their faces, which sometimes freaks me out a bit. A few people have installed shower curtains on spring-loaded bars across their cube entrances to block out some of the noise and distractions so they can work more efficiently. Or maybe so they can sleep undisturbed.

When I pass Faith's cube, I see her sitting at her desk, looking teary and depressed. I'm not really in the mood to hear more about Melvin, but I am definitely curious as to whether Louise interviewed Faith since we left the park. And I suppose the mothering instinct is kicking in again because I can't ignore the crying.

"Faith, are you okay?" I ask.

"Oh, June," she wails. "It's just too much, sometimes."

"Still thinking about Melvin?"

"Well, sure, you know ah'm still sad about Melvin, but it's something else this morning that's got me down. Something…*spiritual*."

"Oh. Something to do with Elvis? Haven't seen him lately? Don't worry about him, Faith, I'm sure he's fine…as fine as a dead person can be."

"No, June, it's my parrot, Sammy. He's departed," she says between sniffles. "First Melvin, now Sammy. Things are just not goin' well in my life right now."

"So, Sammy departed…you mean…he left? Got out of his cage and took off? Maybe he's just hiding somewhere in your apartment."

"No June, he died last night. Took his last little parrot breath right before my eyes," she says glumly, dabbing at her tears with a tissue.

"Oh, I see. I'm really sorry about that, Faith." There is an awkward silent moment as I grope for something to say that might comfort her. "Was he...er...a *good* parrot?"

"Oh, he was the best! Ah shouldn't be cryin', June, because if there is such a thing as parrot heaven, that's surely where Sammy went. Why, he was *so good*...and ah'm such a heathen."

"Uh, Faith, you're certainly not a bad person. Saying shucks or cock-a-doodie once in a while doesn't put you in that club."

"What ah mean is that ah don't hardly go to church anymore, June. But when ah *did* go, ah'd take Sammy with me, tucked in my pocket, and he loved it! He sat there so quietly, ah was sure he must be sayin' his little bird prayers the whole time."

I pause for a few seconds, soaking in the heavenly awesomeness of it all. "My condolences," I murmur somberly. "But I'm sure he's...uhhh...perched right on Elvis' shoulder."

I nod my head and smile like a moron over Sammy's good fortune at being sucked up to parrot heaven. Time to change the subject.

"So, Faith, can I ask...did Detective Freemont talk to you again...after we left the park?"

"Oh, yes, we went over it all again, late on Saturday, but ah really didn't have anything new to tell her. She asked me again if ah was ever in Melvin's house, before you and ah went there, or if ah'd ever seen that gun before, but ah never was and never did, June. So ah'm guessin' that the gun we found belonged to Melvin, even though she wouldn't tell me. And she wanted to know if ah saw in my vision who threw the gun in there." Faith looks at me and raises her eyebrows in an inquisitive gesture, apparently waiting to see if I will corroborate her guess about the owner of the gun.

Should I tell her that the gun belongs to Melvin's father? No, not a good idea. I promised Louise that I won't talk to anybody about Melvin's secret identity. There's no need to get on her shit list yet. So, I ignore the implied question and simply ask, "What did you tell her?"

"The truth. Ah didn't see in my vision who threw it there, ah just saw it lyin' there on the bottom. But ah told her who ah *thought* threw it in there."

"Who?"

"Why, Annuska, of course." She shrugs her shoulders as if the answer is completely obvious.

"Why do you say that?"

"Because of the blood on the trunk of her car. It's *gotta* be her," Faith says, opening her eyes wide and waving her hand as if to swat away any trace of doubt. "Come on June, you *know* she put Melvin in that car trunk!"

"I don't *know* anything. But you sound so certain."

"Well, anyway, it seemed to me that the Detective might be havin' some thoughts that maybe ah'm tryin' to frame Annuska, or somethin' like that, right? But if ah was, like, really tryin' to frame her, then ah would have just said that ah saw her in my vision throwin' that gun in the lake, right? Or even worse, ah coulda' made up a vision that ah saw her shootin' Melvin in the head, right?

S.E. Greco

But ah didn't, cause ah'm just tryin' to be honest about everything, and all."

I nod my head as I try to follow the twists and turns of her logic. "Well, you know, don't take this the wrong way, Faith, but if you told the Detective that you saw Annuska killing Melvin in a vision, I don't think the Detective would just go and slap the cuffs on Annuska. It takes evidence, and…"

"Oh, ah know that, June," she says with another wave of her hand for emphasis. "But even though she asked me if ah had any more visions about Melvin, which ah haven't, ah just didn't get the impression that she believes at all in my powers. Ah just think she was more, like, tryin' to get into my brain, to see where ah was comin' from. Ah think that she thinks ah'm just makin' this stuff up, and she wants to see what else ah make up, you know?"

"What did she say about Annuska?" I ask, even though I already know that Louise won't reveal any of her cards to Faith.

"Nothin', really. Ah asked her if she was going to arrest Annuska, and she said that she doesn't even know if a crime was committed. She just asked me to avoid Annuska, and also to stay away from the park where we found the gun for the time being."

"Oh? Did she say why she wanted you to avoid the park?"

"Because there're gonna be draggin' that pond, and ah think she doesn't want anyone pokin' around there anymore, messin' up the evidence. Least of all me."

"Dragging the pond? What else are they looking for?"

Faith's eyes widen. "Well, apparently…Melvin's body."

Chapter 12

I'm not sure why I feel I have to go over to the park, but a few hours later that's exactly where I'm headed on my lunch break. Maybe it's morbid curiosity on my part?

I remember my feeling of relief when Faith was looking into the trunk of Annuska's car a few days ago and she told me Melvin wasn't in there. But now I'm headed back into a situation where I might catch a glimpse of his dead body being pulled out of a lake, in which case it will probably be super-nasty, like the bloated, mushy little bodies of the dead squirrels I always pull out of my above ground pool when I take the cover off at the start of every summer.

Anyway, perhaps I'm going because I feel some loyalty toward Melvin. He is, after all, my employee. Or *was*. So, I feel that I somehow owe it to him to be there if his carcass is pulled out of the pond. I mean, the indignity of it all. But then again, if he really entered the sweet hereafter, he probably won't give a damn if I'm there or not.

I roll my rattletrap station wagon into the parking lot nearest the pond. There are two big police SUVs already there, both with empty boat trailers attached to them, and one other car, an unmarked, black, big ass sedan with darkened windows that probably gets five miles to the gallon. It looks like the car that Louise was driving the other day. As I walk toward the pond and step around a bank of large trees, I can see a crew that's working the area of the pond where I waded in and found the gun. Dragging the pond, I think Faith called it.

I'm not sure what I expected—maybe radar, sonar, x-ray vision goggles, or laser beams shooting into the water. But all I see are two crappy, old wooden rowboats with their green paint peeling off in a hundred places, revealing bits of at least four other garish colors from prior paint jobs. They look like they were built during the same era when the guy from the *Old Man and the Sea* was out fishing for the big one. And coincidentally, there's an old guy in each boat, and one of them even looks kind of like Ernest Hemingway. They aren't wearing scuba gear like Navy SEALS, or even police uniforms. They're dressed in dirty jeans, flannel shirts, and greasy old baseball caps. Both of them have ropes in their hands.

I watch as one of them pulls on the rope and a vicious looking, three-pronged grappling hook breaks the surface of the water. With a lazy swing, he gives the rope a skillful twirl above his head, launches the hook back into the water, and then starts pulling on the rope again. The guy in the other boat is doing the same. I cringe at the thought of one of these barbed spikes catching Melvin in the mouth, and then one of these guys pulling hard on the rope. It might rip poor Melvin's head clean off.

I stand for a minute right behind the yellow police tape that cordons off the shoreline of the pond, watching the two men. If they saw me, they're ignoring me as they labor, intent on their mission. I spot Louise as she walks around some tall reeds near the shore. She looks up, apparently surprised to see me. And I'm frankly a little embarrassed to be here.

I give her a sheepish greeting: "Uh, hi, Louise."

"June? I didn't expect to see you here." She smiles politely.

"Faith told me you'd be looking in the pond for Melvin's body."

"You felt you had to come and watch? Why, if you don't mind my asking?"

"I just thought, well, you know...if you find Melvin..."

"Well, if we find him in here, it's not like you'll be able to offer him any comfort."

"I know. But why did you decide to look in the pond?"

"Because we found that gun in here. Or rather, *you* found it."

"By the way, you said before that searching the pond is an expensive operation. I see you've got two rowboats out there. No fancy high tech equipment like I expected. It actually doesn't look very expensive, if you don't mind my saying so. I think you said that it would blow your department's budget."

"Well, we have to pay these men. It's actually considered hazardous duty, so they get extra pay."

"Hazardous duty? How's that?"

"They're swinging sharp hooks around, so they could get hurt. Or fall in and drown, I suppose. Anyway, you'd be surprised how much all of this costs. And as far as using high tech equipment, the water is so muddy and full of algae that the sonar equipment really wouldn't work well at all in there. For the same reason, divers would be able to see only inches in front of them. And also, this pond is full of snapping turtles, like I mentioned to you right after you took your little swim. We saw several big ones. The turtles can be territorial. They don't like divers. Or people wading in, like you."

"Yikes, how big exactly?"

She smiles. "Big enough for you to make a large pot of soup for a nice family dinner. Don't think about it too much, June. You survived unscathed, thank goodness. Anyway, unless we find a body, we'll be cut off from spending any more money on this case. We already dropped some money on a visual search of this whole park. We had two uniformed officers on ATVs in here and they did a very thorough job."

"Why did you decide to search the park other than this pond?"

She begins with a reminder, "June, this is all confidential of course."

"Of course," I assure her.

"Well, Annuska is in this park a lot. It's only about two miles from where she and Melvin live, and she's something of a fitness fanatic. Her normal work hours are from noon to five, so a few mornings a week she walks here, hikes around, and then walks back to her house. This park is more than a hundred acres, and it has places to hide something big. There are a number of old stone barns and other buildings and it's crisscrossed with old logging roads and carriage trails. Although it's illegal, you could drive a car in here and park it behind a building or tuck it behind some trees, if you wanted to hide it for a few days or a week. So, if Annuska wanted to hide Melvin's car quickly, this park is a logical place for her to leave it, if only temporarily."

"Hide Melvin's car? That would mean that she…"

She raises her hand, palm towards me, and quickly

says, "Don't jump to any conclusions, June. I just thought it was worth checking out. We also had some officers roaming all over the park with dogs that are capable of sniffing out a buried body. It would be dumb to bury a body in the ground in this park because a hiker's dog would probably eventually find it. But sometimes murderers do dumb things. Anyway, the dogs found nothing. And since these two guys have been swinging their hooks for a good long time now, I'm betting that we're not going to find anything in the pond. So that'll be it. My boss says if the pond search yields nothing, then we give up for now. No further search efforts without clear evidence of a crime. To be honest, June, it's unusual that we would put this kind of effort into a simple missing person case. But things happen to be a bit slow for us right now."

"Hmmm, maybe the nice spring weather is keeping the crime rate down."

"Maybe. By the way, Annuska Hamm is over there, sitting on the grass behind those reeds. She's with her boss, Wayne Chalmers." Louise pointed over my shoulder. "I don't like the fact that she's here, but I couldn't stop her from coming."

I turn my head and look in the direction that Louise pointed, but the reeds completely block my view.

As if she can read my thoughts, Louise says, "They're too far away to hear us."

I turn back to Louise and ask, "Why is her boss here?"

She shrugs her shoulders. "Emotional support, maybe? You tell *me*. Do you know anything about their relationship?"

I remember Florence's innuendo about the two of

them, but considering the source, I'm not about to spread rumors. I suppose that if it *is* important, Louise will ask Florence about it.

"No. He dropped her off at her place that first day I met her. I guess they're friends. Have you interviewed him?" I ask.

"No. Do you have any reason to believe that I should?"

I give her a smile. "No. You're looking for answers or information that I don't have. So, I assume you spoke to Annuska this morning? How does she seem to be holding up? I haven't talked to her since that first day."

Louise nods and says, "She's extremely distressed about her husband. Either that, or she's a terrific actress." She looks straight at me, apparently to see if I agree or not, but I'm expressionless, so she continues, "Annuska told me this search is pointless because Melvin probably threw the gun in there himself. But she came anyway. Maybe she thinks there's a small possibility that we'll find something."

"So, can you tell me what else you found out about the gun? I mean, I'm sure that you must have talked to Melvin's father about it by now. The likelihood that he left the hospice to come over here and toss his gun in the pond is pretty small. Infinitesimal, I'd say. So, Melvin had the gun, didn't he?"

Louise smiles at my perceptiveness and says, "Peter Tremayne told us yesterday that the gun went missing from his house at the time his son disappeared. Mr. Tremayne never reported it stolen. He didn't give a good explanation of why he didn't report it, other than saying he always felt that he might have misplaced it and would find it again, and then he apparently forgot about it. A pretty weak explanation, I'd say. He was a very astute, organized businessman in his day, not the type likely to be careless with a handgun. If his son left willingly, then he probably stole the gun from his father as he was leaving. And maybe Mr. Tremayne didn't want to tell the police that his son might be armed, which could increase the chance of some type of violent confrontation if they found him."

"What do you mean by that? Is Melvin dangerous? Violent?"

She shakes her head. "There's no evidence of that."

"Then why did he take the gun?"

"We don't know. Maybe for one of the same reasons that a hundred million other people in this country want a handgun. He probably had it all these years."

"And did you talk to Annuska about it?"

"Yes, she said she knew Melvin had the gun in his possession, but she never touched it because she's afraid of guns. Also, that she begged Melvin for a long time to get rid of it because she always felt nervous having it around. Maybe she felt especially nervous recently since they've been arguing a lot, according to Florence Shmoo, although Annuska said that her relationship with her husband was very good and that they had only occasional arguments, all minor. *Discussions*, she preferred to call them. Anyway, she says he must have finally tossed it in the pond without telling her, but she has no idea when."

"Do you think she's telling the truth?"

Louise shrugs her shoulders and says, "It's certainly possible. We weren't able to find anyone in the dog park who witnessed someone throwing the gun in the water. Maybe Melvin was nervous, too, about having it around if they were arguing a lot. Who knows, maybe he was afraid that she'd try to use it on him in a fit of rage, so he thought it was better to get rid of it. Throwing it into a pond is certainly a stupid way to get rid of a gun. Better to turn it in to law enforcement, but he might have been concerned that the question of where he got it would be raised.

"So, somehow that gun got from Melvin's house into that pond. The corrosion tests were not very useful. All they could say was that the gun was in the pond for anywhere from a few days to a month. But whatever the real explanation is for that gun ending up in the water, it has to be consistent with the fact that Faith Gelner knew exactly where it was. The obvious question is: Could Ms. Gelner ever have gotten her hands on that gun?"

I give Louise an incredulous stare for a few seconds. She's finally said it, or at least alluded to it. She suspects Faith of killing Melvin. In addition to suspecting Annuska, apparently.

"Are you saying that Faith swiped the gun from Melvin's house, shot him, got rid of the body somehow, and then tossed the gun in the pond? And *then* she tells us where the gun is? To what end? It makes no sense at all."

"At this point I'm not ready to piece together any motives. I'm not saying *anyone* shot Melvin since we don't even know he's dead. But Ms. Gelner knew the gun was in the pond, and if she's *not* clairvoyant, the first question to ask is whether she put it there for you to find. If so, then how did she get the gun in the first place? Perhaps she took it from his house."

"She told me she's never been to his house before we went there together the other day."

"Yes, that's what she told me also. Maybe she's

lying. But even if she was never in his house, that doesn't mean she couldn't have gotten her hands on the gun. Maybe he carried the gun on him. What did he normally wear at work?"

I give her a puzzled look. "Wear? Nothing unusual. A collared dress shirt and pants, usually khakis. But no sport coat, if that's what you're getting at. Nothing that would cover a gun holster."

"Maybe he had it in an ankle holster. Did you ever notice any bulges in his pants?"

"No, and I don't normally scrutinize my employees for bulges in their pants. And anyway, Melvin is the last person on the planet I'd suspect of carrying a concealed gun. He's not the Dirty Harry type, believe me. The guy is mild-mannered, meek, quiet, and even socially inept."

"Oh? Then what do you think Annuska sees in him?" She raises just one eyebrow. I've always wished *I* could do that.

"Honestly, I have no idea what Annuska sees in him," I reply.

"Do you think that Annuska might have married him just to become a U.S. citizen?"

I give Louise a bit of a dumb grin and raise both hands, palms upward, in tacit agreement. But I don't say anything. It's not my style to badmouth people.

"He might have kept the gun in his car," she continues. "Or maybe he had it stashed at work."

"Doubtful. Firearms are not permitted on company property, not even if they're left in a car." This was supposedly an unofficial Fleener policy for decades, long before I arrived, but Fleener sure as shit made the policy official just before the first round of layoffs came, about five years ago. They even put up postings about it on the hallway bulletin boards.

Louise says, "I understand that it's not permitted, but that doesn't mean he couldn't have brought it to work secretly and maybe kept it in one of his desk drawers or somewhere in his workspace."

"I have a key to his desk at work. I could take a look and maybe we'll find some bullets or a holster or something, but I seriously doubt it."

"If you're willing to search his desk and it's not against company policy, that would be helpful. I'd like to search his house but at this point I don't have enough to get a warrant. Not without some evidence of a crime."

"Did you ask Annuska if you can search the house?"

"Yes, I did. She already let the uniformed police officers in there to collect a DNA sample, but they didn't do anything approaching a methodical search. I told her I wanted to thoroughly look for clues as to where Melvin might have gone, if he left willingly. She said it would be pointless because she knows he would not have left willingly since they loved each other, even though they had their occasional *loud* discussions. Then I said that maybe I could find some clue as to who might have *abducted* him. She said that would be pointless too, because he had no enemies. Her theory is that he had an accident, or was the victim of a robbery that ended badly."

"Do you believe her?"

"Should I?"

"You like to answer questions with questions, don't you, Louise?"

"Do you get the impression that I do?" She smiles again. "Here's another question for you: If *your* husband were missing and you had nothing to do with it, would it make sense to deny police permission to search your house?"

"Maybe, if I thought that the police were trying to falsely connect me to his disappearance. Or if I had something else to hide that was not even connected with the disappearance."

"Such as?"

"I don't know, but I can guess…in Annuska's case, she used to be with that sexy Eastern European brides website, right? Maybe she's worried that she violated some law there, even if she had nothing to do with Melvin's disappearance. By the way, did you look into their marriage? Is it legal?"

Louise nods and says, "I did, and it is."

My jaw dropped. "What? Even with Melvin using a false name?"

"Yes. It varies a bit from state to state on how courts deal with getting married under a false identity, but the bottom line is, you marry a *person*, not a name. The marriage is valid until a judge invalidates it, and in the state of Connecticut, which is where they were married, I don't expect that any judge would invalidate it on those grounds. But regardless of the legality of the marriage, Annuska will not get Melvin's father's money, so if she killed him, it was for some other reason."

"Right." I stupidly nod my head in agreement, as if I'm some expert on murderers' thoughts and motives.

Louise says, "There's one more thing. That guy who called you and said that he saw Melvin with a con woman—I have the number he called from."

I stare at Louise for a moment, my eyes wide open. I'm not able to hide my surprise, but I should have figured that the cops have their methods. I simply ask,

"How'd you get it?"

"The Patriot Act allows me to get call logs without a warrant. You gave me the time he called, and I have your number. That's all I needed. I can't track the phone without a warrant. But we could call it. You never know, maybe we'll get lucky and he'll answer."

"Uhh…so I take it you *didn't* try calling it yet?"

"Correct. From what you told me about the conversation, he sounded rather nervous. I'd prefer he didn't know that the police are involved. Would you be willing to call him and ask for more information on this woman? You can tell him that Melvin is missing if you think it will help."

"You want *me* to call him?" I consider the prospect of sinking into even deeper quicksand. I'm already in up to my navel. After staring blankly at her for a few seconds, I say, "Mind if I think about it, Louise?"

She gives me an understanding nod and replies, "Sure, no problem, June." And then she tilts her head and with a thoughtful look as if she were sizing me up, she asks, "June, would you like to go over there and talk to Annuska? Maybe she needs more consoling. Even more than her boss can give her."

I pause as I think about this additional request for help, and this one is a particularly strange one coming from a police officer because she's asking me to talk to a suspect. I say, "It almost seems like you're *playing* me, Louise."

With an innocent looking expression, Louise asks, "What do you mean?"

I shrug my shoulders and, like Louise sometimes does, I answer with a question, in a manner that's more observational than accusatory. "Louise, are you telling me stuff about the case because you think that I can perhaps help you get information from both Faith and Annuska that you might not otherwise be able to get?"

Another slight smile comes to Louise's lips as she says, "I certainly won't deny that I'd appreciate your help, June. Let's face it, this case is unusual. I'm still not convinced that Melvin just didn't get up and leave. Maybe that's exactly what he did. Maybe this is all a big nothing, and I'm wasting my time."

"By the way, is just *leaving* a crime? Like, abandoning his wife, or something like that?"

"Perhaps under some circumstances, but without children in the household, it's not a crime that would normally be investigated or prosecuted. If he's walking out on debt obligations, like a mortgage for instance, then that would surely get him into some trouble eventually, but the police wouldn't be involved in that. And by the way, I haven't told her yet about her husband's true identity, and as far as I can tell, she doesn't know. I *would* have told her if Peter Tremayne had wanted to talk to her, of course. But I'm under no legal obligation to tell her, so I'd prefer to hold off for the time being, to see how this thing plays out."

"Well, if I go over there now and get chummy with Annuska, I think that after I do, you'll want to know what we talked about."

She says, "Well, if I *do* want to know what you talked about, is that so bad? I mean, you want to find out what happened to Melvin, right?"

"Well, sure…but I don't really want to get involved."

"You *are* involved, June. You found the missing person's gun."

"How do you know that I won't tell Annuska to shut up and lawyer up?"

"Because I think you really want to know if Melvin is okay, and that's more important to you than any loyalty you might feel toward your new friend, Annuska."

I give her a polite but firm correction, "She's not actually my friend."

"Okay, but maybe she could use someone to talk to, anyway. So, why don't you just go over there and chat her up?"

Chapter 13

As I walk toward Annuska, my phone chimes. I check it and see that Louise texted me the number of the guy who called me about the con woman. I put the phone back in my purse. I'm not going to worry about it right now. At the moment I'm thinking about what I'm going to say to Annuska.

I am such a sucker. And a hopeless mother hen. What the hell am I doing? Okay, so I'm not going to poke and pry. I'll only try to console her. And only if she's genuinely sorrowful, and not acting. Yeah, like I could even tell the difference, being the great judge of character that I am. But I have to give her the benefit of the doubt, so I'm going to assume that she's truly grieving.

As I come around the bank of reeds, I see them standing side by side at the edge of the water. Annuska's boss at the funeral home, Wayne Chalmers, is closer to me. I barely saw him that first day since he didn't get out of his car, but now I have a good view of him. And he has the look of a used casket salesman.

Wayne is about forty-five, with a neatly trimmed black mustache. His thick hair is greased and parted on the side, and it's an obvious dye job because it's so deeply and uniformly jet black. He wears a dark brown three-piece suit with gray pinstripes, his work outfit I suppose. The lapels are too wide, the pant bottoms are slightly flared, and the shoulders are saggy and baggy. It's probably made of the most durable polyester that money can buy because he must have been wearing it for at least two decades, perhaps sprucing up the outfit with a new tie every five years or so. His face is pale, and his eyes are beady. While Annuska looks straight ahead, focused on the men in the boats, Wayne's head is constantly twisting in short, jerky movements, those small dark eyes darting around in different directions. He reminds me of a rodent after a big meal, sated but on alert for any snakes in the area.

As I get a little closer, I register in his peripheral vision, and he gives his head a sudden ninety-degree twist to fully take me in. His eyes widen and he looks like he's about to crap his pants. I have no idea what he's so spooked about. Maybe he feels guilty at being here with Annuska, and yet here he is, for anyone to see. If he's sleeping with her, well, it's none of my business. Unless of course it has something to do with Melvin's disappearance, in which case I suppose it *is*, maybe, *sort of* my business.

Annuska is still staring at the pond. As Wayne gawks at me, I notice him give her a light nudge with his elbow. Annuska turns towards me very slowly. She has the look of a person saddened and preoccupied, but in control.

I stop six feet short of them and give a polite and consoling smile as I wait and wonder which one of them will speak first. After a few seconds, Annuska breaks the silence.

"June, so very good of you to come. This is my employer, Wayne." She speaks solemnly, without a trace of enthusiasm in her voice.

"Nice to meet you, Wayne," I say.

He gives me a few rapid nods but doesn't extend his hand, so I don't either. For whatever reason, he feels obligated to immediately explain his presence. He speaks in a jabbering manner, fussing with the knot in his tie all the while—loosening, straightening, or tightening it, I'm not sure which.

He yammers, "Just offering emotional support to Annuska, you know? Poor Melvin. What a sad thing, jeezus. Just up and disappeared, you know? God only knows what happened to the poor bastard, but I sure as hell hope he didn't end up in *this* cesspool."

I give a sympathetic nod, but when I don't say something immediately, Wayne seems panicked by the silence. More tie tugging ensues, and then he blurts out, "The grief, you know? It's the grief. Twenty years in this business and you never get used to it, you know? Last Tuesday we buried a rich old broad, in a huge casket fit for King Tut, all steel with marble trim, you know? Shriveled up and wasted away to nothing from cancer, she was, so it had to be closed casket, you know? Pitiful. And cripes, even after all these years, seeing a thousand or more stiffs, I couldn't hold it together that morning, but Annuska was right there consoling me. And three days before that, we buried a poor bastard who'd been dragged by a bus, flattened like a piece o' pita bread, dear God, and holy shit, we *both* lost it, and Annuska and I, well, we were consoling each other. So, we're just...*there* for each other, you know? I don't know what I'd do without Annuska...oh, and my *wife*, of course! And...and..."

I decide I should step into the conversation, to relieve him of the stress of trying to think of something else to say.

"Ah, yes, I'm sure it's a trying business to be in," I agree.

I turn my head toward Annuska, and Wayne thankfully takes one step aside so that I can have a full view of her. She's wearing all black again. Tight black leather jeans and a black blouse, with the same dark makeup she wore when I first met her.

What's up with all the black? Is she in mourning already? Or is black just her everyday color?

Her eyes are red from crying again, or maybe from the spring pollen that's making *my* eyes red.

I suck at consoling people. I did a crappy job with her the other day, and now I'm in for a repeat performance. Here goes.

I shake my head and give her a muted smile, one which I hope conveys the message that I feel her pain. "How are you holding up?" I ask her. "You shouldn't be here, really. This is just all too…emotional for you." How can I say in a sensitive way that in the event they pull him out of this muck, she really doesn't want to see his bloated dead body, probably half-eaten by snapping turtles, as much as *I* don't want to see it either?

So, let's all get out of here now, just in case those old guys hook something big.

She answers in that thick, deep, husky, eastern European voice, which oozes sex appeal even in her state of sorrow.

"June, is good to see your kind face. I thank you again for coming. This is too much sorrow for me." She bows her head and tears flow, somewhere between a gush and a torrent. If she is acting, she is damn good. She squelches the tears and sniffles just long enough to say,

"He is dead, my Melvin is dead. I know this for sure."

"Dead?" I say. "Oh, Annuska, don't give up hope. This search of the pond, it's just routine. But, uh…how do you know for sure?" *Well, of course* y*ou'd certainly know for sure if you shot him…*

"I sense his passing with my Wiccan powers. We are intertwined, Melvin and I. He is passed from this world to the next one. We Wiccans are bonded with nature, and the movement from life to death is a passage of nature." She bows her head again.

"There, there, Annuska. There, there." *Yes, I'm sure that those soothing and totally meaningless words help tremendously…*

I move right next to her and put my hand on her shoulder. Now I have two separate metaphysical predictions that Melvin is dead. Very different techniques, I suppose. Faith thinks she was *born* with her powers. And Annuska has somehow *learned* her powers? From practice? Whatever. But now Faith and Annuska are on the same page. Does this mean it's more likely that he's really dead? Like one prediction backing the other up? I'm more inclined to believe that two loads of hogwash count for no more than one load. Even so, I have a brain fart of a moment where I'm worried that maybe somehow both of them, with their separate but possibly equal psychic powers, can read my mind.

Maybe I should wear an aluminum foil hat like Harold does to block the aliens' telepathy.

"Annuska, if you really think Melvin is dead…can you see if…uh…his body is in this pond?"

She answers in a way that sounds completely sincere, "Such things I cannot see, June. I am only in touch with the passing of life. This I do not know."

Annuska puts her hand on mine and the sudden appearance of those long black fingernails startles me. They look like five vicious daggers. She looks up at me and says, "June, I must have ceremony very soon. Wiccan funeral ceremony. I must honor Melvin's life and ease his passing."

"A funeral? Uhhh…isn't that a little premature? I mean, without Melvin's body?"

She looks at me curiously as if she's teaching a lesson to a small child. "But June, of course you know that to bury or burn the body is not so important as to send the spirit on its journey."

"Oh, of course…the spirit," I respond weakly, nodding my head in agreement. I honestly can't tell if she's snowing me or not. "Well, if you're convinced he's dead.…have you decided…what to do *after* the funeral?"

Staring out at the men in the pond, she says, "I do not know yet. I must go where life takes me."

Will it take you into the arms of this guy in the cheap suit standing next to us?

She turns her head towards me and says, "I wish you to come to funeral, June. And give big speech. What is word…eulogy?"

Oh, shit. Me? Give Melvin's eulogy?

I finish my conversation with Annuska by giving her a gentle pat on the back, which is about as meaningless as the "*There, there*" I'd given her a few minutes ago. And I tell her that of course I would be so honored to give Melvin's eulogy because what the hell else can you say when someone asks you to do that?

Should I have told her the truth, which is that I really don't know him that well, and the only good things I can say about him is that he got his monthly reports to me on time, and kept his cube very clean? Also, I'm pretty sure he wasn't the one voraciously surfing porn websites at work, so that's another positive thing I can mention in the eulogy. But I can hardly say he was a good husband when I know he and Annuska argued quite a bit according to Florence, and I also can't say he was a good son, when I know that he cut ties with his father at nineteen, a father who is now on his deathbed, wishing he could see his son one last time.

As I leave them, I know that Louise wants to debrief me, but I walk briskly past her, saying I really have to get going and that I'll talk to her later.

When I arrive back at work, I pull out my phone and look at the text from Louise. The number is glaring at me. Why not call it right now? I mean, I *am* dying to find out if Annuska is really a con woman. I want to know if I should continue this show of sympathy towards her, or if it's all a farce. Would composing a sappy eulogy be an asinine waste of my time?

I punch in the number on my cell. What the hell, since his phone is a burner, there's a good chance that no one will pick up anyway. The phone's probably been thrown into a drawer or a trashcan by now.

Four rings.

Five.

Six.

I feel a bit of relief actually, when it seems that no one is going to answer, and I haven't thought about what to say anyway, so…

And then, shit, I hear something.

"Hello?" That wary tone again, definitely the same guy.

"Hi, this is June Bloom. Is this the person who called

me…"

"How did you get this number?" he barks in an accusatory tone. "I did the thing to hide it from caller ID."

He's clearly upset. No way should I tell this guy that the police are involved…

My innocent-sounding response, a total fib, comes out with surprising ease, "Well, the number appeared on my caller ID, so maybe you did it wrong, or maybe there was a phone company screw up."

He pauses, and it isn't clear that he swallowed my lie, but at least he doesn't disconnect. He asks rather gruffly, "What do you want?"

"Well…more information, actually. I'm really concerned about Mr. Hamm. And I don't know who this con woman is. Can you tell me her name?"

He answers with scorn, "What good would *that* do? It's surely a false name."

"Can you tell me anyway? Just in case it's not."

He pauses. I hear a few murmurs and a sigh. Even over the phone I can sense his indecisiveness. But a reluctant response eventually comes, "Alice Meeker."

The name is a total blank to me. I say, "I don't know anyone by that name. Maybe you're right, it could be a false name. Does she have black hair?"

"No, but what does that matter? Women dye their hair all the time. I'm certain she could easily change her appearance."

"Does she speak in a thick eastern European accent?"

"No, but I certainly think she's talented enough to fake an accent." Now he's sounding annoyed, and anxious to end the call. I'm losing him. I need some details about her appearance that she can't change.

"Does she have high cheekbones?"

That one flusters him. "Cheekbones? I...I don't know. I don't think I would even recognize high cheekbones if I saw them."

"Okay, well, about how tall is she?"

"Probably a little over five feet, maybe about five-two. But...look, I really shouldn't be telling you any of this. And for all I know, if you have my phone number you might be able to trace this call. I might have screwed myself already. I don't want to get involved, and I shouldn't have called you the first time."

"But it's clear that you called for a reason, that you wanted to be of some help. So, if you could tell me the color of her eyes or her approximate weight..."

He interrupts, his tone turning emphatic, "Don't call again. It won't do you any good anyway, I'm throwing this phone away." He disconnects.

Well, I royally screwed that one up. Should've gone in with a better plan about how to convince him. Begged, groveled, lied, whatever. Too late now. Looks like I'll be giving that eulogy.

In addition to the fact that I consider myself a lousy public speaker, I've never given a eulogy before, so I won't be expecting any standing ovations.

I'm holding out hope that poor Melvin might suddenly show up and this whole complicated mess will vaporize. Maybe he hasn't been shot dead. Maybe he'll wander back to his house this afternoon in a daze, telling a story about getting abducted by extraterrestrials like Harold said, and with nothing more serious than a metal implant in his brain and a sore ass from your standard alien probe job.

****

So, that night I go to sleep thinking about the eulogy, even though I don't really sleep because Darryl snores like a Gatling gun. He must have been exhausted because he fell asleep without putting on his CPAP breathing mask. I try to clamp it on when he's soundly asleep, to stop the snoring, and he doesn't wake up as I struggle with it, but I think I'm putting it on wrong. I don't want to suffocate him, so I eventually pull it off and give up.

And then I just lay there awake, listening to the snores until I hear the robins sing for joy as they start to take their morning dumps on my car's windshield.

Then I get up and make coffee.

When I get to work, I decide that I have to put the whole Melvin thing out of my mind for a few hours so I can buckle down and get the monthly production accounting report done. I don't actually gather all the data for the report myself. I just take the reports that each of my people give me on our different projects, and sort of extract the important stuff, then massage and combine the information into one big report. Faith, Pog, Harold, Verne, Mary, and about five other people all contribute their pieces. And the task of putting together the combined report sucks.

My beef is with the quality of their individual reports. First of all, half of them are written on a third grade level. That's right, I've got a bunch of reasonably intelligent people who can't seem to write an intelligible sentence. Bad grammar? More like no grammar at all. Just a word salad. And they barely use any verbs.

Pog's report always takes the longest to get through. Okay, he has an excuse because English is not his first language, and I understand that and I'm sympathetic. No big deal, I know beforehand that I have to pretty much ignore ALL the words and just look at the graphs and tables and try to pull out what I need. But his graphs and tables are full of way too much technical bullshit that I don't understand, and I'm sure it's all wonderful stuff but I don't need that level of detail. So, I find myself every month telling him that his report is great, but *pleeeeease* can he try to condense and simplify and go for the bottom line in his next report? "Of course, Miss Juney," he always answers cheerfully. And then the next month I get the same bloated mess. Even so, I like Pog and as I've already said, the guy is a workhorse, and the company is lucky to have him.

Harold's reports always read like a bad mystery novel. He's in charge of looking at anomalies in chemical usage. For instance, sometimes in one month the usage of a chemical that's automatically fed into the production line as needed will for some reason go up, even though we're not *supposed* to be using more of it based on the amount of plastic being produced. So, Harold has to figure out what happened. His report this month is *The Mysterious Case of the Overuse of Methylene Chloride*, or whatever, and it reads like a *Goosebumps* novel, with little subplots and descriptions of personality traits of the people he talked to who deliver and handle the chemical, and tantalizing hints thrown in about whether someone might be stealing some of it to sell on the side, based on some rumor he heard in the men's toilet. He describes in detail how he talked to this person and that person, and about every false lead and dead-end he ran down to get to the truth, which always turns out to be something mundane, like a stupid broken valve allowed some of the shit to spill out on the floor and it evaporated. He must be a frustrated screenwriter or novelist who looks for nefarious intentions or conspiracy theories (alien-based or otherwise) in everything, and every month I have to tell him to cut the crap. But he never does.

Some reports have recurring peccadilloes that I've learned to deal with. For instance, Faith's are good except that she has a problem where she sometimes puts in a small double d instead of small double b or double q instead of p. It's some kind of weird mirror image dyslexia or something. She runs spell check which catches a lot of those errors, and she'll fix them, but sometimes a word gets through—for instance there might be the word *rudder* in there where she meant to say *rubber*.

As for Gary, his reports are written perfectly well in terms of grammar and spelling, but he uses *no* punctuation, like he doesn't believe in it or something. So, I have to spend time figuring out where his sentences begin and end, which is sort of like doing a puzzle.

Verne's reports are just total manure. Remember that kid you probably knew in grade school who never read the book before he wrote the book report? He'd just talk to a few people ten minutes before the thing was due, to find out what the book was about in general, and then scribble something on a piece of scrap paper with a crayon or a dirty fingernail, turn it in, and declare success. Well, that's Verne. He puts in no effort all. But he's "protected" in a sense because he hasn't been with the company long enough to get laid off. Fleener has a rule about not laying off people too soon after they're hired, no matter how bad they are, because it might affect our ability to get new people out of college, which is important because they work cheap, and the company needs to have a steady stream of cheap labor so they're able to lay off the older ones who earn larger salaries. Anyway, I've had a few talks with Verne about it, trying my best to be diplomatic and encouraging. He knows that he has to improve, and I hope he gets his act together because everybody likes him.

Then there's the host of usual errors in various people's reports which are fairly common—using the word *fewer* when they should be using *less*, *there* versus *their* versus *they're*, *you're* versus *your*, and so on. Some of these might be considered minor things, but it's another reason that I can't just copy and paste, because I don't feel right about putting my name on a report that's full of these errors, even though my shit-for-brains boss Larry wouldn't be bothered a bit if I submitted a report written at a third-grade level because he writes at a first-grade level.

****

After about four hours, I've pieced together a reasonable report, and I'm mentally exhausted. I took only one short break, to do my little search of Melvin's cube. Now it's lunchtime, so I decide to call Louise. I'm dying to know if the pond search is done. I get her voicemail and leave a message saying simply that I want to speak to her.

She calls me back in about ten minutes.

"Hello, June," she says.

"Hi. So…I searched Melvin's cube and found nothing at all that was gun related. Just the usual stuff I expected. And I assume that you didn't find the body?"

"We finished the search and came up dry on the body. They pulled up assorted pieces of garbage, but that was all. Amazing the crap that people throw in that pond."

I feel relief at the prospect that Melvin might still be alive somewhere. And also some relief even if he *is* dead, because that pond would have been a damn lousy place to end up.

I say, "Okay. Well, I called the guy. The number you texted me. He answered."

"He did? I'm surprised. From what you told me about the first phone conversation, I expected him *not* to answer. So, what did you learn?"

"It was a very short conversation. He was rather hostile this time, and extremely reluctant to talk. The only details I got were the name of the woman, which he said is almost surely an alias, and he also said she's a little over five feet tall. Then he abruptly hung up and told me not to call back. Said he was going to get rid of the phone."

"And what's the name?" Louise asks.

"Alice Meeker. He didn't spell it, but it sounded like M-E-E-K-E-R."

"That's it? Nothing about what she did to him, how she supposedly conned him?"

"No, nothing more. He hung up at that point. Can you trace the call or something?"

"No, but I can at least run the name. Maybe there's an Alice Meeker with an arrest record."

"Okay. Will you let me know what you find?"

"Yes, of course. I trust you to keep all this information to yourself. Will you tell me what you and Annuska talked about yesterday?"

I don't have to think about it because I have hardly any information to offer.

"Sure, but there's really not much to tell, the conversation was brief as you know because you were only a short distance away. She was crying. She told me that she really believes Melvin is dead."

"And how did she reach that conclusion?"

"Her Wiccan powers. Said she's bonded with nature, so she could sense his passing from this world to the next, something like that."

"I see," she says. I can hear the incredulity in her tone. I'm not sure if she's more skeptical of Faith's sixth sense or Annuska's. Probably a toss-up.

"And one more thing, she's going to have a funeral for Melvin. Some kind of Wiccan ceremony. She wants me to give the eulogy."

"A funeral? Without a body?" In my mind I can see her raise one eyebrow in surprise.

"Exactly. Is that legal?"

"Of course. There's absolutely no law against it. She can have a ceremony, she can erect a shrine, she can even bury an empty suit and a pair of his shoes as a symbolic gesture. Whatever she wants. But there won't be any legal declaration of his death until his body is found or until a very long time passes and he doesn't turn up."

"Okay. So, regarding this stuff about the con woman, what do you plan to do now?"

"Nothing, June. What the man on the phone said about seeing Melvin with a woman could have nothing at all to do with Melvin's disappearance. If some woman conned this anonymous man out of money, then a crime might have been committed. If that's the case, I hope he comes to his senses and calls the police. But even if he does, I have no idea where this man lives, and it would be the police in his area that would have jurisdiction in any investigation even if the woman is currently in my area of southern Connecticut. And anyway, I'm putting this case on the back burner for now."

"Why?"

"Because we have a drug-related murder in New Haven that I have to work on, full time."

"How is that more important?"

"I have something with the New Haven case that I don't have with Melvin Hamm's case—a body. In fact, *two* bodies. Both with bullets in them. My chief has taken me off your missing person case until a body turns up, or Melvin is spotted walking around, or his car is spotted, which I believe is the most likely thing to happen in the near future since I'm coming around to think that he probably just skipped town. But, as I said, I *will* run the name you gave me and call you back."

"Well, if Melvin is really out there somewhere, what about the gun we found?"

"Maybe what Annuska said was true, that Melvin tossed it in there at her urging because she was scared of having it around. But of course, I can't rule out the possibility that Annuska threw it in there. Or Faith, for that matter."

Or maybe Annuska tossed it in there and Faith saw her do it? Or Annuska told Faith about it? For reasons that I can't even begin to guess at...

I can't believe Faith would do anything like that, which I suppose means she really is clairvoyant, and I just can't swallow that either.

My head is spinning as I consider all of the convoluted possibilities. I thank Louise and we end the call. I expect the name Alice Meeker will be a dead end. And without the police working on the case, I'm pretty much on my own. So why do I continue to care about it?

I don't have Wiccan powers, I don't get visions, and I can't even bend spoons or read tarot cards, but I just have this feeling that something really bad happened to Melvin.

Chapter 14

As I sit at my desk and sip a tepid cup of coffee, I decide that I have to talk to Florence Shmoo again. I'll go over to see her on my lunch break. I don't want to call her first because she might tell me not to come. Best to surprise her.

I want to know more about the arguing between Melvin and Annuska. I can call Louise back and ask her to give me whatever details about the arguments that she got from interviewing Florence, and maybe she'll tell me a few things. But since she has a new case, I don't want to take the chance of becoming a bug up her ass. Besides, I want to hear it directly from Florence and then maybe ask her a few questions that Louise might not have asked.

I'm not sure what I'll do if Annuska is there because I don't especially want to talk to her again. But maybe she decided to go back to work. If I do run into her, I guess I can tell her that I'm making fantastic progress on writing Melvin's eulogy. She hasn't given me a time frame, but when you don't have a body that's getting a little more ripe as each day passes, does it really matter if you wait a bit to have the funeral?

Anyway, one advantage of doing all this lunchtime investigating is that I'm skipping a few meals. Maybe I've already dropped a few pounds, and it might be worth stepping on the scale tonight. Or maybe I should even stop at the health club to get weighed, and if it's a happy number, then I can tell that snarky young kid, Billy, who wanted to be my trainer, and he can enter the new weight into my file. I'll show him that I'm not on a one-way trip to becoming a blimp for a tire company.

So, at about noon I'm heading out of the cube area and Faith, who sits only a few cubes away from me, notices me leaving.

She quickly jumps up from her chair, runs over to me, grabs my arm to stop me, and asks happily, "Hey June, where are you headed?"

Unprepared with a white lie, I tell her the truth, "To see Florence Shmoo."

Faith immediately raises her eyebrows and says, "Oh, then ah'm comin' with you, June."

"No, no. Annuska might be there," I warn her. "The police told you to stay away from her, right?"

She turns on the pleading voice and the puppy dog eyes again, and says, "When we get there you can go to the door alone, and if Annuska is home, ah'll stay in the car, ah promise."

I really don't want to have Faith come along to possibly do or say something weird or embarrassing. "Why do you need to go?" I ask her.

"Why do *you* need to go, June?" she shoots right back.

I really don't have a good answer because even *I* don't know. So, I give her a wishy-washy one, "I…I just feel that I owe it to Melvin. The police have more or less dropped the case. The detective says they can't go any further without some proof that Melvin's in trouble, because he…" I hesitate, not wanting to say anything about Melvin's disappearance when he was nineteen. "Well, maybe he's out there, and he needs help."

Faith says in a matter-of-fact way, "Oh, no, there' no chance that Melvin needs your help. Poor Melvin's deader'n a tent peg. They'll probably find the corpse eventually. But ah'd sure like to speed up the process, so that wife of his gets what she deserves. You never know, maybe if ah touch more stuff over there…"

"What stuff do you need to touch? You already touched stuff there. You were on the couch, you went into the bathroom."

"But maybe ah touched the *wrong* stuff. Maybe there's *other* good stuff to touch." Faith's eyes brighten as she considers the possibilities.

"Uhhh…so, how do you know what the *good* stuff is?"

"Well, ah surely don't, and that's why ah gotta touch a *lotta* stuff," she explains, as if this was a simple fact that should be self-evident. "Oh, ah surely shoulda' touched that gun, June. Ah probably would have gotten somethin' from it!"

"No, it's good that you didn't touch it because your prints would have gotten on it."

"Well, anyway, ah need to go with you because ah want closure, seein' as how ah had the vision and all. And now, with the police off the case, it's all up to you and me, June."

"*What's* up to you and me?"

"Why, to pin the crime on Annuska, of course."

"Oh, right. You still think she smacked him on the head with a lead pipe?"

"Oh, hell, no. She shot him dead. We found the gun, remember? So, c'mon June, what did they tell you about what Annuska said about the gun?"

I suppose that as long as I don't tell her about

S.E. Greco

Melvin's secret identity, it's okay for Faith to know about the gun. I say, "It was Melvin's gun and Annuska said that Melvin must have tossed it in there because she told Melvin that she's scared of guns."

Faith waves her hands as if to brush away Annuska's lies. "Oh, my Lord, what an industrial manure spreader that woman is! C'mon, let's go over there and talk to Florence and find out just how bad their relationship really was. And ah'll touch more stuff. We need to find that body, and when we do ah'm sure they'll find some real evidence to link Annuska to it."

I instantly have pangs of regret that I told Faith anything about the gun or Annuska's explanation. Not only have I gotten Faith riled up, but I've essentially betrayed Louise's trust.

"I'm not going there to confront Annuska," I explain. "I just want to hear what Florence knows about the arguing."

Faith gives an enthusiastic response, "Okay, so let's go!" She runs to her cube, grabs her jacket, and then starts to walk toward the exit as if it's already decided.

I surrender. Writing the report has mentally drained me and I'm in no mood to argue with someone as persistent as Faith.

We go out to the parking lot and hop into my car.

After we're driving for only five minutes on interstate ninety-five, Faith's body tenses as she notices something in the passenger side rearview mirror.

"June, someone's followin' us. And it ain't just *someone*. It's that crazy bastard, Wally!"

"What?" I look in my mirror and see a small orange SUV. It *could* be Wally's car, but seeing it directly from the front, I can't tell for sure. And I can't make out the

196

driver. The car is too far back.

I try to speak calmly, even though I can feel the cold sweats coming on. "Faith, I think we're still a little spooked from thinking we saw him the other night. That's probably not Wally behind us."

Faith is insistent, "Sure it is! You can prove it by slowin' down. He'll probably slow down too, or he'll pass you real fast."

Trying that would be harmless, so I take my foot off the gas. We're on a slight upgrade, so my car slows down rapidly.

And the orange SUV slows down too.

Faith yells with alarm, "You see? Ah was right!"

Now I can feel the muscles in both shoulders starting to knot up. "It doesn't prove anything," I insist. "Whoever's driving that car doesn't want to rear-end me, that's all. There's no room for him to get over in the other lane to pass right now."

"June, have you got a gun in the glove compartment?"

I throw an incredulous glance in her direction and bark, "A gun? What, are you kidding me? Of course not! Does everybody in Tennessee carry a gun in their glove compartment?"

"Oh, June, it would just be to scare him, that's all. If you *had* a gun, we'd wave it out the window and let him see it. Then you get your car even with his and shout out the window, maybe threaten to shoot one of his balls off. He'd get the message real quick, June. Ah *know* he would."

"Even if I had a gun, I wouldn't be waving it out the window. Now *calm* yourself, Faith," I order.

Faith continues to track the SUV in the rear-view

mirror. After another minute, she hits me with a second frantic suggestion, "He's still there. Try speedin' up. Lose him, June, take it up to about ninety."

"No way. This old car can't go ninety. You feel that vibration now? And we're only doing sixty-five. It'll start to shed parts when I hit seventy-five. And anyway, I'm getting off now, this is our exit." I signal, slow down and veer onto the exit ramp. In my mirror I see the SUV pass by, and I feel immediate relief.

I give Faith my told-you-so look. "You see, that wasn't Wally," I say. "He didn't get off the exit."

But Faith is undeterred, "Ah got a look at the driver, June. It surely *was* him."

"No, it wasn't. I'm *sure* it wasn't."

Was it?

"Bald, June. That driver's head was bald and shiny, like the prize-winnin' watermelon at the county fair. He didn't want to get off probably because there's a stop sign at the bottom of the exit ramp and he would have to pull up right behind us, you know?"

"Well, he's passed now, so we'll never know, but I'm betting it wasn't him."

Faith points at me to emphasize her warning, "He's playin' with you. He'll get off the next exit and double back to try and find you again, and maybe try to run you off the road. You really should tell the cops about him, June."

"No way. They couldn't do anything, anyway. I can handle this myself. *"*

Uhh...Can I?

My sweaty palms feel like they're glued to the steering wheel. I pull them off one at a time and move them down to where the wheel is dry.

Faith crosses her arms and makes her disapproval evident with what I call her Tennessee pout. "Ah'm just trying to look out for ya, June," she assures me.

"I'll be fine," I counter.

Keep saying it. I might eventually start to believe it.
****

We reach Melvin and Annuska's place with no further signs of the orange SUV. The house looks quiet, and the only car in front is the one that Florence calls her Japanese shoebox.

I park at the curb and immediately notice the van with the big red ant on top about a block down from us, also parked in the street. So maybe Filbert is here de-lousing the place again. Either that or he's at one of the neighbor's houses. Maybe the whole block is infested. I make a mental note to avoid sitting in any chairs, assuming I get inside.

"There's the exterminator van," Faith says. "Ah wonder if he's here again workin' on this house. Oh, my Lord, they must be overrun with vermin."

Faith and I walk up the cracked pavement and I ring the doorbell. I'm not sure if we'll be greeted with a puff of insecticide when the door opens. As we wait, I suddenly recall that my plan is to have Faith wait in the car.

I quickly turn to her. "Faith, you were supposed to wait back in the car until we know if Annuska is here."

She looks contrite and says innocently, "Oops, ah'm so sorry June, ah forgot, but don't you worry, ah'll just stand next to you real quiet, ah surely do promise." She raises her hand as if she's testifying in court.

I consider ordering her back to the car but then relent. Instead, I give her a firm command, "Just let me

199

S.E. Greco

do *all* the talking."

The door springs open with the harsh squeal of rusty hinges and Florence stands in front of us. A bluish-gray gas plume hits me in the face but it's fortunately only noxious tobacco smoke as opposed to noxious insecticide. She's wearing the same lounging outfit she wore when I saw her before, but this time her trashcan-sized curler is lime green instead of pink. She eyes us with suspicion.

"Hmmph, so you're back," she grunts with a scowl. "Haven't seen you two since you chased down that car." She takes the cigarette from her mouth and points it at me. "You recovered from that nasty fall you took, toots?"

I give her a polite smile because I know that I have to be nice to have any chance of my questions being answered. "Oh, we're fine, thanks for asking. Uh, is Annuska home?"

"Nope. That why you came by, to talk to her?"

"Well, no, I actually came to talk to you."

"Me? My lucky day." She waits for me to continue, making no move to invite us in.

"Um…first of all…if Melvin and Annuska rent this place and you're the homeowner, I'm just curious, if you don't mind…I mean…why do *you* answer the door? I don't quite understand the living arrangement."

"Oh, so you're losin' sleep at night wondering about that? Well, there's only one front door, toots. When I hear the doorbell, I come up from my cave and answer it if I think they're not home. That's the agreement I got with Melvin and Annuska. Yeah, I guess you could consider that to be an intrusion on their privacy if I make a mistake and they're here. But so far, so good. I never walked in on 'em having sex on the coffee table or anything like that."

I just nod my head and don't say anything because I am suddenly nauseous at the thought of Melvin having sex on *that* particular coffee table. Melvin's bare butt on the plate glass, the naked lady mannequin below, and Annuska on top. A Melvin sandwich, basically.

Florence continues, "Anyway, we don't get too many people ringin' this bell. Got Crumm, that incompetent exterminator. He just left an hour ago. This place is like his second home now. And once in a while we get some people preachin' that ol' time religion. I tell *them* where they can go. And now you."

"I see. So…as the homeowner, why aren't you living in the upstairs part and renting the downstairs?"

She looks at me with scorn and says, " 'Cause the upstairs can get more rent, bein' that it has more room and more light and all my beautiful palatial furnishings. But that's not even important when the renter doesn't pay the rent, is it?"

"I suppose not." I smile politely as if to sympathize with her predicament.

Florence pulls a new cigarette from the pocket of her robe and lights it from the one that's almost burned down. But then she apparently makes a snap decision that she can get one last mighty suck out of the short one and she sticks both in her mouth. One for each lung.

I continue my questioning, trying to sound casual and friendly. "Actually, I just wanted to ask you a few more questions about Melvin."

"Yeah, well I assume he hasn't turned up then, has he? I haven't seen a hair on his freeloading ass since he was reported missing."

"Well, no, he hasn't."

"What about his corpse, did *that* turn up yet?"

"Well, no…thank goodness."

"Too bad. Do you know how complicated it will be to evict him when he's missing, as opposed to dead?"

"Evict him? But…Annuska is still living here. Won't she want to stay here…I mean, if Melvin doesn't come back?"

Florence gives an abrupt wave of her hand at my suggestion, and says, "Ah, Christ, there's no way she'll be able to afford the rent. That woman spends money like it comes out of a spigot."

"Well, uhh, getting back to their relationship… Annuska and Melvin…would you mind telling me, how well do they get along?"

She tilts her head, closes one eye, and gives me a mistrusting squint with the other. "Why do *you* care, sweetie?" she asks. "You're just his boss, right?"

"Yes, but…well, we're also his friends." It's a little lie. And I'm pretty sure she isn't buying it.

"He's got friends? Well now, that's just precious."

"Yes, well, I mean, not super *close* friends, but…close enough to be concerned. So anyway, do they get along?"

"If you call screamin' at each other gettin' along."

"Okay, well since they were married, I guess at *one* time they must have been happy together. Do you think they have a lot in common?"

"Yeah, they both scream. They share a love of screaming."

"I see. Well, maybe it's better to ask how they're different?"

"He screams in English. She screams in Romanian.

That's *one* difference."

"Uh, do they ever get violent or anything?"

"I never saw any violence. But I don't like to pry, you know?"

"Of course not. So…what do they argue about?"

Florence pulls the burned down cigarette from her mouth and tosses it just beyond the edge of the front step where I stand. It joins at least two dozen other dead soldiers. It's a skillful toss, no doubt coming after years of practice flicking cigarette butts, but even so, it barely misses my leg.

"They argue about money, for one thing," Florence answers. "Annuska spends money they don't have. I think that when she married him and became a U.S. citizen and all, she musta' thought she hit the lotto jackpot, set for life and all that. That's gotta be why I couldn't even get my damn rent money out of him."

"So, they…Melvin and Annuska…apparently had money problems. And what else—"

Florence interrupts, maybe from a need to let off more steam. She isn't ready to let go of the rent issue. She says, "Christ, that Melvin is such a freeloader. Never paid the rent on time. I didn't think I was gonna get it last month. First, I get excuses three days in a row. He says he has the money, but he ran out of checks. So, I tell him to do a wire transfer to my account. Then he says his bank is having some problem with their website and he can't do the transfer. Finally, I say to him, 'Well shit, no problem, let's go right over to an ATM and get it.' So, we get in his car and go to his bank, and I have to lead him over to the ATM by the ear and stand right next to him as he takes the money out. You gotta do that with Melvin. Is that the way you treat him at work? Do you have to lead him around by his pecker to get him to do his job?"

"Uh, well, no, in our department you need to be able to work independently. So, what else do they argue about?"

She stares at me as if trying to read my mind. "You're kinda nosy, aren't ya, toots?"

Faith blurts out from where she stands behind me, "Can we come in? I need to use the powder room if you don't mind."

I turn around and give Faith a stern look that Florence can't see because Faith isn't supposed to say *anything.* She gives me an innocent look back as if to say that asking to go to the bathroom doesn't count.

A huff and a grudging answer comes from Florence, "Yeah, sure. You know where it is."

"Thanks," says Faith as she steps around me.

Then Florence walks inside, and I follow. I'm not all that happy about hanging out in the living room where the smoke is much worse. Across the room I see on the ceiling a smoke detector hanging down by two wires, apparently having been disabled long ago. I can easily imagine Florence falling asleep in bed some night with one or two burning cigarettes hanging from her mouth. When a few red embers drop onto the blanket, Florence and this entire dump with its cheap carpeting and nineteen-thirties construction, will go up like a box of dry matches.

Before I can get out my next question, Florence asks one, "Did Annuska tell you she's havin' a funeral for her beloved?"

"Well, yes. Actually, I'm supposed to give the eulogy."

Florence gives me a sarcastic grin and nods her head. "Oh, so you're the lucky one who's gonna spew all those compliments about Melvin and say how he was such a fine human being, and the planet will be a much worse place without him? I'm sure you're a great speaker, toots, but regardless, I'll be bringin' a barf bag if I go."

"Well, I'm really not sure if I'm supposed to give a...er...*conventional* eulogy. It's a Wiccan ceremony, and I haven't researched it yet."

She rolls her eyes and snorts. "Christ on a ten-speed bike! A Wiccan ceremony? You mean that cult she belongs to? Well, then, count me out. You might end up having a pretty small audience, especially considering how unpopular that moron was."

"It's definitely not a cult, it's more like a nature-based religion or a spiritual way of life. You should really keep an open mind about it. In any case, do you have any idea why Annuska wants to have the funeral so soon? I mean, Melvin hasn't even been—"

She points her cigarette at me again and cuts me off. "I *know* why, honey. So she can get on to the job of finding someone with more money than Melvin. Hopefully a *lot* more. Or, maybe right after the funeral she'll do us all a favor and get herself a ticket on the cattle boat back to Romania. Either way, I'm okay with it because she'll be out of here and I can get a paying tenant."

"Well, actually, I don't think she can legally marry someone else until Melvin is declared dead. This situation is complicated, and..."

"Oh, yeah? Well, can she legally screw someone else and take his wallet out of his pants in the middle of the night?"

"My goodness, you're rather…cynical. She's grieving for her lost husband, and—"

"You think she's some kinda Girl Scout, don't ya?"

Faith comes out of the bathroom and stands next to me, smiling politely. It's clear to me that this conversation is going absolutely nowhere, so I decide to wrap it up.

"Okay, well, thank you for your time, Florence, we have to get back to work now. I'm sure you'll want to know if we get any information about Melvin."

She nods and gives me that familiar sarcastic grin. "Oh yeah, I'll be waitin' by the phone night and day."

Faith and I walk out silently as Florence stands in the doorway and watches. When we reach the car, I jump at the sound of the screen door slamming shut. It makes a bang as loud as a damn gunshot.

Regaining my composure, I say to Faith, "Wait here, I'll be right back."

I walk to the exterminator van, which is facing away from me. As I get closer, I expect that I'll be noticed, and maybe the engine will start up and the van will roll away.

Nothing.

When I reach the back of the van, I can see through the open passenger window that Filbert is asleep, his head slumped back against the headrest.

I approach the window and with my cupped hands I give one mighty clap, about two feet from his head, and simultaneously shout, "WAKE UP, FILBERT!"

Well, the guy must have been wound up like a spring because his ass jumps a foot off the car seat and his head whacks the ceiling, crushing his bright red baseball cap.

"Why are you here?" I demand.

With his eyes wide open now, Filbert's head whips around wildly as he tries to figure out if a nuclear bomb just went off and if he should duck under the dash for cover. When he recognizes me, he looks embarrassed. He takes his hat off and starts rubbing the top of his head.

"Oh, Ms. Bloom, how are you?" he says sheepishly, still rubbing his head and wincing. "I…uhh…I just finished fumigating Ms. Schmoo's house."

"Oh, yeah? Well, she said you finished an hour ago."

"Well…I, uh…maybe it *was* about an hour ago. Time just seems to fly when you're doing…important stuff."

"If you finished an hour ago, why are you still here, Filbert?"

I look in his eyes and I can see that his little bug brain is working frantically, trying to dream up excuses. He comes out with a simple one, "I don't have anywhere to go. I mean, I don't have another job at the present time."

"Well, then shouldn't you be out trying to drum up business? Offering free inspections? Driving around with that big bug on top should remind people they could have ants or termites or whatever eating at their foundations."

"Well, I decided to wait here until I get a call from the dispatcher. I'm staying here to…to save gas. Because this might be a hot zone, you know? Heavily infested. That's the technical term we use in the business. Maybe I'll get a call for a house in this neighborhood."

"No, actually, I think you're trying to do your detective thing by watching Florence's house." His countenance goes from defensive to guilty to pouting as

I watch.

After looking down at the floor with his pouty face for a few seconds, he says, "Okay, I admit it. There's no pulling the mosquito netting over your eyes, you figured it out. But with all due respect, Ms. Bloom, you standing at the window here is drawing attention to me. I need to remain discreet and inconspicuous."

"Are you kidding me? Inconspicuous? In a van with a giant ant on top?"

"Ms. Bloom, did you ever hear of the phrase, 'Hide in Plain Sight'?"

I think, *did you ever hear of the phrase: Dumb as a Stump?*

"Filbert, this is *not* hiding in plain sight. There is no hiding, in any sense of the word, when you have a six-foot ant with flashing green eyes on top of your van."

"But they're not flashing when the engine is off."

"Doesn't matter. This van screams, *Look at Me, I'm Right Here,* even when the engine is off."

He turns sad and pouty again like I've hurt his feelings. I think he might cry. Why do I feel sorry for the guy?

Yeah, I know. My mother hen complex.

I relent and strike a conciliatory tone. "Okay, look, you can come to my place this evening when I get home and do your exterminator inspection thing. But since you were just crawling around Florence's place, which is infested, just make sure you change your clothes or de-louse yourself or whatever, before you come into my house, okay?"

Instantly a proud smile flashes across his face, and he chirps, "Fantastic! And please don't be afraid that I might carry some tiny vermin into your domicile from a prior job. We at *Don't Bug Me* are highly trained to take extreme precautions against cross-contamination. For instance, they make me completely change in the back of my van before I go to the next job. I mean, totally naked, I even strip off my underwear!"

"Too much information there, Filbert. I don't need to hear anything about you being naked."

"Sorry."

"Right, so just be at my place at five-thirty. See you then. And don't hang around here. Don't surveil Florence's house, and don't worry about Melvin and Annuska, got it? I know you want to be a private detective, but there's nothing here for you. Melvin probably just left because he and his wife had some problems, and that's that. Happens all the time. So, it's really none of our business."

So why the hell am I here?

Filbert nods obediently at my order, and I give him a farewell wave and walk back to my car. Faith is standing by the driver-side door, and seeing her reminds me that something Florence said in there is bothering me. But I can't remember what…

"Oh, my Lord, June, ah am just standing out here savorin' the fresh air. The smell in that house reminds me of my uncle's roadside shack in Tennessee. He had his own business smokin' country pork butts. Sorry ah had to go to the powder room. Ah touched everything in there, but ah got no visions, unfortunately. Ah just wish ah coulda went into Melvin and Annuska's bedroom, but ah think Florence woulda seen me duck in there. So, what'd ah miss? Did you get any information from her?"

"You didn't miss anything. It was a waste of time coming here."

S.E. Greco

Faith had asked Florence if she could use the bathroom...

Faith lets out a sigh and says, "Can't say ah'm surprised. That woman is just plain ornery and uncooperative. Oh well, then, let's go." She walks around to the passenger side door. "Hopefully we won't run into Wally again. There's a chance he coulda followed us here, and he might be waitin' close by. But if we *do* see him again, ah'll have my phone ready to snap a picture of him. You just gotta get your car close enough to his. Just a picture of the plate would prove it's his car, though ah'm not sure how to prove he's been followin' you. Unless we live-stream some video, maybe."

Faith's babbling is barely registering with me because I'm thinking about what Florence said to Faith: *"You know where it is."*

Faith has been in the bathroom before.

It was *before* the cops came. Before the day Melvin disappeared.

Chapter 15

We make it back to work with no further Wally incidents. Faith goes right to her cube, and I go straight into a break room and shut the door. I pull out my cell and dial Louise's number again.

She picks up immediately. "June? I didn't expect to hear back from you so soon."

"Uh, well I didn't expect to have to call back so soon."

"Is it about the name, Alice Meeker? I ran it, nothing turned up. So, she probably used a false name."

"Okay, thanks. I guess that's what I expected. But that's not why I called. Can you tell me again how you got the DNA sample from Melvin that identified him as being Max?"

"From hairs on a brush that was in the bathroom. Hairs with follicles. Annuska said that only Melvin uses that brush."

"Okay, that's what I recall. Well…I remember that Faith used the bathroom while we were waiting for the police to come. What if she…" I pause, unsure of how to phrase my accusation.

"What if she…what?" coaxes Louise.

"Look, the man who called me said he saw a woman who was maybe a little over five feet in height. So, it could've been Annuska…but Faith is about the same height. I mean…I'm sure you've given at least a *passing* thought to the notion that there's a slight chance it might have been Faith he saw?"

"What exactly are you saying?"

"I'm saying that maybe Faith put those hairs on the comb."

"Just a short while ago you were defending her vehemently. Why would Faith do that?"

"I...I don't know. I'm like you, trying not to draw conclusions before all the facts are in."

"I see. Turning into a detective, are you?"

"Not really. I just...sometimes when I get involved in solving a problem, I can't let it go, I just plug away at it. Personality flaw, I guess. As far as motive...who knows? This is complicated, I just don't know what to think."

"Where would she have gotten the hairs?"

"You're asking questions I don't have the answers to. Not even speculative answers. I'm probably way off base with this suspicion. But...can you somehow get another DNA sample from Melvin...just so we can be absolutely certain that he's Max Tremayne?"

There's dead air for a few seconds. I half expect her to say that I'm nuts.

"Fingerprints," she finally says.

"What?"

"We'll do fingerprints instead of DNA. It's much cheaper. Everything costs the department money, remember? And I'm not even supposed to be investigating this disappearance anymore, but a simple fingerprint check will essentially go under the radar. We have Max Tremayne's prints on record. They were taken from his father's house after he disappeared. And I assume Melvin's prints are all over his cubicle at work.

I can come to Fleener and lift the prints myself, off-hours so it doesn't draw a lot of attention. I'm not a fingerprint technician, but as long as the prints are on standard surfaces, smooth metal, or plastic, I should have no problem."

It sounds doable to me. The cube farm is a plastic paradise.

"Uh…is it legal?" I ask her.

"As long as you get me a proper visitor's pass if it's required and escort me into the cube area, I won't be doing anything illegal in lifting the prints. Of course, they would never be admissible as evidence in a court of law because even though you brought me into the cube area, you don't own Fleener. But the prints will tell us if Melvin is Max. That's really all we're after at this point."

"Okay, let's do it, please," I say.

"By the way, June, there's something else about the hairs that I didn't tell you. There were also some *red* hairs on that brush. So, they weren't Melvin's or Annuska's, or Florence Shmoo's, for that matter. Ms. Schmoo has reddish hair, but hers is frizzy and these were straight. There were no follicles on these hairs so we couldn't do anything other than establish they were human hairs."

"Red hairs? So…what does that mean?"

"Well, maybe it's all innocent. A brush like that can have hairs that are years old. I wish that I could have searched their bedroom closets for a red wig. Maybe Annuska wears one sometimes. She seems like maybe the dress-up type to me. But if they're not from a wig belonging to her then another possibility is that Melvin had very close contact with someone with red hair."

Close contact? Like…maybe…SEXUAL contact?

Could Melvin have been cheating on Annuska? I never thought of him as the sex machine type. I thought it would have been Annuska who cheated on Melvin, perhaps with her boss. But if Melvin was a cheater and Annuska knew it, then it certainly gave them a reason to argue.

And maybe Melvin wanted that gun out of the house before Annuska got any ideas about castrating him with it.

****

Later that day I sneak out of work early again. I need to get back to the house so I can be there when Filbert arrives, but before that, I want to stop at my brother's place. I won't call him first because I want it to be a surprise.

A really *big friggin' surprise*.

Part of the reason for not giving him any advance warning is that I want to see how he's living. Paul's home is a dumpy little one-bedroom apartment, and the last time I stopped in unexpectedly, it was in a state of utter squalor. I go over there about once a month. Even if I call ahead, I don't expect him to clean up because, after all, I'm just his sister. But the guy is a total slob. To get his place even back to the point where you could just call it *unkempt,* he'd have to hire some people to come in wearing hazmat suits, and they'd no doubt use power washers filled with bleach or acid. Maybe one of those companies that specialize in cleaning up murder scenes.

I worry that if he ever does find some nice woman suitable for marriage, taking her to his apartment will put a stake in the heart of any budding relationship, but he's too dull to realize that. And you might expect that any intelligent woman starting a relationship with a man would have her biggest concerns in the area of avoiding sexually transmitted diseases, right? But not in this case. One look at Paul's apartment and she'll be a lot more worried about picking up stuff like cholera or typhoid fever. And God forbid he should try and cook a meal for her. In that case, watch out for hepatitis A.

When I reach his apartment building, I park in the lot and climb the outdoor staircase to his second-story walk-up. I give ten hard raps on the door.

I'm not sure why I feel obligated to check up on him like this. But since Mom and Dad died, I feel like I'm the only one around to take care of him. I worry about Paul a lot. I just wish he would get married. I only hope he has the financial resources some day to do it. I have no idea how much he has in savings because he won't discuss it with me. He just says that he's doing fine. But how much could a fast talker make?

The door opens and Paul stands in front of me, a sheepish smile on his face.

My brother is not bad looking at all. Thick sandy hair, medium height, dimples, a decent physique, a pleasant smile. And he's intelligent, except when it comes to women and career choices. In those areas, the guy is a dunce, but a dunce with a pleasant personality. I got the sarcastic genes; he got the meek and passive ones. But there's no reason he shouldn't be able to land a wife. I just don't want it to be Abbey. I don't think she'd marry him anyway, she'd just suck him dry before moving on to the next rube. Maybe I should be hoping he's completely broke, in which case she'd tell him to take a hike as soon as she found out.

Geez-o Pete, he's in his pajamas! And it's five o'clock in the afternoon.

I know that I should really start the visit with a nice

sisterly hug instead of a confrontation—but I can't help myself. I immediately blurt out, "Are you kidding me? You're still in your PJs? Do you know what time it is?"

I've seen him wearing these *Star Trek* pajamas at least a hundred times before. They're maybe twenty years old, tattered at the bottoms, ripped at the side seams, threadbare everywhere, but I can still make out the images, on each of Paul's thighs, of the Captain firing his laser or phaser or ray gun, or whatever the hell they call it, at some big green alien dude with a lizard head.

Paul is pretty much always perky and cheerful, and by now fairly impervious to the shit I give him.

"Hi, Juney, great to see you. I do most of my work at home, remember? So, I work in comfortable clothes. It helps me channel my creativity."

Creativity?

Okay, I have to remember that Paul considers himself an artist. But how much creativity does it take to talk really fast? He fancies himself to be as much of an actor as those people doing voiceovers for animated films, I suppose.

I nod my head, and despite his cheerfulness, I can't hold back a cynical response, "Ohhhh, I see…you were *working.*" I look over at his nineteen-inch computer screen and I see some kind of medieval war game going on with goblins, archers, swordsmen, dragons, and scantily dressed damsels. At least it isn't hardcore porn.

I walk past him into the living room, carefully stepping around various food stains on the greasy carpet. I don't want to track anything into my car, which is sixteen years old, but the carpet in it is cleaner than what I'm stepping on now. The apartment is filled with various overlapping smells, the two dominant ones being fry grease and mildew. The first thing that visually registers is the pile of pizza boxes. No way can I miss it because it's five feet high, standing grandly like a war monument except that it's slightly tilted. I point to it and say, "That was here last time I came, but maybe half as high. Planning on getting rid of it sometime this year?"

"Oh, yes, well, those boxes are recyclable, of course, so I can't just throw them away in the regular trash. And I haven't yet figured out where the recycling…"

I cut him off and ask, "Cripes, do you eat *anything* other than pizza?"

"Well, of *course* I do," he answers, pointing at the various empty takeout containers and food wrappers scattered around on the sofa and tables. From scraps of food and labels on the sides of cartons, I can make out Mexican, Chinese, Thai, and classic American drive-in fare.

"Well, thank God you're rounding out your diet with nachos and hot wings. Do you attempt to cook at all? You *do* have a fully functional kitchen, I believe."

"Well, I don't want to waste time cooking. I choose to spend my time doing other stuff."

"What stuff?"

"Oh, you know…various important and creative stuff."

I change my line of questioning. "Do you remember that I bought you new pajamas last Christmas? Calvin Klein."

"Right, Juney, I have them, they're great, thanks again. I just want to get my last bit of use out of these. And I was just going to get dressed."

"Okay, so you've sat around in your pajamas for *this* long. For what reason, at five o'clock, are you going to get dressed? Going out?"

Maybe with Abbey?

He ignores my question, pretending he hasn't heard it and asks, "Would you like a cup of tea?"

"You have a clean cup?"

"Well, no. But I could wash one."

"You have dish soap?"

"Well, no, but..."

"I'll pass. So why are you really still in your pajamas?"

"Uhh...I had a late night."

"Oh yeah? How late?"

"Well, not really very..."

"You slept with Abbey, didn't you?" I blurt out. "Was she here?"

"Oh, no, certainly not."

"No to which question?"

Eager to avoid a confrontation, he spreads his arms diplomatically, sighs and says in a calm voice, "Juney, I *do* appreciate your interest in my romantic life, and I'm also grateful for you having introduced me to some very nice women. But what happens after the introductions is really none of your business, is it?"

"It *is* when you sleep with Abbey. You don't understand her."

"What about her don't I understand?"

I point my index finger straight at his nose and ask, "Did you wear a condom?"

He looks aghast. "Juney, please, I'm thirty-six years old! Why would you ask such a question?"

"Because you need to protect yourself, Paul. Who the hell knows what rugby team she dated last week."

He holds up both hands and says, "Okay, I think

we've crossed the line here, and we should just end this conversation, Juney. Let's talk about something less antagonistic and…

"Look, let's just get right to it. She's *not* good for you. Gotta trust me on this, brother. Okay, so you slept with her once. You got it out of your system. That's fine. That's enough."

"Actually, I'm taking her to dinner tonight."

Shit!

"Excuse me, but what the hell does she see in you?"

"Hmmm, if I didn't know better, I'd say that sounds rather like an insult, Juney."

"Okay, take it as an insult."

"Well, I'm intelligent, good looking—"

"Yeah, yeah." I give him a dismissive wave of my hand as I take a step away from the pizza box tower, out of fear that my footsteps will cause it to collapse. "Whatever. Intelligence and good looks is *not* what she's after. Does she think you have money? Has she seen this dump?"

"No, we went over to *her* place after the party. It's beautiful."

"I'm sure it is. But if you continue on this path, you're gonna be just another ornament on her tree. One more charm on her bracelet."

"Oh, I don't think so. She's very nice. And after all, *you* introduced us. I forgot to thank you for that. Thank you, Juney." He smiles.

"I *didn't* introduce you. Darryl invited her without asking me, and you pounced on her the second she walked into the living room. No introduction was needed. And she's *not* nice. She's evil."

Paul chuckles. "What? Evil? Oh, come now, how

can you say that?"

My phone rings. I touch accept and hear Darryl's voice, "Hi, hon, it's me. There's a guy here. Says he's a terminator."

"You probably mean an exterminator."

"Right. My mistake because he's all dressed up like some kind of futuristic soldier. Did you ask him to come?"

"Yes, hon, sorry I forgot to tell you. Let him in, he's not dangerous. Just keep the kids away from him. Let him go into the basement to look around. Tell him that's where the silverfish are."

"Okay. Do you think he can be trusted in the basement by himself?"

"You mean trusted with all that valuable shit we keep down there? I hope not, maybe he'll steal some of it and haul it away. I'm at Paul's place. I'm leaving now. Could you get dinner going? Just heat up the leftover stew and mashed potatoes."

"Sure. See you soon, hon."

I put the phone back into my purse and give Paul my wise but stern sister look. "Gotta go, brother. Just take my word for it, she's not for you. We'll talk about this again."

I skitter out the door and down the stairs, convinced that my visit won't change a thing. Paul is about to jump right back on the idiot express and go out to dinner with Abbey. Probably some expensive steakhouse where she'll order the *steak au poivre* and the waiter will finish it table-side with cream, butter, and flaming cognac, and she'll no doubt order the most expensive bottle of wine on the menu, and she'll get Paul to pay for it all.

My brother is such a putz.

****

When I get home, things are under control. Darryl is stirring the stew, and the boys are doing something other than trashing the place because I don't hear any sounds of fighting or explosions from upstairs. I step over the various items of sports equipment which litter the floor—cleats, baseballs, gloves, caps—and go down to the basement to check on Filbert. When I find him, all I see is a fulsome ass and a pair of stubby legs sticking out of the crawl space.

I call to him, "Filbert, you still breathing in there?"

A muffled response, "Uh…yes, Ms. Bloom, I'm fine. Just inspecting everywhere for vermin. We at *Don't Bug Me* pride ourselves on being very thorough."

"Well, you've got me a little worried. No offense, but you're a few pounds overweight, and I'm thinking that you might get stuck in that crawlspace."

"Oh, no problem. I'm coming out now."

Grunts and groans ensue as he pushes himself backward towards me, slowly coaxing his corpulent frame out of the cramped opening. I watch as he backs out, holding my breath, anxious that with every little push he might get himself tightly wedged in.

The crawlspace is elevated, and his feet are off the ground. If he falls, I sure as hell can't catch him or even break his fall. I'd be nuts to even try because his bulk would squash me like an army boot on a ladybug.

After about a minute of watching him struggle, I sigh with relief as his feet safely touch down.

Filbert turns around to face me, and his unearthly appearance gives me a jolt. He has some kind of eye goggles on, with round lenses that are fogged up on the inside. He also wears a tightly fitting plastic helmet, apparently to guard against head bumps. His generous ears protrude from holes in the helmet, and one of them has a Bluetooth earpiece wedged into it. I assume he's in constant contact with the home office or the mothership or whatever.

"Nice getup, Filbert. You look like one of those spaceship fighter pilots from sci-fi movies. Find anything in there?"

He removes the goggles and rubs at his sweaty brow. "I sure did, Ms. Bloom. You were right, you've got a battalion of silverfish."

I wince with disgust. "Oh, dear God. Can you get rid of them?"

"Yes, of course. I have several chemical options. Some chemicals are more powerful than others. The less powerful ones take more applications."

"Are these chemicals safe? I've got kids in the house."

Filbert puts his hands on his hips as if to emphasize his expertise and says, "Well, now, *safe* is a relative word, isn't it? Do you feel *safe* having millions of insects invading your domicile?"

I point my finger at him and say sternly, "Don't you try and bullshit me, Filbert. I work at Fleener Plastics, where bullshitting people is a way of life. I've heard it all. Just answer my question."

He pulls his earpiece out and checks to make sure it's shut off. He then leans towards me, and says in a near whisper, "Sorry. I don't mean to be evasive. That's what we're trained to say when customers ask us about chemical safety. What I *can* tell you is that *Don't Bug Me* has never successfully been sued for causing anyone harm through the use of these chemicals. And by that, I mean we always settle out of court, with no admission of wrongdoing."

"Well, gee, that's reassuring."

"As far as my *own* knowledge about the safety of our chemical agents, I'm very confident that they won't harm your children. But let me ask you this: Are you beyond your childbearing years?"

"That is waaaay too personal a question, Filbert."

"Sorry."

"Look, I want you to use the least toxic stuff. Even if it doesn't kill all the silverfish, just make sure you annoy them enough so that they'll move over to my neighbor's house."

"Okay, will do," he says happily, giving me the thumbs up.

"But I don't want you to start the first application until a few days from now. Wait till you hear from me."

As he packs up his huge duffle bag, I get the name of the chemical from him and tap it into my phone's notepad app. I'll research it on the internet and if I come up with any red flags I'll tell Filbert to forget the whole thing.

As he gathers up the last of his weapons for waging his bug wars, he says to me in a casual tone, "You know, Ms. Bloom, you have such a nice house here, you really should protect it with some kind of a security system. Or at least get some surveillance cameras for outside your house. Even Florence Shmoo has cameras outside her house, front and rear. They're tiny, but I'm trained to spot them."

"Florence put cameras up? I don't see her as the techie type. Maybe Melvin put them up."

"Maybe. They offer some protection against

invaders, and you can view them on your cell. I can put some up for you if you want. I'm highly trained in all aspects of surveillance because of the courses I've taken in how to be a private detective, and—"

I put my hand up to stop him before he can get too far into his speech. "Look, right now I'm just interested in getting rid of the silverfish. Let's take care of the tiny invaders first, and then I'll give some thought to the big ones. Okay?"

"Oh sure, no problem." He zips up his bag and then says to me in an easy conversational manner, "I saw Mrs. Hamm leaving this afternoon, just before I came here. It sure looked like she was moving out. She was taking a lot of stuff with her."

I snap to attention and ask, "What kind of stuff?"

"Like, everything she needed to move permanently. Lots of suitcases, some boxes that were taped shut, some bundles and bags. She threw everything into a rented minivan, then she drove away. She stopped first at a UPS shipping place and dropped off the boxes and bundles. Then she went straight to New Haven airport with the rest. At the airport, she returned the van to the rental place. I couldn't go in there because it had a low clearance barrier, and my roof ant was too high. I lost her there."

"You *followed* her? When was this?"

"Just this afternoon. And I also noted this morning that there was an orange SUV following *you* after you left the Shmoo residence."

My jaw clenches. "What?" I bark. "You're kidding me, right? You were following *me?*"

Filbert's eyes widen with alarm. He gulps and says, "Well, there was nothing going on at the Shmoo residence. So, I just thought I'd tag along behind you when you left there. I was just sort of going in the same direction anyway. And I noted the SUV that was obviously following you. I took an internet course in mobile surveillance, you know. It covered how to follow cars and also how to spot when you're being followed, or when someone you're following is being followed by someone else. Just thought I might be of help." He sports a stupid looking grin of feigned innocence.

I move in close to him, invading his personal space, and give him my royally pissed off look, poking my index finger into his fancy thirty pocket vest. I say with as much menace as I can muster, "Filbert, now you listen to me *very carefully.* You are *not* to follow me again, do you understand?"

His skin goes gray as he turns sheepish and gives me his third apology in as many minutes. He looks as if he thinks I might smack him in the face.

"Sorry, Ms. Bloom. Just trying to be helpful," he blubbers. "Just thought I'd…keep an eye on you. Faith Gelner told me there was a man threatening you because you fired him. She saw him the other night hanging around outside your house during a party."

"I didn't fire him, I had to lay him off. There's a big difference. You're *not* being helpful, Filbert. First of all, I want you to forget *everything* about Melvin and Annuska Hamm. Forget about this case. In fact, there is no *case*. Melvin just left. And Annuska…well, okay, so I guess she left too, for whatever reason. Marriages fall apart all the time. And secondly, I can take care of myself. Got it?"

His demeanor is that of a bad dog with his tail between his legs. "Yes, yes, of course, Ms. Bloom.

I'm…so sorry," he whimpers.

So that is, I think, the fourth apology. The dejected exterminator picks up his bag and starts walking toward the stairs.

But of course, I now have an itch I have to scratch. I need to know a little more. Faith and I saw an orange SUV when we were driving to Florence's house, but I'm not convinced it was Wally's. And now Filbert says he saw a similar car following us when we left Florence's, even though Faith and I missed it. Too much of a coincidence.

Shit, which means…

Wally might really be following me.

Filbert is still wearing his pouty face. He is somberly shuffling his bug-busting bulk up the stairs to the kitchen. I say reluctantly to his back, "Filbert, wait. Did you get the plate number?"

His glum mug dissolves in a flash and his face lights up with a proud smile. I hate to encourage him at all, but I want that number if he has it. I have to know.

"Absolutely!" he sings out, vindicated that his surveillance mission was a noble and worthwhile one. He stops and pulls out his phone and reads the plate number to me. It isn't a personalized one, just a random string of letters and numbers that I don't recognize, but that doesn't mean anything because I don't even know my own damn plate number. I'll check it out in the company's database.

Filbert finishes his trip up the stairway with a happy bounce in his step. Maybe he's having daydreams of being the next Sam Spade.

I follow Filbert up to the kitchen, then quickly usher him out the front door. Grabbing my laptop, I go to the kitchen table, plop into a chair, and log onto the Fleener Plastics employee portal.

As I navigate to the website page with the personnel records of the people I manage, I wonder if I'll be in time to get the info I need before it's erased from the corporate database. All traces of the existence of every employee that was shit-canned in the most recent purge will soon be gone if they aren't already. Fleener upper management always orders the data erasure to be done pronto, in order to get the people who remain to forget about their former colleagues as soon as possible. Don't speak of the fallen ones, erase them from your minds, and in fact pretend they never existed. Just have the survivors go on toiling away, hopefully distracted by their even heavier workloads resulting from the personnel reduction, until it's time for the next layoff, and then it might be *your* turn, sucker.

After a few clicks, I'm glad to see that the data purge hasn't been done yet (probably due to laying off a good number of the IT people who'd be given the task of actually doing it). Wally is still listed as working for me. Next to his name and job title is his ID picture. His scary and serious mug stares out at me. I've never looked at this picture of him carefully before, but I now see that the company photographer indeed did a remarkable job of capturing those psycho killer eyes. Probably Wally's visage will be gone from this website by tomorrow or the next day, but for now there he is, still glaring at me with that *cross me and I'll rip your face off* expression.

With a few more clicks I pull up the plate number of the car he drove to work. I compare it to the number that Filbert just gave me, and…

Oh, crap, it's a match.

Wally is definitely following me.

Chapter 16

Remain calm.

That's what I tell myself all night while I toss and turn, thinking about what I should do.

Tell Darryl? Tell Fleener security? Tell the police? Buy a gun?

Finally, I decide to do what I pretty much always do when I have trouble deciding.

Not a damn thing. Not yet, anyway.

As far as telling Darryl…well, I love him lots, but he's not exactly a rock to cling to in times of crisis. I'm more concerned that he'll panic if I tell him about it, and maybe go out and buy a gun on his own, in some manly gesture of protectiveness. I sure as shit don't need to worry about getting accidentally shot in the derriere one night when I'm coming home very late from work. It's better for all concerned that Darryl remains his usual oblivious self for now.

As for Fleener security, they're worthless, and in fact, I'm pretty sure they'd only make the situation even worse by pissing Wally off without having any means at all of restraining him or protecting me. That leaves the possibility of telling the police, and I figure they'll just tell me that I have to get a restraining order, which will require some proof to bring before a judge that Wally is following me. I don't really have any, except maybe for some testimony from Faith and Filbert, not the two most levelheaded characters that I'd choose to accompany me to court. And anyway, I'm reluctant to get involved in any type of legal mess.

However, there *is* another possibility. I can tell my detective friend, Louise, and maybe she can suggest something less drastic than getting a court order. Like, maybe she could have a nice friendly talk with Wally?

I'll have to think about it.

****

I drive into work, and as I walk down the aisle toward my cube, I catch all of the familiar fragrances of corporate life which, given my state of unease this morning, are somewhat comforting in that they reinforce some sense of normalcy. I'm referring to the smells of whiteout, stale coffee, burned-up toner cartridges in a desktop printer, cheap lemon floor cleaner, the metallic tang of toxic mercury vapor from a broken fluorescent light tube, a smoking lithium-ion laptop battery, and general body odor.

I dump my stuff in my cube and without even opening my laptop I head to the snack bar before any of my people can catch me for their morning bullshit or piss and moan session. Certainly, it's part of my job to listen to them patiently, but not before I've had my coffee.

At the snack bar I immediately spot Faith in line at the coffee dispenser, with one person in front of her. She is swiping and tapping furiously at her smartphone the way young people do. I stand back behind the bagel bar and wait since I'm not especially eager to have a conversation with her.

In just a few seconds she's at the dispenser. Faith places her phone on the countertop, grabs a cup, and fills it. She steps aside to add some cream and sugar, then goes to the cash register without noticing me.

And she's forgotten to pick up her phone.

I move to the coffee area, and I'm the only person around.

Okay, so I'll pick up the phone and give it to Faith…

But then I notice the screen is still on. The phone is unlocked, but it will probably lock in seconds, so I have that much time to decide whether to do something that I've never done before, or at least not in my semi-respectable adult existence: To sneak a look at the details of someone's private life.

I reach over and touch the phone's screen, just a tap, but of course it's enough to keep the screen from locking until whatever wait period that Faith has it set for is over. I leave the phone on the countertop, still afraid to pick it up.

Okay, so I haven't made my decision yet about snooping…but I have more time to think about it now, maybe another thirty seconds.

There's still no one around me. I steal a glance at the register and see that Faith is gone. When she left, I saw her talking with Mary, and maybe that distracted her a bit, but even so, she might return any second for the phone. If I'm going to do this, I have to act fast, immediately in fact, and what the hell will I say to her if she comes back right now and catches me looking at the phone?

One possible reason for Faith knowing that the gun is in that pond is that Annuska threw it in there and told Faith about it…for God only knows what reason…but that would mean that Faith and Annuska were somehow…what?

I want to get a look at Faith's call log.

If Faith comes back and sees me, would it be better if I'm facing the entrance to the snack bar, with the phone visible, which will look more innocent, and I can see her coming in? Or facing away, with the phone hidden behind me?

I make my decision. I grab the phone and face the entrance. If she comes back right now and sees me, I'll say that I didn't know whose phone it was and that I was looking at the screen saver picture to see if I recognized it. Some people, after all, have as their screen saver a picture of their spouse, their kids, or if they're really vain, themself. Faith's phone is open to some fitness app that counts steps. I go to the calling app and hit the *recent* button, opening the call log. I swipe…back, back through lots of calls…

Shit, I can't believe I'm doing this…

And then I see it. A call to Annuska' cell, made the day before Melvin disappeared. It doesn't have a contact name associated with it, but I recognize the number since I looked it up to call her the morning that Melvin disappeared. I want to check further back to see how extensive their communication was, but I feel that I've already pressed my luck. I go back to the fitness app and then hit the side button and the screen goes black.

And that's when Faith and Mary come back and see me. They approach me immediately, both of them smiling.

In the most casual tone I can muster, and I think I'm reasonably convincing, I look at them and say, "Ladies, does this belong to one of you? I saw you leaving here earlier."

Faith speaks up, happily gushing her gratitude as she takes the phone from me. "Oh gosh, thanks, June. Ah just don't know where my head is today. Ah surely am glad that someone didn't send it to lost and found, 'cause that place is a serious mess. Ah lost a good scarf once, and someone told me they sent it there, but when ah went there, they didn't have it, can you imagine that? And ah'm just bettin' that somebody there with sticky fingers kept it for themselves and if they know what's good for 'em they better not be wearin' it around here, let me tell you!"

Mary holds up her cup of coffee and says, "I wouldn't get the blueberry coffee if I were you, June, it's pretty bad."

I nod my head in agreement. "I think they need to scrub the sludge out of these big thermoses. None of the coffee here is very good. That's why I stop every morning on my way to work at the Main Street Beanery. So does Darryl."

Mary asks, "You coming back to cube city, June? We'll wait for you."

"No, I have to go the other way, I need to stop at the production manager's office. You ladies go ahead without me."

They wave and leave.

And I let out a sigh of relief.

I suck at this cloak and dagger stuff. Deception is not my strong suit. But I pulled this one off. I learned something about Faith.

And now…what the hell should I do about it?
****

Back in my little cube, I sit, think, and sip bad coffee.

Should I contact Louise now and tell her about Faith calling Annuska? And what do I expect Louise to do about it anyway? Yes, there's a very slight possibility that Faith knew where the gun was because she and Annuska had colluded for some reason, but Faith calling Annuska isn't a crime. It doesn't *prove* anything. And Louise will of course ask me how I got the information and I have to be honest with her...

Is peeking at someone's phone a crime? Well, not really, I guess, but since Faith works for me, I committed a severe violation of her privacy, and I'd be crucified if what I did somehow got back to Fleener upper management. Even if I don't get fired, I'd be strongly reprimanded...by my immediate manager. That over-inflated gasbag Larry will have a field day with me.

Okay, I won't call Louise now. I'll mull it over until the end of the day, when I expect a call back from her anyway about the fingerprint report, and if that raises suspicion that Faith might have put those hairs on the comb for God's knows what reason, well then...I'll tell Louise about the call to Annuska.

Sounds like a plan. So, shake it off for now.

I really have to get some work done. I have a presentation to get ready for tomorrow, and I haven't even started making the charts yet. And of course, I'm expecting more distractions and interruptions because that's just the way it is around here.

When you work in a cube farm, constant interruptions are part of your workday. You've got a report due, and someone walks by your cube, they see that you're in there, and they have to stop to talk to you because of course you'd be more interested in hearing about their kid taking oboe lessons than in getting your report done. Or why wouldn't you want to halt everything and listen to them rail about how that contractor working on finishing their basement tried to screw them over because instead of installing the authentic reclaimed barn wood paneling, he used some cheaper kiln-dried shit wood and assumed you were too much of a rube to know the difference.

I'm always too nice to tell them I'm busy, and so I stop what I'm doing and listen. If they're talking about their troubles, I try to look sympathetic, but not *too* sympathetic because they might get the idea that I want to know more and they might be inclined to give me their whole life story, starting with how they were jaundiced at birth. And if they're talking about their successes or their good times, I try to look happy for them, but not too damn happy, for the same reason—that would be positive reinforcement to keep them jabbering.

As they chatter away, I'm smiling and listening and nodding my head, but I'm thinking, *Please go the hell away because if you don't, I'll just have to do this report tonight, when I'm home, after I do the dinner dishes and get the kids into bed and maybe have a short conversation with my husband about how our days went and how the kids are doing in school. And then I'll have to open up my damn laptop and start pecking away until the stupid report is done, which makes me lose sleep and come in the next morning looking like even more of a zombie than usual.*

I know a few people around here who keep their earphones on all the time when they're in their cubes, and if you stop to talk to them, they tap the earpiece to indicate they're in a telecon. Maybe I should start doing that, although I think a lot of people recognize it's a ruse. I wonder if upper management realizes how much more work they could get out of employees if they would just put a cheap sliding panel on everyone's cube, a simple door that closes you off from distractions. Even if the tall people can look over it, that'd be okay. You'd still have to put up with all the disgusting and distracting sounds, the belches and farts, the sniffles, sneezes, coughs, and wheezes, and also the smells of simmering fish heads and spoiled roast beef sandwiches. Whatever. But just having a cheap door there in the closed position politely indicates that you should have a damn good reason before disturbing me. At least a better one than telling me how your kid Roscoe totally knocked 'em dead at his oboe recital.

About a year ago, before this new cube farm was installed, the company had actually considered the open space concept, like some of those California high tech companies have. I lobbied heavily against it, not that my opinion counts for shit around here, but thank God the idea was killed. Open space? Just a hook to hang your coat on and a bean bag chair to flop in? I don't think so. Maybe I'm too damn old-fashioned but I like my own private squatting spot, even if it's only this three-by-three-foot chicken coop.

"Hi June," Faith says as she enters my cube. I pause on the e-mail I'm composing and look up from my laptop.

Shit. I really don't want to talk to anyone right now because of the work I have to get done, and Faith is at the very top of my *don't want to talk to you right now* list because of my suspicions about her. But I can't just jump up from my chair and tell her I have to run to the ladies' room. That would look too weird, and anyway she'd probably be waiting for me when I get back.

I say to her as casually as I can, "Oh, hi Faith." But

I can't keep my anxiety completely hidden. My *tell* when I'm anxious is impulsive ring twirling. So, there I am, twirling my ring, and Faith notices.

It's the ring that Darryl gave me for our tenth anniversary. My Darryl is pretty darn lousy at picking out gifts for me like clothing, jewelry, purses—basically anything to wear or any personal stuff. But this one he got right, and I can only assume that he got lots of counsel from some wonderful person with fabulous taste at the jewelry store. When he gave it to me, he told me the story of how he was so conflicted about whether to even get a ring because he had another fabulous gift idea—A weekend for me at one of those colon cleaner ranches where they give you tea enemas every hour as a way of flushing and rejuvenating your ravaged body, while you listen to soothing harp music and drink triple-filtered wheatgrass juice and maybe if you're lucky they give you a little tree bark to eat for fiber. I remember watching him tell me how tortured he was trying to make this decision. He had his two hands out, palms up, and moved them up and down in opposite directions like he was weighing two things on opposite sides of a balance scale, saying how he just couldn't decide: *diamond? enema? diamond? enema?* Until finally, painfully, he settled on the diamond ring. And I remember, when he was telling me this story, how I was grinning and shaking my head and thinking how lucky he was that he decided on the diamond because I'm not sure how I'd have reacted had me handed me a gift certificate for the never-ending enema experience.

So, I unconsciously twirl the ring, and Faith notices. Her eyes brighten and she leans forward to look at it. The ring is really a beautiful piece. It has three diamonds—a larger central one and two little ones on either side. Of course, they're not high-quality diamonds, but so what? So far, no one has pulled out a jeweler's eyepiece to examine them.

"Oh, that's just a gorgeous ring, June. Did Darryl give that to you?"

"Yes, for our tenth anniversary. Picked it out himself."

"May ah?"

She reaches out and takes my hand. Gently holding the tips of my fingers, she elevates them so she can see the ring better. The diamonds are facing slightly off to the side because of my nervous twirling. She touches the ring gently with her index finger, rotating it so that the stones face straight up.

And what I see next totally startles me.

Still touching it, Faith's gaze goes blank for a moment, then she looks up and her head suddenly jerks backward very slightly and both eyes start blinking rapidly. The whole thing lasts only about two seconds, but I can tell that something is wrong. I think she might be having a stroke or a seizure.

"Faith, are you okay?" I say with alarm, my eyes locked on hers.

She comes back from whatever momentary trance she was in and looks straight at me, wide-eyed. She releases my hand and says in an anxious whisper, "June, ah saw Darryl."

"Darryl? How? He's away. On a business trip. He drove to Boston this morning with a colleague."

"Ah mean…ah just had a *vision* of him. Ah saw him…up here." She taps the side of her skull.

My initial feeling is one of relief that Faith is okay.

I say, "A vision? Of my Darryl?" I don't mean to be a wiseass, but I can't hold back a sarcastic comment. "Was he jammin' with Elvis?" Darryl used to play the accordion, mostly polkas, and he's pretty damn good. I suppose he could manage a decent duet with the King.

"June, this is serious!" she admonishes.

I lose the smile immediately and say, "Okay, I'm sorry, I'm sorry. What about Darryl?"

She bites her lip and leans in even closer. "June, he was in a car, and it's off the road, and he's lyin' slumped against the wheel."

My spine stiffens and I sit bolt upright and stare at Faith. "What? What do you mean?" My alarm bells went off at the phrase *slumped against the wheel.* I know that even though Darryl went on this trip with his co-worker Henry, it's Darryl who must be driving because he took his own car.

"That's all ah can see. Ah don't know if he's conscious. You gotta call him, June, to see if he's safe. Right now!"

"Faith, you're scaring the shit out of me, so…"

"June, please, just call him," she pleads.

"Is he hurt? I mean…is there blood?"

"Ah don't know, ah really don't, all ah see is a vision of him slumped over the wheel. June, just…"

"This is nuts! Now you're having visions about my husband? I thought you said that you get visions about people that you're emotionally attached to, right?"

"It's *you* ah'm emotionally attached to, June. You're my friend, and Darryl's your husband, that's how we're connected. And ah just touched the ring he gave you."

I think about the two-second trance Faith was in. It looked like her mind was somewhere else. Like she was traveling.

She continues her urgent plea, "Look, maybe it's nuthin. Ah *hope* it's nuthin, but humor me, please! What does it cost to just give him a call?"

Despite my skepticism about her visions, Faith is right. It won't cost anything at all. I take out my cell and tap Darryl's image on my favorites list.

Four rings.

Six rings.

Eight rings.

I know his phone is set to go to voicemail after ten rings. I'm mentally composing a message to leave him and I'm wondering what I should do next after leaving it.

And then suddenly he answers. I hear his voice, but it's bleary and slow, not his normally upbeat tone at all. It sounds like he's trying to say hello, but it's more of a soft moan.

I blurt out a frenzied response, "Darryl, are you alright? Did anything happen?"

I hear nothing for a few seconds. My breathing stalls. I remain completely silent so I can pick up even the tiniest of sounds. Finally, he says in a soft, halting voice, "Hon, I…yeah, something just happened. But I'm okay. The car's probably banged up a little, though."

I freeze. Faith stands above me, also frozen, but visibly relieved that Darryl is talking.

"What? What happened?" I sputter.

"I…I must have fallen asleep at the wheel," he moans. "I…don't know how…I…was on the highway."

"When did it happen?"

After another few seconds of silence, he answers, "Just now, hon. I mean, a few minutes ago. I don't recall drifting off the road. Just woke up here, in the driver's seat, with the car off the road, at the edge of a field. I have a little bump on my head. I'm still sitting in the car. Henry's next to me."

"Darryl, did the airbag open?"

"No, no. I didn't hit anything hard enough for that. Just a few small bushes. I sort of knocked them over. It was enough to stop the car. I'm in a bit of a ditch. Might have to call a tow truck to pull it out. I'm about thirty feet off the road."

"Are you bleeding?"

"No. Just a bump, hon."

"Maybe a mild concussion?"

"No, really. I'm fine."

"Is Henry okay? Let me talk to him."

There's no response from Darryl, just a delay as the phone is apparently being handed off. In a few seconds I hear Henry's deep voice, "June? We're fine, don't worry. I didn't even bump my head like Darryl did. I just got jostled around a bit." Henry's voice sounds normal and calm.

"Henry, that's good, but can you tell me what happened?"

"It's like Darryl just said, he must have fallen asleep at the wheel. We're on a long straight stretch of road. There were no other cars in sight when it happened. I was just trying to get some music on the radio, and next thing we're off the road before I could grab the wheel or do anything. This is a rural side road that the navigation app diverted us to because of some pileup on the interstate. We're somewhere near Sturbridge, maybe sixty miles or so east of Boston. Nothing much around here but fields and forest."

"Okay, I'm glad to hear you're not hurt. Can you hand the phone back to Darryl please?"

In a few seconds I hear Darryl's halting voice again, "Hon?"

"Darryl, are you going to call the police?"

He sounds aghast at that suggestion, "Oh, God no, hon. We don't need an accident report for this. We may not even have to tell the insurance company about it. We don't want our rates increased. Maybe the damage is under our deductible anyway. I'll be fine. I'm feeling better already."

"If you feel well enough, step out of the car now, but stay on the line with me."

"Okay, hon."

I hear the creak of a car door opening.

"Anyone around there you can ask for help?"

"No, I can't see anything on this stretch of road, no buildings and at the moment no cars. I'll just call the auto club. They'll send a tow truck eventually and we'll get a ride in it."

"That could take a long time. Can you call a taxi or some ride service?"

"Wait, there's an eighteen-wheeler on the horizon now. These guys usually are willing to stop and help people. It's a few hundred yards away, give me a minute, we'll try to flag him down."

"Okay, but you need to get to a hospital and get checked out to see if you have a concussion. Or at least go to one of those urgent care places if you can find one. And if the car is drivable, let Henry drive."

I extract a promise from Darryl that he will call back as soon as they have the car situation figured out, and then we end the call.

I look up at Faith as she stands over me. Her eyes are huge, one hand resting on her cheek, and she stares at me anxiously. I give a hard swallow to try and clear the lump in my throat as the realization sets in that Faith's prediction was dead on.

"Is he alright?" she whispers.

"Yes, he's fine," I assure her. "He fell asleep at the wheel. His car drifted off the road and he hit a bush."

Her shoulders sag with relief, the tension apparently draining from her body, and she says, "Oh, my Lordy Lord, thank goodness he's not hurt. Ah'm so sorry that ah scared you, June. If ah hadn't told you about my vision, y'all woulda' found out about it when Darryl told you eventually, and you woulda' been spared the worry. Ah'm just so sorry for alarmin' you." She looks distressed, as if she somehow caused the accident instead of just seeing it in her vision.

"No, no, I'm glad you told me. I mean, it's best to know. It's just…spooky, you know? How did you…?"

Faith shakes her head, as if despairing of her lifelong burden. She's nearly in tears. "Oh June, like ah told you, ah really don't know. Ah've never known why ah can see stuff. It just happens."

I nod my head slowly, mechanically. I am in a daze as I mull over the implications…

It just happens.

Holy crap.

Faith really is clairvoyant!

And that means Melvin really is…dead.

Chapter 17

In about an hour Darryl calls back and I learn that the truck driver stopped, and they all examined the car. There was some minor damage to the front, including a broken headlight. They tried to get the car free from the ditch, apparently with Darryl behind the wheel and Henry and the trucker pushing or rocking the car, but without success. Darryl is now in the cab of the eighteen-wheeler, being taken to the nearest urgent care clinic, which is fortunately less than ten minutes from the accident site, and he'll contact me after getting the medical report. Henry is with the car, waiting for the tow truck.

I'm reeling from the double jolt I've just received—first, that Darryl was in an accident…and second, that Faith *saw* it.

By touching my ring.

Too weird. My head is spinning.

I decide that I need to splash some water on my face, so I drop my laptop off at my cube, grab my purse, and head to the women's room. I'll wreck my makeup, but I have some mascara in my purse, so I'll be able to do a touchup.

Before I reach the restroom, Verne appears from around a cube corner, notices me, and decides to snag me. One of his hands shoots up and he says, "Hey, June."

I stop and face him. He looks uneasy. He puts both

hands in his pockets and starts shifting his weight from one foot to the other.

"Have you heard anything about Melvin?" he asks.

"Unfortunately, no. The police are still digging into it." And that is a blatant lie, but I'm not ready to tell anyone that I now know he's dead, thanks to Faith's spiritual guidance.

"So…why can't they just find him by tracking his cell phone?" Verne asks.

"Well, the cops said it's not in contact with cell towers anymore."

"Hmmm. Maybe it just died. I know the battery was bad because it was always running out of juice. If he was away from his desk at a meeting or something and he needed to get in touch with his wife, he would sometimes borrow my phone or Faith's to make the call."

"Wha…what was that?" I stammer. "He borrowed …"

Faith's phone? Oh Geez, and I almost had a heart attack sneaking a peak at Faith's phone in the cafeteria! What the hell am I doing? I suck at this spy shit!

Verne's eyes narrow and he continues in a thoughtful tone, *"Or maybe…he just turned his phone off."*

"Uhhh…why do you think he would do that?" I ask.

Verne answers my question with a hesitant one of his own, as if he were stepping into dangerous territory, "His wife, Annuska…do you know if they're questioning her?"

And then I find myself doing the same thing. I give him back a question. But I have a good reason. I want to spill as little as possible about the investigation so as not to violate Louise's trust. At least not more than I already have.

"Do you *know* Annuska?" I ask.

"I met her once at a party. I just think…well, that they should question her carefully. About their… relationship."

"Why?"

"Well, they weren't the happiest couple, you know." More foot shuffling. He's concerned but evasive. His body language is easy to read.

"I've gotten some mixed signals about that," I respond. "Pog says they were very happy, at least when they got married. But lately they argued, according to their landlady."

"I mean, maybe Melvin just left because their marriage got a little too…troubled, you know?"

I tilt my head and look carefully at his eyes, trying to read them. "Verne, you're being very…indirect. Is there something you're trying to tell me? Something important?"

"All I'm saying is…the police should look into…marital strife, you know? Sometimes it causes people to *do* stuff."

I remain silent, hoping that he will feel obliged to fill the void with more information. It works.

He looks around to make sure there's no one within earshot, and then he says in a soft voice that I am shocked to hear High Volume Verne is even capable of, "I probably shouldn't tell you this. I don't mean *you* specifically, June, I mean anyone. Because it's really no one's business but Melvin's. But now that he's missing…well, maybe it's important…

Here it comes…

In an even softer voice, nearly a whisper, he leans

toward me and says, "I think that Melvin cheated on his wife. At that conference that he and I and Faith went to two months ago, I saw…well, one of the three nights that we were there, I couldn't sleep. I stepped out of my room at about four in the morning to get some ice. For my *water*," he quickly adds, as he studies my eyes to see if I have a shocked look because one of my employees might be drinking in the middle of the night.

But I don't, so he continues, "My room was at the opposite end of the hall from Melvin's, and I caught a glance from behind of a redhead leaving his room. But maybe it was just a one-time thing, June. Melvin was drinking a lot there, too. And you know how conferences are, right? He probably just met her there, and people get crazy at conferences sometimes. You're away from home, and…oh, but not that *I* would!" He pauses and stares at me apparently to gauge my level of shock, as if he's himself just confessed to adultery in addition to that prior confession to nighttime binge drinking. "Holy smokes, I didn't mean that like it sounded. I love my wife, and I *never* would…"

"Relax, Verne, this isn't about you," I assure him.

My comment calms him a little. His shoulders drop an inch or two, but he continues to shift his weight, showing his nervousness.

"Maybe I shouldn't have said anything about Melvin, but, you know, considering that he's missing…I felt like I had to tell somebody. I sure hope he's okay."

"Me too, Verne. Me too."

And now I know where the red hairs on Melvin's brush came from.

****

A few hours later, Darryl calls me back and says

they gave him a clean bill of health at the urgent care center. They apparently didn't even feel the need to x-ray him or anything. They just put a piece of ice on his bump for a few minutes, gave him a lollipop and a bill for four hundred dollars, and sent him on his way. I'm hoping that we met our medical deductible already and also that our insurance will even cover the exam because it's an out-of-state one. If not, then Darryl is sucking a four-hundred-dollar lollipop, so hopefully they at least gave him his favorite flavor, which is grape.

Darryl also said that the auto dealership checked out the car almost immediately. They were going to replace the smashed headlight, so the car would be street legal again. The rest of the damage was minor, just cosmetic. Darryl talked about getting the little dents and scratches fixed at some local body shop near us where they'd do the work on the cheap, but I know that we'll probably just let it go, because body work done anywhere always seems outrageously expensive to me. Parking in Fleener's lot, I'm always picking up door dings, and the last time I got an estimate to have a bunch of them fixed, I almost stroked out when I heard the number. Needless to say, those dings are still there, and new ones get added to the collection every month.

It's time to call Louise. I sneak into a break room and take out my cell. She answers quickly.

"Hi June. I don't have the fingerprint report yet, if that's why you're calling."

"Thanks, Louise, but it's something else. Something really remarkable." I explain to her in a few minutes, and as calmly as I can, the entire incident with Darryl. I start with Faith touching my ring and getting the vision, and finish with the results of the medical check. She is silent as I speak. Either she's listening intently or perhaps she zoned out as soon as she heard me mention the vision at the beginning. I hope it's the former.

When I finish, there are about ten seconds of silence. Then she asks, "Is that it, June?"

"Pretty much. What do you think?"

"I think I have a few questions."

"I knew you would. Fire away."

"You said the airbag didn't deploy, but the car was disabled."

"Right. In a ditch, so he couldn't drive it out."

"Why didn't he call the police?"

"Uh…well…he didn't…think it was that bad."

Her reply to that is a disapproving, "Hmmmmm," and then she asks, "They're absolutely certain that another car didn't run them off the road?"

"Yes, absolutely sure."

"Has Darryl ever fallen asleep at the wheel before?"

"No. But he has sleep apnea. He wears a CPAP mask every night."

"Was the mask working last night? I mean, I'm no expert on those things, but I know they have to be cleaned regularly."

"To prevent bacterial buildup, yes. But normally they don't clog up unless you really neglect them. Darryl takes good care of his CPAP unit, and he's a mechanical engineer, an expert on pumps, so believe me, he knows what he's doing. As far as I know, it was working last night. I saw him sleeping soundly with the mask on when I went to bed, but I can't be certain that he got a full night of sound sleep."

"I see. And Faith…when did she come to work this morning?"

"Same time I did, about eight o'clock. That was about an hour before Darryl left the house to drive to Boston."

"Alright, so let's think about this calmly. There may be some reasonable explanation."

We are both silent for about fifteen seconds.

Finally, I ask her, "Come up with anything? An explanation?"

"Only one. Faith is clairvoyant."

"I thought you said that you didn't believe in this stuff, Louise."

"I never said that, June. I said that I'm extremely skeptical. I think there are a lot more fakers out there than genuine psychics, but there *are* some genuine psychics."

After another brief silence Louise says, "Faith could be tested. A scientist at Yale has a battery of very rigorous and carefully controlled tests for ESP. He's documented several cases in which he claims to have validated genuine psychic powers."

"But how? By putting a playing card in an envelope and the person has to identify it? That would be useless because Faith says that with her kind of clairvoyance, where she touches an object and gets some sort of vision about a person, you can't prove or disprove anything by a test."

I hear Louise sigh. "That's convenient. All right, so we can't test her, I accept that. But...if she has more visions about Melvin that she tells you about, call me immediately. I still can't get officially back on this case without a body or evidence of a crime, but maybe she'll see something that I can follow up on. And also, I'd like to have your husband's car examined. Where is it right now?"

"At a dealership in Sturbridge. They left it there and rented a car because they had to get to Boston right away."

"Okay, good. I have a friend on the force at Hartford headquarters who knows cars and he owes me a favor. I'll ask him to go over to the dealership to examine the car himself, right away if possible."

"What will he look for?"

"I don't know. Let's just say anything out of the ordinary. Something that might have caused the car to drift off the road. He'll check the steering of course, but also the car's computer brain and everything else. I'll ask him to go over every square inch."

"I understand. But I just want you to know that...well, because Faith knew about Darryl falling asleep, which has never happened before...and she knew it at the exact moment it happened...I believe she really *is* psychic."

After I give Louise the car information and we end the call, I sit back and shake my head in wonder.

We have a genuine clairvoyant working right here at Fleener.

I want to run over and talk to Faith about her powers, now that I know they're real. The same powers that I scoffed at just a few short days ago. But now is not the time. I am just so grateful that Darryl is alright. Even so, I told him to call me once more toward the end of the workday. I just want to make doubly sure he isn't passed out on the floor of the hotel bathroom due to an undiagnosed injury.

I try to push it all out of my mind for now. I just *have* to get some work done. If I don't start the charts for the meeting tomorrow, I'll be doing shadow puppets in front

251

of the upper-level managers during my fifteen-minute time slot.

****

When I finish up a crappy first draft of the charts, I'm startled to see that it's already four o'clock, the time for the meeting with a rep from the information technology department. So, I have to do a crappy second draft tonight at home, and then make my final changes in the morning, when I'll be working on six other things at the same time. Putting together this presentation will be a complete rush job, so the end result will no doubt be…well, total crap.

I close my laptop and head to the meeting. Our area has been tasked with coming up with a scheme to tackle the porno internet browsing problem since we have by far the greatest number of infractions. Thankfully this meeting with IT will be a small one—just myself, my moron of a boss Larry, and one IT rep.

I walk into the meeting room, and I'm the first one there. I sit down, hoping the IT rep will show up before Larry. I'd rather have a root canal without painkillers than talk to Larry anytime about anything. But making small talk alone with him before a meeting is the absolute worst. The last time it happened, maybe six months ago, he asked me when the baby was due, and when I told the asshole I'm not pregnant, he asked me how my diet was going and recommended a starvation regimen for at least a week.

So, I'm relieved when I see Randy the IT geek walk into the room before Larry, despite the fact that Randy is weird. And young.

Really young.

And we're supposed to discuss this sex stuff with

him?

I know Randy is twenty-one years old, but he looks twelve. He just reached drinking age but he'll probably be carded at bars until he's fifty, so I'm jealous. Last time I got carded was fifteen years ago when some jerk of a bartender glared at my driver's license and said that it must be fake because I looked way older than twenty-five.

Randy has a beanpole frame, perfectly round coke bottle glasses with thick tortoiseshell rims, and greasy hair (not sure if it's mousse or natural grease). He's barely shaving but nonetheless trying to cultivate a mustache, which is basically nine hairs growing out of his upper lip. Today he wears Nantucket red pants that are six inches too short above his fire engine red canvas sneakers. The pants are so tight, you'd think they're painted on if it wasn't for the little blue lobsters all over them. His arms, white and skinny like two birch twigs, stick out from beneath a gray tee-shirt with a picture of Einstein on a bicycle.

Seconds later, Larry walks in, raises his arms over his head, showing off his yellow pit stains, and barks, "Okay, let's talk about sex!"

Randy says, "Well, first of all, I've done a drill down, if you guys would like to hear it. I've divided the porn sites that are being accessed by your employees into categories and subcategories, and this may give you some insight into the motivation of—"

I interrupt him, "What exactly to do you mean by categories, Randy?"

"You know, for instance, bestiality, sex with vegetables, sex with cured meats, sex under—"

I chop at the air to cut him off midstream. "You can

stop right there, Randy. We don't need those details, thank you."

Larry says with bluster, "Okay now, June, we're all adults here. Don't feel bad about this, it's not your fault that you've got a bunch of pervs working for you, although I suspect there might be something about your management style that brings out the baser instincts in people. Or it could be just *one* perv with a lot of free time on his hands instead of a bunch. So why can't you tell who it is, Randy?"

"We can only narrow it down to Ms. Bloom's department since all of her employees use the same IP address under our rather antiquated system. To drill down further, we'd need to do some software upgrades to her people's computers."

"Do it!" orders Larry with pompous authority.

"It will cost you money, of course. The IT department would have to charge it to your department's budget."

"*Don't* do it," Larry fires back, knowing full well that he'll score brown-noser points with his manager if his expenditures come in under projections.

"Whatever you say," Randy responds with a confused look.

"We'll have to think of some other way to identify your offending deviant," Larry says to me with a stern look. He turns to Randy and asks, "So, can you block these porn sites?"

"Yes, I can use a commercial software product that erects a firewall to porn sites," Randy explains. "We basically just input all the URLs that we want to block. A lot of these sites periodically change their URLs by one or two characters to get around these kinds of walls, but the software is designed to anticipate this and uses a mathematical algorithm to identify and block the changed URLs. It also constantly scans the internet for brand new porn sites. It costs money to license this software of course, but you really need to get the licenses so that you can get the frequent updates."

"Sounds expensive," sputters Larry, in fear of his budget and what the cost might mean to his personal appraisal. "Updates? Why do we need constant updates?"

"Because there's a small army of coders in Macedonia constantly writing hacks to breach this type of firewall. So, the software company has its own army writing patches to defeat the hacks. And you have to upload the new patches at least once a week."

Larry jabs his finger at Randy. "Okay, but…you said we have to put the websites into the software. Aren't there *thousands* of these porn sites?"

"No, more like *hundreds* of thousands. We'll start with a standard list that comes with the software. Then we'll add more every day as the software identifies new ones."

"And to decide if new sites should be added, will you have to *look* at them?" Larry asks.

"Some of them I may have to quickly scan, to see how objectionable the content is."

I immediately add, "Are you qualified to do this scanning, Randy? And does your mother know that this is part of your job?"

"June, he's an adult," scoffs Larry.

"Right," I say. *But he looks like he should be playing on the T-ball team with my son.*

Larry asks Randy, "Uhh…is this software product

really good? I mean, would it block *you*?"

Randy gives Larry a look of disbelief at the question, and answers, "Seriously? *I* can get through anything. But for the people who work for you, yes, it should be fine."

The meeting then drifts into a conversation about what other sites we should block while we're at it, like perhaps social media ones because the recent IT analysis also indicates that our people spend a huge amount of their work time on the popular social media sites.

I have to confess that I don't really get the obsession with social media, and by that, I mean I'm baffled by some people's complete willingness to put all the details of their private life out there for anyone to see, or at least for a thousand of their closest friends to see.

As for me, I have two social media accounts, but I don't use them much. I check them maybe twice a month, not every ten minutes like some of the fanatics around here. And if you want to be my social media friend, that's fine as long as you understand that the flow of information goes pretty much one way. In other words, I consume information but don't produce much of anything for you to look at because I don't feel the need to share. And what the hell business is it of yours anyway? You can look at my profile picture all you want if that makes you happy since it was taken seven years ago when I was a few pounds lighter and the crow's feet around my eyes were much less obvious.

So, at the end of a long discussion, we decide to embrace the social media storm and *not* block those types of sites. The managers like me are in fact encouraged to submit to our public relations department cool stuff to post on the official Fleener Plastics social media sites that would make our old, creaky, polluting, environmentally unconscious, rust bucket of a company look totally hip to millennials and gen-z-ers, so they'll be tripping over themselves to friend us. Add *that* one to my list of impossible tasks.

Then Larry puffs up his chest and goes into his, *I'm the big boss man,* authoritative routine. Pointing both index fingers at Randy for emphasis, he says with a snap, "Okay, then! We'll just have to bite the bullet and cough up the money to pay for this porn blocker firewall. Make it happen, Randy!"

The meeting ends when Larry asks Randy about the actual dollar cost of the firewall and Randy responds with an estimate, which causes Larry the lamebrain to gasp and then have a spasm that contorts his whole body for a second or two. Then he runs out, I assume to the men's room to scrub the mess out of his trousers.

As I stand to leave, Randy asks me if I would stay behind for a few minutes to talk about another IT issue, this one concerning Wally.

"Sure," I say, and I plop back down in my chair, thinking: *Oh geez, NOW what about Wally?*

I'm pretty sure that my blood pressure will shortly be spiking.

"Ms. Bloom, as you may know, we're supposed to scan the laptops of everyone who gets laid off. Mostly we check to make sure there's no indication that they tried to introduce any viruses into the company intranet around the time that they were being let go. I mean, some people somehow know ahead of time, and they might be pretty good with computers, you know?"

"I don't think Wally was much of a computer geek," I say.

Oh damn, I didn't mean to use that politically incorrect term in front of Randy, the head computer geek.

I correct myself, "Uh, I mean, not a knowledgeable computer person. Also, I don't think Wally knew what was going to happen until it actually happened. I literally told him to come to the conference room five minutes before the…uh…bad news."

"If you're all set up on your laptop to make trouble, all you need to do is hit one key."

"So…are you saying he infected us with a virus?"

"No, I didn't find a virus or a worm, or anything like that."

"What's a worm?"

Randy's eyes brighten because I've apparently raised a subject that he is passionate about. "It's *like* a virus, you know? But better, cooler, sneakier, more insidious."

I nod my head. "Ahh, I see." *Okay, so I guess he thinks any deeper technical explanation would explode my forty-year-old brain.* "So, what exactly *did* you find on his hard drive? Was it porn?" I ask hopefully. My mind races as I consider what kind of weirdo porn Wally the psycho ex-marine would have downloaded—no doubt some militaristic, sadistic stuff, girls wearing camouflage lingerie, pole dancing on Patriot missiles, or maybe…

"No, I didn't find any of that, and the porn sites are still being accessed after the layoff. But there were some e-mails on his hard drive that I don't think should have been there."

"Why don't you think they should have been there?"

"They're from Gregory Cantor."

Uh-oh, not good. Cantor is the functional manager of my division, three levels of management above me, and not too far from the guy at the very top.

"Are you sure they aren't just e-mails that Cantor sent to everyone in the division?"

"I'm sure. They're addressed to specific people. Not to Wally."

I gulp. "Uhhh…how many e-mails, roughly?"

"About two thousand, sent over a period of a few weeks. Some sent *to* Cantor, and some sent *by* him."

Yikes!

"Two thousand? Uhhh…subject matter?" I ask, fighting off a hot flash.

"All kinds. But some were quite sensitive, certainly. Some stuff about the layoff."

Oh, geez.

"What about the layoff?"

"The ranking lists for people to get laid off, for one thing."

Double geez!

Hot flashes are coming in waves now. I try to remain outwardly calm and ask, "How did he get these e-mails?"

"He hacked Cantor's mail file. It's not difficult."

"How?"

"There are lots of ways. First of all, you could guess someone's password."

"Oh, come on Randy, Cantor's password can't be that obvious. He's not that stupid." *This comment coming from the woman who's first Fleener password was 12345, before I changed it to my second, less obvious one which I think was 54321…*

Randy says, "What I mean is, you can often get someone's password by using a program that cycles through billions of possible passwords randomly created by combining words in the dictionary with numbers and symbols."

Randy leans a bit toward me and continues, whispering with his hand cupped beside his mouth, "Between you and me, Ms. Bloom, computer security at Fleener is *pathetic*. The entire security team is me and one other guy, and the other guy is worth shit. I'm excellent of course, but they're *starving* us for resources. We need to buy protective code, and they keep turning down my requisitions because of budget constraints. Bottom line is, a determined three-year-old with a game console could eventually get into anybody's e-mail here. Except for mine, of course."

"Of course."

"Getting into Cantor's e-mail would have been easy, believe me. Despite what you think, Cantor's password is pretty weak."

"How do you know?"

Randy raises his eyebrows and looks at me as if I were a fool for asking such a stupid question. He answers, "Because I know Cantor's password. I know *everybody's* password."

Great.

I quickly think about my own e-mail...is there any sort of personal information on my drive that I don't want this twelve-year-old kid sitting next to me to read? Probably, but I have bigger problems at the moment. The thought of someone at Cantor's level being somehow tangled in my Wally problem is giving me colon contractions.

So, Wally stole the layoff list for my group. Everyone is on the list, and it's really just a ranking list, with the worst-performing employee at the top. And Wally was at the top, the first choice to get the ax, and he knew it.

"Randy, there must have been another note to Cantor which said how many people in my group were to be *remaining* after the layoff."

"Yup, Wally had that note too. It said that the post layoff headcount target was fifteen people."

Staring up at the ceiling, I begin to think out loud (which doesn't matter because Randy apparently knows everything about everybody anyway). "So…before the layoff, I had a total of sixteen people in my group including Melvin. And then when Melvin went missing, if we assumed that he wasn't coming back, the number was already down to fifteen, so I wouldn't have had to lay anybody off, and in fact I got the word from Larry that we weren't going to axe anyone in my group at layoff time because if we did and Melvin didn't come back, we'd be short-handed. But then, the day before the layoff, the bean counters got greedier like they usually do. They decreased the post layoff headcount targets for many groups, including mine. They dropped my target to fourteen, which meant that Wally was once again on the chopping block even with Melvin out of the picture. And that's when I was told to let Wally go."

I look at Randy and ask, "Gregory Cantor should have gotten another e-mail, the day before the layoff, with new headcount targets for a lot of groups, including mine. The new target for my group was fourteen. Did Wally steal *that* e-mail too?"

"No. The last stolen e-mails he had were the ones from two days before he got laid off. He was hacking Cantor's e-mail file once every three days."

So Wally thought, right up until the end, that his job would be saved if just one person, any person, in the group disappeared...

Which means...

Wally had a motive to get rid of Melvin. Wally thought it would save his own job.

Okay, okay, so...just because Wally had a motive doesn't mean...well, what the hell DOES it mean?

He had a clear motive for murder...AND he's a psycho.

Chapter18

I thank Randy and tell him we're done for now.

Jumping out of my chair, I scurry back to my cube. My racing thoughts are interrupted by my cell ringing. It's Darryl, giving me the one last callback today that he'd promised me, and of course I answer immediately.

"Darryl, how are you feeling?"

"Perfect, hon. I feel great now. Don't know why I fell asleep at the wheel. I had my coffee with an espresso shot this morning at the usual place before I left for Boston. But it's weird that I had two car incidents in two days, you know?"

"Uhhh…what do you mean, two? When was the other?"

"Yesterday on the way to work."

"You didn't tell me about it. What happened?"

"I got a flat, and I didn't have a jack. You know, hon, we bought my car used, and I never bothered to check if there was a jack in the trunk, and I never needed one until yesterday. Probably the auto dealer took it out to inspect it when they were prepping the car for sale and forgot to put it back."

"So, if you didn't have a jack, what did you do?"

"A guy stopped to help me when he saw me pulled over onto the shoulder with the trunk open. I had the spare tire, and he let me use his jack."

"Well, that's fortunate. Did you know the guy?"

S.E. Greco

"No, never saw him before. But it's nice to know that sometimes you can still receive kindness from strangers. He was an intense-looking guy, had kind of an icy stare, head shaved bald, so it goes to show you that you can't judge a person's character by appearance. You know, I remember when—"

My heart rate kicks up and I interrupt him. "Did you say...shaved bald?"

"Yes, completely."

"Did he give you his name?"

"No. After he left, I realized that we didn't even introduce ourselves. I wish I could send him a thank you note or a gift card or something. Why do you ask, hon?"

"Darryl...about how old was he?"

"Ohh...I'd say about sixty."

Now my ticker is galloping and the hot flashes that momentarily abated when Randy left the room are back. "And...Darryl...what kind of car was he driving?"

"I don't remember the model. It was an orange SUV, small and sporty looking."

Wally!

I sit bolt upright. The phone becomes slippery in my clammy hands. I take a moment to compose myself, to think how best to word this to my husband.

I speak with a deliberate calmness. "Darryl...I know him. He works for me, or I mean, he *used* to work for me, and I had to lay him off recently. You've never met him, and I'm sure it's just a coincidence, but just do me a favor and if you do happen to see him again, give me a call right away. And it's best not to speak to him or even approach him, because if he realizes you're my husband, well, it just gets kind of awkward, you know? But I'm sure it was just a coincidence. Okay?"

Coincidence my sorry ass.

Darryl is very intelligent but way too trusting, the complete opposite of a cynic. He wouldn't believe for a second that the guy held any grudge against me personally for being laid off, because that's part of life, and me being his boss, well I was just the messenger, just a tiny cog in the huge corporate machine, so why would he blame *me*? Darryl doesn't understand that when people get screwed, they're angry and they look for someone to blame. And look for revenge. That's human nature.

So, Wally was following Darryl, and when he saw that Darryl got a flat, he stopped to help, just to mess with my head. To let me know that he could get to me. Through my family.

Well, NOBODY messes with my family!

Luckily, Darryl is his usual oblivious self. He agrees to do as I ask. I tell him it's best to stay in his hotel room for the remainder of the evening and rest because of the bump on his head, and he agrees to that also.

We end the call. Darryl is safe in Boston for now.

Next, I call Emily, the teenage girl who stays at the house with the boys from the end of their school day until I get home. When she answers I tell her to take the boys over to my neighbor Mona's house immediately.

Then I call Mona and tell her to expect the boys and Emily, and not to ask me any questions now because I'll explain everything later.

Then, I decide that I need to contact Louise about Wally's encounter with Darryl, even though I just talked to her a short while ago. This will be the umpteenth time I'm going to bug the shit out of her about a case that she isn't even supposed to be working on, which technically isn't even a case because there isn't even evidence of a crime yet. I know that she can't arrest Wally or even detain him for helping Darryl fix a flat. So, before I call Louise, I'm going to see if I can get more information about Wally for her to work with.

Information from Faith.

Like maybe where Wally stashed Melvin's body?

On the outside chance that Faith might get a vision about something, Louise might be able to check it out in a rush, and maybe she'll find something that will link Wally to the crime, in which case she'll have a reason to pick him up.

And if Faith sees *nothing*…well, then I'll call Louise anyway and tell her about Darryl's flat tire and Wally's motive for killing Melvin, even though she'll probably be able to do squat, other than arrange to have, *I Told You So,* carved into my gravestone after Wally decapitates me.

I know Faith finished her workday a while ago, so she should be home by now. Her apartment is not too far from Melvin's place.

And I have a plan of action.

Under my desk is a box of all kinds of wonderful shit from Wally's cube—papers, pens, binders, a pencil sharpener, an old raincoat, a baseball cap, a pair of winter gloves, a scarf, some small bags of nuts and candy, and so on. It's a mix of Fleener supplies and personal stuff that Wally left when he stormed out the other day. It's my job to look through it and sort out Wally's personal stuff and then contact him to ask if he wants it back.

I've been dreading it and was trying to figure out how to have some neutral person who doesn't know Wally contact him instead of me, like perhaps someone from that lovely Human Resources department that had a hand in perpetrating all of this downsizing carnage. But it's fortunate that I delayed this unpleasant task because now I'm going to have Faith touch all this stuff and see if she can get a signal or a vision or whatever. And while she's at it, I'll have her touch whatever property of Melvin's was left in Florence's house. Faith wanted to do that since the last time we visited Florence, before I was a believer in the visions, but the opportunity didn't present itself.

Now, the situation is different. Annuska is gone, according to Filbert, and it sounds like she left in a rush. So much of a rush that she didn't bother to tell me that Melvin's funeral is canceled. People in a rush usually leave things behind, and I can't imagine Florence having any objection to Faith touching whatever is left. So I'll take the box of Wally's junk over to Florence's house and ask Faith to meet me there and we'll do it all at once, as quickly as possible. Assuming Florence agrees.

I saved Florence's number in my contact list the day I first met her. I hit the call button and after six rings I hear a click and then a single raspy word, like a file on a wrought iron railing, "Yeah?"

"Hello. Florence?"

"None other. Who's this?"

"June Bloom."

"You again? Ain't you grown tired of chasin' that dead horse yet, toots? Either he's dead or maybe he's back in Romania with his blushin' bride. But if I was bettin', I'd bet on dead."

"Uh, yes, I heard that Annuska left."

"That's right. Never to return, I hope. Packed her stuff up in a rush and snuck out when I wasn't home, so

I couldn't hassle her about the money Melvin and her owe me. I'm lucky that hustler didn't clean me out when she left since I have shit around here that's worth a lot. Like this chandelier made from deer hooves, it's an original—"

I interrupt, "How do you know she went back to Romania?"

"She left me a handwritten note. Said she was sure her true love Melvin was dead, and there was nothing for her here, and she saw no point in hangin' around here. So, she was headed back to the homeland to explore her gypsy roots, or some such hogwash. Said she'd send me the rent. Yeah, right. I have about as much chance of seein' that money as that Romanian sweet tart has of being elected pope. But at least I can get a paying tenant now."

"Did she leave any things behind?" I ask.

"Yeah, a mountain of worthless shit."

"Uh…are there any *personal* items?"

"I saw one of Melvin's jockstraps in there. Is that personal enough?"

"Okay, well I have a rather strange request to make of you. It has to do with Faith's…powers. You see, Faith is a genuine psychic. She sometimes gets visions about people she has some type of connection to…from touching their things."

"She touches their thing?" she barks. "What the hell kind of a sick game is that?"

"I meant things, as in personal belongings."

"Ohhh, I see. Visions from touching stuff, ehhh?"

At this point I suspect Florence moves the phone away from her mouth because I hear some muffled chuckles followed by assorted snickers and snorts.

I ask, "Florence? Are you still there?"

"Oh yeah, I'm here, toots. Just havin' myself a good laugh, that's all. You and that little girlfriend of yours are just precious, you know that?"

I brush off her ridicule and say, "What I'd like to do is have Faith touch whatever they left behind, if that's okay with you?"

After a few more laughs she answers, "Sure, whatever. She can touch all their stuff, she can rub it, she can pleasure herself with it, whatever she wants. On one condition, though: You gals haul it all out of here, except for the few things I think I can sell. You'll be savin' me the hassle of throwing all this lovely shit out. I gotta pay three bucks a bag for throwing out non-recyclable trash if you can believe that. And there's some big stuff, pieces of cheap plastic furniture. You got a car big enough to haul it away to the dump?"

"Yes, I have a station wagon," I assured her.

"Okay, everything I *don't* want is all yours then…all for just a hundred bucks."

"You want me to haul all the worthless stuff away to the dump, and *I* have to pay *you*?"

"Well, sure, but there might be some very valuable crap in there that I didn't recognize the value of, and now you get to keep it. You know the sayin', one man's trash and all."

I tell her we'll be over as soon as possible, figuring I can get her down to thirty or forty bucks once I get over there.

Next, I call Faith and tell her to meet me at Florence's. She sounds puzzled but excited.

"Meet at Florence's house? Are we gonna check more cars, June? 'Cause oh my Lord, Melvin's body's gonna be really ripe by now, but I'm game. Let' *solve* this case, let's do it!"

"No, Faith, there are no more cars to search. Annuska has left, maybe to go back to Romania. But she left some of their things in the house, and Florence is going to let you touch them all. Plus, I'm bringing a box of Wally's stuff from his cube, and I want you to touch that too."

"Wally's stuff? Why?" she asks.

"I'll explain when I see you at Florence's place."

****

I pull up to Florence's house and park in front. Only Florence's car is close to the house, so apparently Faith isn't here yet. I take the box of Wally's stuff out of the back of my car and lug it up to the door. The box feels like it weighs at least twenty pounds. Maybe after a month or so at the gym, the new buff me will have an easy time carrying it, but for the current slightly flabby me, it's a bit of a struggle.

I knock on the storm door hard with my foot. My arms are already getting tired but there's no way that Florence can *not* hear that nasty bang and rattle of the old door, even if she's in her downstairs suite.

Thankfully, she opens the door within ten seconds. I'm surprised to see that she isn't wearing the bathrobe and fuzzy slippers. But it's after five, so she's apparently moved on to the evening wear stage, which is a baggy gray sweatsuit with pink stripes on the legs and arms, and a pair of old white sneakers. The big curler is still in her hair. I can only assume she's eternally curling.

She eyeballs me suspiciously and says, "That was quick, sweetie. You're really anxious to get your hands on all this good stuff, yeah? And what's that you got there?"

"Just a few other things that I want Faith to touch while she's here."

I enter the living room and plop the box on the floor. "Yes, I'm rather anxious," I add. "Can I see what Annuska left behind?"

I follow Florence into Melvin and Annuska's bedroom. Things are strewn about on the dingy carpet in no discernible order, and *stuff* is too generous a word. Assorted debris or just plain crap are more accurate terms for describing what Annuska has left: clothes, shoes, books, magazines, curtains, towels, pictures, two clothes hampers, an old broom, empty wine bottles, an enormous pile of yellow and moldy papers, some plastic end tables, toiletry items, over the counter medicines, and on and on. There's a pair of scissors on the floor, along with two empty packing tape dispensers. Annuska obviously left in a big rush.

It looks like she took all of *her* clothes but none of Melvin's, which makes sense since every time I saw her, she was dressed in a style I'd call *Italian Leather Chic*, whereas Melvin's workday wardrobe was *Garage Sale Glam*.

Florence pipes in, "You know, I think I'll keep his clothes, toots. They might buy 'em at the consignment shop. At least the ones he didn't sweat through."

I'm looking for personal stuff, things which Melvin might have had very close contact with. But then again, Faith got a vision from touching a work report that Melvin wrote, which was just paper. Faith said it was so completely unpredictable what she'd get a vision from, so we'll just have to try everything.

I turn around to Florence and say, "I'm really sorry

to have interrupted you around dinnertime."

"No big deal, kiddo, dinner's not a major event for me. I eat by myself. I don't exactly get the white tablecloth and candlesticks out every night."

"Okay, well there's nothing we can do until Faith gets here. I'm sure she'll be here very soon," I assure her.

I'm not overly thrilled by the prospect of having to make polite conversation with Florence as we wait. She's five feet from me and smoking like a wet campfire. I'm hoping to get some space between us for at least a few minutes so I can take some deep breaths. And then my phone beeps.

It's a text from Louise:

—*Fingerprints confirm that Melvin Hamm is Max Tremayne. Also, Darryl's car checks out, my friend found nothing suspicious.*

My phone quickly beeps again with another text from Louise:

—*Also, Peter Tremayne died this morning. His will is now public record, here's a link to it if you're interested. I'll call you in a little while.*

Out of habit, I click the link and the first page of the will appears on my screen. I scan it quickly and at the bottom of the page something catches my eye, and...

Holy Shit.

Double ho-leeeee shit!

I immediately look up at Florence and say, "We've got to hide."

"Hide?" she barks between puffs. "What are you talking about? This is my house, toots. Hide from what?"

I am in panic mode.

I grab my purse and laptop and jump up from the couch, swiveling my head back and forth, looking for a safe place. Or maybe an out. "Is there a back door?" I ask.

"Well, yeah, sure, but…"

"Please, let's get away from the windows."

"Why?"

"I don't want to see Faith," I whisper. "Maybe if we hide, she'll go away."

Florence doesn't take the hint about turning the voice volume down. "Go away?" she bellows. "You're talking about your little southern fried girly friend, right? Are you nuts? *You* told her to come here, didn't you?"

"Please, we've got to get away from the windows!" I run into the kitchen and Florence waddles in after me and asks, "What the hell is wrong with you?"

It's a tiny eat-in kitchen with grimy oak cabinets, stained lime-green linoleum, and an ancient refrigerator that wheezes and groans like it's going to die any instant. But luckily there's only one window, and it's over the sink, and I know that if we get under the kitchen table we won't be seen. I push a chair aside with my foot and dive onto the floor.

"C'mon!" I plead. I motion with one hand for her to join me under the table.

"You gotta be kidding, lady. I ain't sat on a floor in twenty years. I could break a hip or rupture a kidney. This is *my* house, *my* palace, and I ain't movin' until you tell me what's up." She puts her hands on her hips and waits for my response.

My mind races as I consider how to explain things to her in fifteen seconds, and in words which will magically make her fully cooperate. I start babbling, "It's *very* complicated. Melvin is not Melvin. What I mean is, his real name is Max Tremayne, and he's due to inherit a lot of money when his father dies, which in fact he just did this morning. I just looked at his will, and I know this sounds crazy but I'm certain that Faith wrote it. I don't know how, but I know her writing style, I've read many reports that she's written, and she has this weird dyslexia thing that's really rare, she switches small double b's with small double d's, and I just saw it in the will because it has the name of his beloved cat Mister Tabby which instead reads Mister Taddy."

"What? Mister who?" she barks.

More words spill out of me in a confused and frantic sputter, "And I'm sorry, this must sound totally weird too, but a man called me twice and told me that Melvin was mixed up with some type of con woman who had screwed him out of money. I thought it was Annuska, but now I know it had to be Faith. Somehow Faith found out that Melvin is Max and she's angling to get that inheritance money, and holy crap, maybe she killed Melvin! I mean, Max. Listen, you're just going to have to trust me on this. It could be a matter of life and death. If we hide maybe she'll think we're not here and go away."

And I'm certain I sound like a flaming idiot…

My heart rate is up to at least a hundred and sixty now, my breathing is shallow, and my ass is firmly planted in whatever sticky shit had spilled on the floor eons ago and was never been mopped up. I'm thinking maybe cream soda.

Florence stands there and looks at me like I have six heads and three tails. She takes a long, slow, deliberate drag on her cigarette and says with a cynical sneer, "You know what you sound like, toots?"

I just stare at her and think: *Why yes, of course I*

do…an idiot, imbecile, moron…take your pick.

She continues, "You want *me* to trust *you*? On a matter of life and death? I wouldn't trust you to clip my toenails."

Oh, shit! Faith will know I'm here because my car is out there! She could pull up to the curb any second.

I command myself to calm down as my mind races through my options. But there are no *good* options now that I've stupidly given Florence that information dump. I can still try to convince Florence to cooperate…maybe promise her money, or a lifetime supply of smokes, or whatever it takes.

But first I have to call Louise and tell her about the will.

Still sitting on the floor, I open my laptop so I can look at the will while I speak to Louise. I quickly connect to Melvin's wireless router, which Annuska apparently neglected to take or even deactivate in her rush to leave. Opening the text message program on the laptop, I find Louise's message, click on the link to the will, and I'm ready to go.

I take out my cell to make the call, but as I do, it rings.

Must be Louise calling me back like she said. Thank God she's available.

Without looking I push the accept button and put it on speaker so that my hands are free to use the laptop.

"Hello? Ms. Bloom?"

That's definitely NOT Louise.

I recognize the voice. It's the guy who I've talked to twice about the con-woman he saw with Melvin. He didn't even bother blocking the caller ID function this time. Bad timing, but I'll make it quick.

With my heart still pounding so hard I think it will crash through my chest wall, I say, "You didn't throw out the phone like you said you were going to."

He ignores my statement and says, "I have to tell you something." His tone is different than in the other two calls.

He sounds worried, guilty, maybe scared.

He continues, "That woman, she was living in a small apartment during the time I knew her. I went over there this morning. She had cleared her belongings out in a huge hurry, according to the landlord, who said she accidentally left one small suitcase behind. As I expected, the landlord had no forwarding address to send it to. I told him I was her nephew, and he gave me the suitcase. I looked in it, hoping to find some clue to this woman's real identity. I want to get my money back, and—"

I interrupt him, blurting out, "Wait. Did you say nephew?"

"Yes."

"How old was this woman?"

"In her seventies, I'd say. Sometime after she took off with my money, I spotted her and Mr. Hamm at an ATM."

In her seventies? What the hell?

"Are you certain she's that old?" I exclaim. "I mean...could she have been wearing some kind of makeup that made her look much older than she is?"

"I'm *sure* she's a senior citizen. I could tell from the appearance of her hands. And the way the skin hung on her arms, you know?"

"And how'd you identify Melvin Hamm?"

"I work at the bank. Not that particular branch, I live

far away from Mr. Hamm's area. But I have computer access to customer information at all the branches. I just looked to see who had accessed their account on that outdoor ATM at the time I saw them together. So, this woman, she had posed as my aunt, my father's sister whom I'd never met. My father died long ago, but I knew he had a sister somewhere. This woman, she contacted me, said she found me with an internet search, and when we first met in person, she showed me a birth certificate and a driver's license. They looked authentic. She had information about my father's childhood that I thought only a family member would have. It was enough to convince me, and…unfortunately I gave her quite a large sum of money for her medical expenses. Ms. Bloom, I called to tell you that there's a gun in the suitcase. She's probably dangerous like I thought. Capable of violence. So, you need to be careful if—"

A hand reaches around and hits the disconnect button on my phone. From behind me Florence says, "If he calls back, you tell him he can keep the gun, toots. I have another."

She pushes the cold metal barrel into my back.

And then Faith walks in, looks at us, and says, "Don't shoot her, Mom. Not yet."

Mom?

Florence says to Faith in a matter-of-fact manner, "She knows you wrote the will. She saw your d's and b's switched."

I am stone-statue rigid. I have no idea how steady Florence's gun hand is, but I'm not going to do anything to startle her and make the weapon go off accidentally. I'm just hoping that the vibrations caused by my heart crashing against my chest wall won't jar her trigger finger.

I stare at Faith in disbelief as she stands in front of me. I've never had a gun pointed at me before. The closest thing was when one of my kids shot me in the forehead with a suction cup arrow. This situation is a bit more serious, but at the moment I'm feeling more amazement and curiosity than fear. I want to know more than anything what the hell is going on. There's plenty of time for some good gut-wrenching, colon-cleaning fear to set in later.

If they let me live till later.

Chapter 19

Faith walks over to us, and Florence casually hands her the gun. It's startling to see the thing. A revolver, shiny and nasty looking. With a few silent waves of the weapon, Faith motions for me to get out from under the table. We all walk into the living room where she signals that I should sit down on the grimy couch. With her free hand, she takes my laptop and phone. She closes the laptop, throws it on a chair, and then puts my phone in her pocket.

Faith now looks me in the eyes with a stern expression on her face. She is definitely not looking like the cheery little Faith I know so well. She stands with the gun pointed squarely at my face. I think it's best to wait for her to speak.

Florence pulls out her own cell, taps it a few times, then puts it away. After that, she seems completely relaxed, even bored, and happy to be relieved of the weapon, apparently because it frees up her hands, one for a fresh cigarette, the other for a lighter. She sits in a chair, reclined, legs crossed, looking at me with an expressionless face.

Holy shit. These crazy bitches are going to snuff me. Okay, now think. I'm a first-level manager, I deal with crises every day, not quite the same as this one, but there must be a way out. What are my options?

Faith thankfully breaks the silence. She says, "You

know, I *like* you, June, I really do. You've always been good to me. That's why this is painful for me."

"Painful?" I reply. "No problem, let me spare you the pain. Just let me go."

She shakes her head. "Can't do that, June."

"Faith…uhhh…what happened to your cute southern accent?"

She smiles. "Did you like the accent, June? Made me sound really sweet and friendly, didn't it?"

"So, you're not from a crappy little town in Tennessee?"

"No, I'm from a crappy little town in New Hampshire."

"Is Faith even your real name?"

"Oh, I've got lots of names, June. My real name? It's been such a long time since I've used my real name that I can barely remember it. But I've used the name Faith Gelner before, in fact for a long stretch of time when I was younger. You can keep calling me Faith if you like."

Keep them talking. If they're talking, they're not shooting. Then, when the time is right, I'll throw them off guard by faking an epileptic seizure or something.

I turn to Florence and ask, "Are you really Faith's mother? I thought Faith's parents were dead."

Florence answers, "Yes, I'm really her mother. True flesh and blood. And sure, I've died lots of times. Whenever I get in a tough spot, I go right on through those pearly gates. And then I miraculously get reborn, with a new name and social and a clean record."

The gravelly edge in Florence's voice is gone. She speaks slowly and clearly and sounds in control. So, her elderly white-trash persona is apparently all an act, too.

Except for the chain-smoking, because she still puffs away.

Faith says, "You're probably really curious about how you were suckered, June. Well, you're right, I wrote Peter Tremayne's will. Florence and I had just finished a job and we were looking for a new mark. With some fake credentials, I got a job in a law office as a paralegal. The practice dealt mostly with messy divorces and wealthy people's wills. That's where I met Peter Tremayne. He was perfect for us because he was lonely, old, dying, and rich. And I wasn't going to let his fortune go to some stupid dog training charity.

"So, I got friendly with the old coot, even went to his house a few times to go over some paperwork with him. It was easy for me to slip into his son's bedroom, and I found hidden behind a picture frame something the cops had missed: a photo of his son and a girl."

Faith stretches her legs by taking a little stroll around the living room as she continues to speak, but all the while she keeps the gun pointed straight at me.

"When I found her name in his high school yearbook, I was able to track her down. She was living in Florida with her parents and Max followed her down there and lived near her for a little while, trying to woo her, but eventually he gave up and left. I gave her a bullshit story about being his cousin and wanting to find him. She didn't have an address or a phone number for him, just a P.O. box number here in Connecticut.

Faith stops and moves to switch the gun to her other hand, and I instantly have crazy thoughts of springing up from the couch like a ninja during the switch, grabbing the gun in my teeth and wrestling her to the ground. And then in a blink, the hand switch is done, the opportunity gone. Probably just as well…

"So, I came here and took a job in the post office and sorted mail for two weeks until I saw Max walk in one day to check his box. I followed him and it was easy to find out where he lived and that he was now Melvin Hamm and worked at Fleener. But my original plan to marry him, then get him to write a will leaving everything to me, and eventually have him fall victim to some tragic accident after his father died, was totally blown up because that moron had already taken himself an internet bride. He couldn't wait any longer, I suppose. Poor, frustrated Melvin. I suspect he was a virgin when he married Annuska. I don't think that little Florida girlfriend ever gave him so much as a hand job.

"At that point, the first thing we did was make an extremely generous offer to the owner of this shithole house where Annuska and Melvin were living. Florence bought it and moved in as the new landlady, to keep tabs on our fifty-million-dollar investment. And I got a job at Fleener so I could be around Melvin."

I say, "Uhhh…so, I assume you're not an accountant?"

"That's right, June. Just like I'm not a paralegal."

"Amazing. Because you outshine most of the other people in my department, who I'm pretty sure really *do* have degrees."

"I never took a college course of any kind in my life, but I sailed through that job interview with you, didn't I? I can fake my way through pretty much anything." Faith puts her free hand on her hip and smiles at me as if to congratulate herself.

I bob my head up and down in obsequious agreement. Somewhere I heard it's not a good idea to contradict someone pointing a gun at you.

Faith continues, "I worked on seducing Melvin, but that putz had such an idealized concept of marriage. Happily ever after and all that. He barely gave me a glance. Finally, I got him shit-faced drunk at that conference two months ago and got him into bed. Even so, he was a mess afterwards, sobbing about being unfaithful to Annuska, swearing he'd never do it again and that he was going to confess everything to her. I worked on him, trying to convince him to leave her, but he wouldn't go for it.

"Then last Monday night he confessed his infidelity to Annuska, and I gotta give her credit, she did what I suppose any self-respecting Eastern European internet bride with a really bad temper would do. She shot him in the head. And man, at that point our plans were doubly screwed."

Speaking of getting shot, I think that since the hand switch, Faith's gun is now pointed at my left eyeball instead of my right. Just an observation. I don't really have a strong preference about which eyeball I get shot in...

"We didn't actually witness the murder, June, if that's what you're thinking. That's why Annuska thought she'd get away clean. But when Florence first moved in, we put some tiny motion-activated surveillance cameras outside the front and back of the house that send video to our phones, so we could monitor comings and goings, and an audio bug in their kitchen. We also put GPS trackers in Melvin and Annuska's cars. It paid off because the night Annuska shot Melvin, Florence was out, but we got video of Annuska behind the house, dragging out something big wrapped in a sheet. The GPS history showed that a few minutes later, Annuska drove straight to the funeral home where she worked.

"That's where Florence caught up with her. By then it was late at night and the place was closed but Annuska had the keys to the building. Florence got there in time to see Annuska leaving, and Florence eventually got a look in her trunk later that night and saw that the bundle was gone, so she'd obviously left it at the funeral home. We knew exactly what had happened when we listened to the recorded audio from the kitchen microphone for the few minutes before Annuska dragged out the bundle. We heard a muffled argument followed by two bangs.

"Oh my God," I moan. "Annuska did it. He's really dead. Poor Melvin. I mean, Max."

Faith shrugs and says, "Yeah, well, Florence was right, the guy had it coming, one way or the other. Lowest on the evolutionary ladder, and all that.

"Anyway, we checked what was going on at the funeral home that week, and there was only one possibility for permanent disposal of that body. There was a closed casket ceremony the next day for a woman who'd died of cancer. The woman was light, she'd wasted away to nothing. The casket was big and heavy, and Melvin was a small man. Annuska got away with stuffing Melvin's body into that casket with the dead woman and sealing it for burial the next day. It was a gutsy decision to do that. I mean, she could have just run, but she really wanted to stay in the States. If she'd buried the body somewhere, there was a decent chance that it would have eventually been found."

"But…his car…how'd she get rid of his car?" I ask. I shift in my seat so as to relieve the pain I'm getting in my ass from the worn seat cushion, and I notice the gun barrel shifting position slightly to follow my head. I'm guessing that Faith has probably held a gun before, and she's probably damn good with it.

"The next morning she just drove his car away at the normal time he left for work, but she took it to Balmer Park. She drove up a logging road and parked it in one of the old carriage barns and then walked back to her house. The only thing she forgot to do was toss the gun into the casket. So, she threw it into that pond on her way back from stashing the car. Florence saw that too, because she followed her and watched with binoculars from that dog park next door.

"We knew that as soon as Annuska reported her husband missing, we wouldn't be able to keep Melvin's real identity a secret from the cops. So, we needed a new plan and that's where *you* came in because the plan started with me getting a vision of Melvin's body in the trunk of a car and telling you about it."

"Then you're not…uhhh…clairvoyant?" I ask.

She snickers and looks at me like I'm a dimwit. "Hardly, June. Disappointed?"

"Yeah, in myself. I'm an idiot to have ever believed in that hocus pocus."

"Oh, June, don't be so hard on yourself. There *are* some *genuine* psychics, I'm sure. But I'm not one of them."

"How did you know that there was blood on the trunk lid of Annuska's car?"

"Well, obviously, there wasn't until Florence put it there."

"But you didn't kill Melvin…so…where did you get the blood?"

"Well, that was easy June, because that fool had three nosebleeds an hour. Christ, he'd turn his head too fast, and it would trigger a gusher. I just pulled some bloody tissues out of the waste can in his cube. But we didn't want the cops to have the car yet because we didn't want Melvin's body found right away. So, we made it look like the car was stolen."

"What do you mean by 'made it *look* like the car was stolen?' It *was* stolen. You and I *saw* it being stolen. By that old guy."

"Oh June, come on." Faith admonished, as if she was addressing a hopelessly dull student. "That old fart was my father."

"What? Your father! Your whole family is in on this?"

"You might say it's a family business. Florence and I are the brains, Dad is just an imbecile who does things for us when we need him to. We throw some money his way and he's content as long as he has enough to buy his whiskey. He doesn't ask many questions and he would never squeal on us. And he's got an old eighteen-wheeler that comes in handy. Dad went over to the park right after Annuska stashed Melvin's car in the carriage barn, and before she got a chance to move it out of there to a safer hiding spot. He hot-wired it and drove it into his truck. Annuska's car is also in his truck now. Dad will get rid of Melvin's car, but Annuska's will be found about ten months from now, sitting abandoned in some parking lot. It will look like it's been stolen. It'll be a little banged up and there will be some additional miles on the odometer. And in the trunk, the cops will find more of Melvin's blood and also under the trunk carpet there'll be some spent shell casings from Melvin's gun that Florence found in their bedroom. Annuska actually did a tidy job, not leaving any obvious evidence in that trunk. But we'll give them plenty to work with. We'll make it a very rich crime scene. And when the cops find that the car belongs to a person who fled the country shortly after her husband went missing and whose gun was fished out of a pond, they'll open a murder investigation and they'll be salivating to find that body."

Faith pauses and grins at me as I squirm in my seat. I can tell she's enjoying this.

"I know exactly how they think, June," she confidently says. "They'll want to interrogate me again because I saw the inside of that trunk before the car was stolen and because I found the gun. I'll insist on touching the shell casings and I'll get a vision, June, a vision as clear as a morning sunrise, of Melvin lying inside that buried casket. With my recent history of accurate visions about this case, it will all come together for the police. They'll have the casket exhumed and they'll find poor Melvin with a few holes in him, and they'll know that Annuska is the only one who could have put his body in there."

I glance over at Florence again, and she looks relaxed and settled in. Is she proud of her daughter? I guess so. And I'll bet she's glad that her acting job is done and she'll be moving out of this dump soon, and on to the next con.

Faith continues, "Unfortunately for the cops, it will take at least two years to extradite the murderer from Romania if they can even find her. Florence and I decided it was best to send her back there. Even though we think she didn't know anything about Melvin being Max, she was too much of a wild card. Florence

S.E. Greco

convinced her that she'd better leave, or we'd turn her in. It was either send her away, or plant *her* in the ground too, and we don't do that sort of thing unless there's no other way."

"*You* told Annuska to leave the country? At one point I thought maybe you were somehow scheming with Annuska. I saw the call log on your phone."

"You looked at my phone when I accidentally left it in the cafeteria, didn't you? I figured you might have. You don't think that if I was really scheming with her, I'd be stupid enough to use my own phone to call her, do you? Melvin just borrowed my phone a few times to call his wife."

I'm still confused. "So, Melvin...or Max...will be declared dead about ten months from now. So what? How does that benefit *you*?"

"Oh, C'mon, June, you're smart. You're my boss, after all. *Think* about it. You have all the important pieces of information. You read the will, you know that Melvin's widow can't inherit the money directly from Melvin's father, only Melvin's child can. And you know I screwed Melvin at the conference."

My jaw drops in shock. "Holy shit! You're pregnant? With Melvin's baby?"

Faith smiles. "That's right, June. At the conference, I let that slob impregnate me. And it's a good thing I was ovulating at the time because we only had the opportunity to do it twice, and I'm amazed that microscopic pecker of his could even manage two times in two days, but somehow it did the job. I'll be having Melvin's baby in seven months. A few months after that we'll set things in motion so that Melvin's body is found. And then, after a respectable time passes, I'll contact

Peter Tremayne's executor and explain how Tremayne's son and I had an affair at the conference, and that I became pregnant and had a child. A DNA test will verify it. The baby will have a genuine-looking birth certificate and a social security number. Florence is good at getting socials, she has eight of her own."

"But…you'll never get away with it," I protest. "When Faith Gelner tries to claim that money…"

"Ah, but it won't be Faith who contacts the executor. It'll be a woman named Rita Bremer who lives in Seattle. Rita is a lonely single person who had a conference tryst like many people do. Rita has red hair, bulky eyeglasses, and wears very high heels which make her look taller than Faith.

"You see, I attended the conference as Faith, but also as Rita. I'll explain to Peter Tremayne's executor how Melvin unburdened himself to Rita about being Max Tremayne when he was totally shit-faced from liquor and lovemaking. If the executor decides to check carefully, there will be a record of Rita attending the conference, and there will even be hotel security camera footage of Rita at the front desk. The shots of her face won't be very clear of course, because I'm careful. I even put on my red wig, glasses, and heels when I left Melvin's hotel room on those two nights, in case there were any witnesses. Melvin of course had sex with Faith. He never met Rita. He was passed out cold both times when I left his room. The booze combined with the twenty seconds of sexual thrusting were too much for him.

"And so, the baby will inherit the money, and I'll manage it, of course, being the legal guardian. I'll be able to quickly siphon it off into overseas bank accounts."

Holy crap. Fifty million bucks, theirs for the taking. These two ladies...are GOOD.

Chapter 20

I am struggling to find a hole in Faith's plan. I have some far-fetched idea that if I somehow show them it won't work, they might let me go.

I say, "But...the DNA test on the baby...it will show that Max is the father but also that Faith Gelner is the *mother.* *Y*ou gave the cops your DNA after you found the blood on the trunk latch."

She chuckles and dismisses my consideration with a quick swat of her hand. "Don't be silly June, I would *never* give the cops my DNA. I scraped the inside of my cheek, but I switched swabs before I handed it to the forensic technician. You saw the technician flirting with me, didn't you? It's all about distraction. I made the switch when he was looking at my chest, not my hands. It was so easy. I assure you that *my* DNA isn't on file anywhere."

I shake my head in defeat. "Cripes, you thought of everything. Every base covered, I guess....except...you were lucky Annuska didn't get pregnant."

"We don't leave *anything* to luck, June. We didn't think Annuska had any interest in having a baby, but even so, one of the first things Florence did when she moved in was snoop in their bedroom, and she found Annuska᾿s birth control pills. If we weren't sure she was protecting herself, we'd have figured something out. Maybe drugged her and given her a contraceptive injection. We're pretty resourceful."

Faith gives me another sinister smile.

"Uhhh…then I guess you *did* think of everything."

"You were a key part of it, June. You talked to Detective Freemont about us finding the gun and about my vision of Darryl falling asleep at the wheel. I'm sure you've got her convinced that Faith is a genuine psychic, so she'll be anxious to exhume that casket when I have my vision ten months from now."

"But…Darryl's accident…how did you…?"

"Oh, June, that was easy too. You told me that Darryl stops at the same place every morning to get coffee, and that he was going to Boston this morning. Florence went to the coffee house and slipped some sleeping pills into his drink at the creamer bar. She's great at it, she's been doing that kind of thing for fifty years. She also put a GPS tracker on his car when it was in the coffeehouse parking lot, a military-grade unit accurate to within three feet. I was notified on my phone when his signal went twenty feet or more off-road, and if there were no buildings or parking lots at the location, it was very likely he'd fallen asleep and drifted off the road. Dad was following in his truck about five miles behind Darryl. When Dad stopped to help, he removed the GPS unit from under the bumper. We couldn't be *certain* that Darryl would fall asleep and go off the road, but if it hadn't worked, we'd have thought of something else to convince you I was a genuine psychic."

I squeeze the edges of the grimy cushions so tightly that my knuckles go white, and the cheap material begins to tear like tissue paper. Staring at Faith in horror, I hiss, "What if Darryl had been killed?"

Faith scowls and replies, "Oh, don't get all dramatic

on me, he's fine. But if he'd been killed, maybe run head-on into a telephone pole, or gone off a cliff, or something like that, then you would have seen me shed some tears. I would have consoled you and bawled my eyes out at his funeral, June, with all of Faith's southern sorrowful charm, you can be sure of that. It would have been a very convincing act.

"Hell, June, I've earned my fifty million, don't you think? How long do you think you could play a role like I did? How long could you act like a complete airhead? Could you do it for a month? Five months? Could you let some disgusting slob impregnate you? Could you have his baby?"

Aghast at the thought of the baby's fate, I say, "The baby…oh my God, are you going to…?"

"Oh, June, calm yourself down, I'm not going to murder the baby," she admonishes as she shakes her head. "I'm not a monster. Faith will very shortly quit her job at Fleener and move away with her boyfriend Ralph, who will think the baby is his. Ralph is as much of a clueless putz as Melvin, but at least he'll be good for changing diapers. Eventually, I'll leave, and Ralph can keep the baby if he wants to, but if not, I'm sure it'll end up being adopted by some couple who don't mind raising an ugly baby, which it no doubt will be since it'll have Melvin's genes. I'm not cut out for motherhood, anyway. The cops may get suspicious after I abandon the baby, but Florence and I will be long gone by then."

I look over at Florence, hoping that maybe I'll see just a tiny smidgen of sympathy in the eyes of the older woman. But she looks totally bored.

Faith continues, "And June, do you know why I'll leave Fleener? Do you know what excuse Faith Gelner will give for quitting? Emotional devastation at the sad death of her manager. That's right June, it will unfortunately be a tragic ending for you. That crazy bastard, Wally, who you laid off, is going to get even by murdering you. And then he'll kill himself, of course. No suicide note will even be needed because everyone knows he's a nut job. You and he will just be two more unfortunate victims of today's heartless corporate culture."

I know a lot about heartless corporate culture. How many people have I told that my job's going to kill me? They should have taken me seriously…

Faith looks down at her watch and says, "Dad's been following Wally, and Florence gave him the go signal before we started this chat. Dad's a bit older but Wally's not expecting to be ambushed by a geriatric trucker with a stun gun. Wally should be tied and gagged shortly and laying in the trunk of his SUV in the parking lot of that supermarket that you often stop at on the way home from work. We'll meet them there in your car. It'll look like Wally followed you and ambushed you."

Faith sighs and adds, "Can't say I'll miss my job at Fleener, June. I thought being a paralegal was bad but working for Fleener is the most boring job in the world. Production accounting? Sitting in that little cube all day? There were many times I thought about slitting my wrists when I was writing those reports for you. The only thing that got me through was the thought of those fifty million bucks. But even though I hate the job, June, I don't hate *you*. So, we'll make it painless. A bullet to the head."

A bullet to the head? Okay, June, time to step up your game, you've got to somehow talk your way out of this one…

I pant with desperation as I give it my best shot, "But…but…you said…you don't like to…uh…kill people, you know. That's what you said… and…Faith… or whatever your real name is…I swear I won't say anything…I swear."

It's difficult to be persuasive when you've got no cards to play…

Faith shakes her head and says, "Can't take that chance, June. I partly blame myself, since I let that spelling mistake slip by in the will. If you hadn't seen it, this might have ended differently."

Just keep her talking until help comes. Yeah, that's right, I'm sure the cavalry will burst in here any second and save my sorry ass.

But I know that won't happen. No one will be saving me today.

This is it, then. They have it all figured out, every detail, all sewn up and tied with a big friggin' Christmas ribbon.

I stare at the gun that Faith is pointing at me, almost unwilling to believe that the thing is real. It feels like we are all in a scene out of a movie.

And then I glance at the front door.

If they're going to shoot me anyway, why shouldn't I try and make a run for it before they tie me up? Or drug me? Or stun gun me? If I could do a flying leap up from the couch right now and give Faith a Karate chop, she might drop the gun, and then I might be able to make it out the door, and…

I take a quick peek at the front door again, judging the time it will take me to get there…

But Faith notices my darting pupils. She says with authority, "Don't even think about it, June, because if you decide to give us any trouble here, I can make sure it *won't* be painless." She raises the gun a little higher, pointing it now at what appears to be a spot in the middle of my forehead.

Yup, that did the trick. I immediately stop thinking about escaping. Painless is good. NOT painless is bad.

And she's right…she WILL get away with it. And I'm toast. I just hope…Oh, dear God, I just hope she doesn't do anything to Darryl and the boys. Thank God, I told Darryl nothing. He knows nothing about this at all, nothing of my suspicions about Faith or about Melvin being murdered. Should I tell Faith that? Yes, I'd better tell her that Darryl is oblivious, for what it's worth.

I open my mouth, but I can't form any words. It's like trying to talk after you've stepped out of the dentist's chair and your mouth is still numb from the Novocain. I am essentially scared stupid, as they say…

But there's really no need to shoot me…I'll croak right here…my ticker is racing from fright like I'm a hummingbird on speed, so I'm sure I'll blow out an artery any second…then this wacko can just sneak my carcass into my shitty little chicken coop sized cubicle at Fleener Plastics after hours and plop me in my chair, slump me down so that my head is on the desk, put a pen in one hand and a coffee cup in the other and that's it, job done, because who the hell is going to question one more employee being worked to death by that crappy company?

Hot flashes are coming in waves now.

I feel dizzy, faint, peripheral sight shutting down, and…and now, I'm looking out the window and…

I see a vision.

A vision of…

DEATH.

I gawk out the living room window in my delirium. I'm losing it. I feel almost giddy…and don't they say that when you're near death, you accept it and get very calm and even happy?

With what little perception I have left, I see the eyes of God approaching me and…*Hey, whad'ya know, they're green!*

Go figure, you'd think they'd be blue or brown, since those are much more common colors, and God made us in his image and all that, right? And hey, am I getting all religious now? Just in time, I suppose.

And as I watch, those big green eyes grow larger and then pulsate once, twice…

And then the world EXPLODES.

The huge picture window and the section of wall below it bursts inward, directly toward the three of us with an ear-shattering BOOM and a shower of plasterboard, splintered wood, and glass shards, each of which twirl and spin and tinkle, seemingly suspended in the air before my eyes like snowflakes on a crisp winter morning. I think a bomb has gone off, but a nanosecond later I see the green eyes of God flying through the air and then, holy crap, God's whole body comes sailing through, following those eyes, and who would have figured that God would have two long antennae coming out of his majestically pontifical crimson cranium, and a huge red body in three sections?

The almighty creator sure as shit looks just like one damn big bug to me.

My eyes lock onto that gigantic bug body as it glides gracefully through the living room air with its six legs spread-eagled, parting the billowy clouds up near the ceiling which remind me of the heavenly white ones that Michelangelo painted on the canopy of the Sistine Chapel, except these clouds are grayish blue and were belched from Florence's smoky lungs. Gravity soon does its job and the otherworldly thing careens down and crashes squarely into Faith's chest, flattening her little body like Dorothy's house squished the Wicked Witch of the East. The gun skitters across the floor and then all I can see of Faith are two skinny white legs sticking out beneath that big red ant body, and they aren't even twitching. She is out cold, and unless she's wearing an armor-plated bra, she'll wake up as sore as a matador who's been gored in the chest by a raging bull.

As my vision begins to clear and the fog which engulfed my brain disperses, I see the front grill of the white exterminator van that plowed six feet into the living room before stopping. I glance sideways and catch a glimpse of Florence running towards the kitchen, trailing smoke behind her. Filbert's bulky frame bursts out the driver's side door into the fog of plaster dust which fills the room, and he immediately barrels after her and past me like a madman on a mission, his insecticide gun drawn and ready to fire, his utility belt slipping down a little more with each stride, down below his generous gut, which jiggles and bounces like a big bag of gelatin dessert.

Stunned and wide-eyed in disbelief, I raise both hands to get the deranged exterminator's attention, but I only get one word out as he charges past me. "Filbert?"

"Right back, Ms. Bloom!" he says without giving me a glance or even slowing down.

I feel like I died and was brought back. I tilt my head forward and brush some of the plaster dust off my hair.

I'm not sure what to do next. Call someone? The police? An ambulance for Faith? Before I can muster the will to walk to the kitchen and look for a landline phone, Filbert marches Florence back into the living room, holding her from behind by both arms. I'd expect the light and wiry Florence to give Filbert more of a run for his money despite his age advantage, but for a heavy guy, Filbert can move pretty well. And the insecticide gun is holstered, so it appears that he got his woman without firing a single shot.

I say in a halting voice, "Filbert, you…saved me. How did you know? How did you…?"

He beams with pride and says, "There's bugs here, Ms. Bloom!"

"I know. You've been trying to get rid of them for a month. But what does that have to do with…"

"No, I mean *bugs*." Still holding Florence with one hand, he goes over to the deer hoof chandelier, reaches up and pulls out a black disk the size of a nickel, with some kind of a short wire antenna sticking out of it, and he holds it up in front of me.

"I've been listening," he says.

Epilogue

Three Weeks Later

As I walk over to Verne's little workspace in Fleener Plastic's cubeland, I think about dinner tonight.

I need to get one of those rubber mouth appliances that prevents you from grinding your teeth. But I won't use it when I'm sleeping. It's just for this evening when I'm having Paul and Abbey over for dinner.

That's right.

ABBEY!

I'm sure I'll be sitting there during dinner with a shit-eating grin while she chats away about the color of her electromagnetic aura or some such bull, probably while she's stroking the back of Paul's neck or blowing in his ear. And if I don't have that rubber mouthpiece in, my teeth will be ground down to little nubs by the end of the meal. And I know that I won't be able to eat with that thing in my mouth, but that's okay because you can't gag and eat at the same time anyway.

The reason I'm having Abbey over is that Paul told me he likes her and he's going to continue seeing her, despite what I think about her. I have to admire him at least for standing up to me. Maybe he's growing a spine. So, I figure that if he's going to see her, I should at least get involved because, spine or not, he's my only brother and I still need to look out for him. I want to see how they interact, and maybe I can tell if she's totally using him and maybe not, but at least I'll have his back if he needs me.

And there's something else. After many months of me talking to Paul about doing something other than just his fast-talking job, he's finally taking some action to branch out. But he was never the nine-to-five type, so he says that maybe he'll enter the world of…get this…*competitive eating.*

Paul is one of those guys who can eat like a pig and not gain an ounce. He's got a metabolism that just melts away the calories like ice cubes in a cast iron pan. He says there's too much competition in the usual areas of eating hot dogs, chicken wings, and pies, but Paul thinks he can be a champ and earn big bucks in the much less popular and vastly more disgusting areas of competitive butter and mayonnaise eating.

Okay, so it's completely gross but at least he's thinking about doing *something* other than fast talking, so I've decided not to give him a hard time about it. At least not yet. And anyway, there's also the possibility that Abbey will find it so offensive that she'll call him a loser and tell him to hit the road.

I think again about how lucky I am that Filbert blatantly disobeyed both me and the police by persisting in his surveillance of Florence's house. Not only was he listening in when Faith had the gun on me, but he recorded the whole damn thing, which was essentially a confession.

Faith and Florence (or whatever their real names are) now face charges of conspiracy, fraud, kidnapping (holding that gun on me and telling me not to move is considered kidnapping, go figure), assault (because they drugged Darryl), reckless endangerment, and a few other things which escape me. They didn't actually murder anyone, but those charges are enough to put them away for a long time.

They're being held without bail because of the judgment that they're an extreme flight risk, a conclusion which was reached after the cops searched Florence's house and found her eight different passports. She apparently left a trail of hapless victims across at least a dozen states. The one victim who called me several times decided to testify against her. The cops are still trying to trace down all of her past confidence schemes, some of which involved Faith. Louise says it's like tracing the strands of a spider web, and it's kept a trio of detectives busy for a week.

The cops were able to get a court order to have the casket of that poor woman who died of cancer exhumed, and when they dug her up, sure as shit they found poor Melvin, lying with his face in her crotch and her face in his. The bullets they found in Melvin's body were a match to the gun that Faith and I pulled out of the pond. Louise said that an extradition request for Annuska had been drawn up and sent to the government of Romania, but they couldn't even begin the long extradition process until they located her. Surveillance cameras caught her catching a bus out of Bucharest Airport in Romania, but from there the trail went completely cold. They have no address for her, no record of her checking into a hotel, and no list of friends or relatives. So, I think it will be a long time before they find her, if they ever do.

Did Annuska love Melvin?

Doubtful.

He was her meal ticket, her way to get American

citizenship. No evidence ever turned up that she knew a thing about Melvin being Max. She plugged him because he was unfaithful to her, and she had a wicked temper. Some people get really pissed off at rejection, even from someone they don't love.

And was Annuska screwing her boss, Wayne? Well, we don't know for sure. He denied it, but even if they were having horny Transylvanian vampire sex in one of those big caskets every day, having an affair is not a crime. Louise said that Wayne nearly crapped himself when she brought him into the interrogation room, and she concluded that he was too weak-willed to have had anything to do with the murder. So, he's back running his funeral business, and without Annuska's organizational skills, he's probably quickly running it into the ground (pun definitely not intended).

Faith's father's truck was found abandoned somewhere in upstate New York, with its forged registration papers still in the glove compartment. He hasn't been located yet, but the cops expect to eventually catch up with him even though he has no listed address, or driver's license, or passport, or anything. That's because Faith and Florence gave the cops a good description of him, and also a list of his friends and favorite watering holes that they know of. The two women were more than willing to sacrifice his flaccid ass to give the sentencing judge even the slightest of reasons to go a little bit easier on them.

And as for Wally, Faith's father indeed tased him, just as she said he would, and the cops found Wally delirious and tied up in his SUV in the back of the supermarket parking lot. Faith's father panicked and took off because he assumed something went wrong

303

when Faith didn't answer her phone, which was flattened at the same time that Faith was flattened.

The actual tasing took place as Wally walked out of a diner and was about to get into his SUV, and one of those razor-sharp little taser darts hit him right in the scrotum. Well, when those ten-thousand volts entered his testicles, he apparently saw God. It was a real, *hallelujah, come to Jesus,* moment for ol' Wally, and it changed his outlook on life, I'd say.

His doctor claimed that the experience may have char-broiled the part of his brain that processes anger, but I don't think so. I think he just felt so lucky to be alive after what he went through that the hate was simply sucked right out of him. He dropped his plans for revenge against me and the company, and after his release from the hospital, he profusely apologized to me in person for scaring me.

The cops didn't charge him with anything, but since he admitted to intimidating me, Louise has been keeping track of him. She told me that after his recuperation from the tasing, he drove down to Florida and he's currently on a two-week guest trial stay at one of those enormous all-inclusive retirement villages where it's non-stop fun for seniors. She said he'll probably buy a condo there and do some part-time maintenance work for the facility. And since he's only sixty and the average age there is about seventy-eight, the guy is supposedly a rock star at the recreational activities, a real sex pistol with the blue-haired ladies. So, I guess his tool is still working after getting zapped. And he's learning to country line dance, too. I'm a little jealous about that part because *I* can't country line dance.

And then there's my buddy, Filbert. How do you

adequately thank someone who saved your life? I'm not sure, but I've started by having him over for dinner once a week. He's coming over tonight in fact, and who knows, maybe I can get Abbey interested in him. Filbert's just an awkward, lonely guy who needs more contact with two-legged creatures as opposed to six-legged ones. He's not a private detective yet, although he very much wants to be. Still an exterminator, just a little bit happier one now that he has me and Darryl and the boys to chat with.

For now, I'm asking around to help him get more bug business. At the moment he's all excited because tomorrow he'll be setting off one of those massive fumigation stink bombs in Mona's house, and he doesn't often get the chance to use his heavy ordnance.

So...the reason I'm walking right now over to Verne's cube is the porno investigation.

And I have to thank that young IT geek, Randy, for his ingenuity (*okay, there I go again using the politically incorrect term "geek", sorry about that*).

Well, it turns out the little geek is just amazing at writing code. He wrote a sophisticated program that snoops on the people who work for me, and he did it just for kicks, in his spare time, to *see* if he could do it. He told only me about it, and he remotely loaded it onto my people's computers. It gives a little pop-up message on my screen every time one of my people go to one of those porno websites.

Is it ethical to snoop like this? Maybe not, but as long as the other managers keep calling me the porno queen behind my back, and I know they still are, then I feel okay about using Randy's program.

I was honest with him and told him that with his

abilities he shouldn't be working this dead-end job at Fleener, where he's obviously underpaid and under-appreciated by everyone except me. He should be working on his own software start-up which he would eventually sell for billions so that he can retire at twenty-eight and then hopefully bestow his financial beneficence upon the few people like me who made it all possible by encouraging his entrepreneurship when he was just an unknown little IT geek.

So, he loaded the program a few hours ago and I just got my first pop-up which said that Verne was accessing some porn site. I never would have thought Verne to be the one. He seems too nice to be a porn addict, but who knows?

The message listed the URL, which looked to me like just a bunch of gibberish, but it also gave a short descriptor of the filth that's on the website. And oh, dear God, I took a look at that and after I saw the words *unicorns* and *naked fairy princesses*, I stopped reading because I really don't want to know any more details. I just hope that Verne's zipper won't be down when I confront him.

As I come within a few aisles of Verne's cube, I decide to approach him from the unoccupied cube directly behind his. That way, I'll probably be able to get a look at his computer screen and be absolutely sure he's gawking at smut before pointing my finger at him and shouting *J'accuse*! or whatever other dramatic phrase pops into my head.

And now I'm sneaking up quietly to the adjoining cube. Quiet. Quiet.

The first thing I see, over the top of the cube wall is...oh dear God, on the screen there's a naked fairy, and you'd think that they'd have tiny little fairy breasts, but no, this one is a really stacked fairy. And I move a little closer, and now I see the top of Verne's head...

But...IT'S NOT VERNE.

"YOU PIG!" I scream at my boss Larry. "You've been sneaking onto Verne's computer! Why can't you watch porn on the public library computers like all the rest of the perverts?!"

Larry stares at me wide-eyed, fearful, and totally BUSTED!

In a complete panic, he slams the screen of the laptop shut.

He launches himself from the chair, raises both hands, palms toward me, as if he's afraid I might hit him or spit at him, and he yelps in a frenzy, "Now, now, June, just calm yourself! I would encourage you to look at this unemotionally instead of through a fog of female hormones. The pornography thing is, well...a man has needs, you know? And anyway, I'll deny everything, so it'll be your word against mine, and who are they going to believe? Me, of course. I have more years with the company. And do you know what they'll do to you for falsely accusing me? You'll probably get fired! At the very least, you'll lose your management position."

I lean closer to him and bark, "They won't have to fire me. I QUIT! I wouldn't work for a pig like you a minute longer, or for a company that puts sexist pigs like you in positions of authority."

Wow! That felt damn good.

And then I storm out.

I'm hoping that the good feeling will last for at least thirty seconds. But I only make it to about twenty, before

I think: *Oh, shit. I sort of* need *this job. What did I just do?*

And...what am I going to do now?

A word about the author…

S.E. (Stephen Edward) Greco grew up in the Philadelphia suburbs and studied science and engineering at Cornell University. After a career at a major tech company, he pivoted from writing patents and technical papers to penning fiction. His mystery, suspense, humor, and science fiction short stories have appeared recently in Suspense Magazine, The Dark City Crime and Mystery Magazine, Literary Hatchet, Scarlet Leaf Review, CommuterLit, Bards and Sages Quarterly, Society of Misfit Stories, Suspense Unimagined, Strange Stories, Mysterical-E, and Going Down Swinging: Pigeonholed. His work has been nominated twice for the Pushcart Prize anthology and his story "I Called to Say You're Dead" was a runner-up for the Short Mystery Fiction Society's 2020 Derringer Award for best mystery novelette. "Downsized or Dead" is his second novel; His first is a work of mystery/suspense titled "A Patient Enemy." Steve lives in New York and divides his time between writing, reading, and oil painting.

Visit him at segrecoauthor.com.